BLOOD AND ILLUSION

HISTORICAL PARANORMAL ROMANCE — WITH A STEAMPUNK EDGE

ANN GIMPEL

Edited by
ANGELA KELLY

CONTENTS

BLOOD AND ILLUSION

COVEN ENFORCERS, BOOK THREE

Historical Paranormal Romance—With a Steampunk Edge
By
Ann Gimpel

Tumble into a supernatural version of the Old West with heart-pounding romance

Not all witches join the Coven. Fiercely independent, Isla heads up her own small band in the San Francisco area. She's never needed help before, but dark sorcerers drive her and her group into hiding, trapping them.

Sam's worked for the Coven as one of their enforcers forever. He's been there so long, the Coven is the only mistress he knows. It's a lonely life on the road thwarting wickedness and Black Magick with his guns, his magic, and his horse, but it's been enough to satisfy him. Until now.

A group of witches is in deep trouble. They're not part of the Coven, but Sam is sworn to protect all witches and he rides to their assistance with several of his brothers. Nothing prepares him for the outspoken spitfire who ends up riding double with him. She's forthright, opinionated, and downright hostile, but he's drawn to her self-sufficiency—and her undeniable beauty. Soon, Isla is all he can think about.

Dark forces are on the move. Protecting the woman he's falling in love with is at the very top of Sam's list. If they manage to survive, he'll tame her. Claim her. Make her his.

CHAPTER 1

Sam Jennings made his way to San Francisco's docks through muddy streets teeming with people, horses, and every variety of wagon and carriage imaginable. The odors of food and sewage mingled in an unpleasant brew, with the food smells predominant near saloons, hotels, and restaurants, and the raw, acrid stench of human waste nearly overpowering from every alleyway. Smoke billowing from wood and coal fires thickened the air, making it difficult to see very far ahead.

Despite all that, a sense of excitement permeated everything. San Francisco was a young city, boisterous and bustling. Everybody seemed to be in a rush, and Sam pulled magic about himself hoping it would speed his journey. His horse, unused to crowds and traffic, shied whenever anyone or anything got too close, so he wound his power around the animal to create a buffer zone.

Tom and Cory, two other Coven enforcers just like him, were also headed for the docks. They'd split up on the outskirts of town so they wouldn't draw undue attention to themselves.

They had a job to do, and being waylaid by the local sheriff, who was sure to recognize them as trained killers, wouldn't help matters. Humans maintained a healthy distrust of nearly anything that smacked of magic. While the Coven had established a fragile détente with law enforcement back east, Sam suspected tolerance for his kind hadn't made it too far west of the Mississippi.

"Now's not the time to test it," he muttered to the accompaniment of nickering from his horse, who seemed to agree.

Sam glanced around. He'd been to the city when it was still called Yerba Buena, but it had grown by leaps and bounds since those days. Still, if he followed the scent of water, he was bound to find the bay. A group of threatened witches had gone to ground beneath one of the many warehouses lining the docks. As a Coven enforcer, part of his sworn duty was to protect witches. This group wasn't officially affiliated with the Coven, but they were close friends with Hester Thorne, a witch who'd been one of the original founding members hundreds of years ago.

Hester had intercepted the witches' distress call back in Salt Lake, and Sam and the others hastened to offer aid. They'd been on the road for many days, riding hard, only resting when their horses went into full rebellion.

Every enforcer had a telepathic connection to every other enforcer, and Sam had reached out to others in their brotherhood who were close enough to San Francisco to help the witches. Fifteen men were presumably on their way. He kicked himself for not checking on their location when he was at the edge of town. To do so now wasn't wise. Sending power spiraling outward would surely alert any dark sorcerers in the area, and he wanted to maintain the element of surprise as long as he could.

He, Tom, and Cory had agreed to avoid mind speech until they met on the docks for just that reason—unless one of them ran into unexpected problems. The enforcers riding to swell their ranks could find them through the link they all shared. Because each of them went through the same training regimen, even enforcers who'd never met before meshed well in battle situations. The only problem was they wouldn't have an opportunity to craft a coordinated attack plan.

It wasn't ideal, but it couldn't be helped.

His bay stallion crested a hill, its hooves clanking loudly on cobblestone streets that took a definite downward slant on the far side. Sam studied the horizon, taking in waves crashing on the shore. The brisk salt tang of the sea, mixed with rotting fish, stung his nose.

Almost there.

He tightened the shrouding around himself and hunted for the particular taint Black Magick held. Better to rid the area of dark sorcerers before they drew the witches out of hiding. The women would be weak from their enforced seclusion. They could sink into a kind of stasis where their needs for food and water diminished greatly. Not surprisingly, that particular casting carried a hefty price. Witches had good recuperative skills, but it would take at least a day or two for them to bring their power back to a full charge. They'd need him and the other enforcers to protect them until they were up to snuff again.

His horse shied violently, snapping his head upward and yanking him out of his thoughts. At first he didn't see anything, but then a pervasive chill moved in from all sides, surrounding him. An opaque, gray cloud rose from nowhere, cutting him off from the surrounding city.

Shit!

What would come at him out of the mist? Wraiths? Mad wolves? Other turned animals? Dark sorcerers?

While he still could, he raised his mind voice and called for Tom and Cory.

Amid whinnies and shrill neighs, the stallion crab-walked, stumbling on the uneven surface. Sam slid from his back, hands raised as he summoned power, focusing it with the opal that was his power stone. Multihued fire streamed through the gem, slicing through the gray and illuminating two men wearing badly tanned leathers. Both stank of Black Magick and its peculiar combination of sulfur, ozone, and brimstone.

"You killed our leader," one growled in thickly accented English.

"Your turn to die," the other grunted in the same guttural dialect.

Were these some of the crew from the Far East who'd cut a swath through San Francisco's witch population?

Sam narrowed his eyes. It didn't matter a good goddamn who they were. Or where they'd come from. He was sworn to eradicate evil, and these two qualified. Kill first, ask questions later had always been his creed.

Before he killed them, though, maybe he could glean information. "I'm sure I have no idea what you mean," he said smoothly as he balanced power, ready to loose it at a moment's notice. "Who was your leader?" He grinned viciously. "If I'm getting credit, I like to know what it's for."

Instead of answering, black-tinged fire flew from the taller man's hands. It bounced off Sam's warding. With a furious cry, the dark sorcerer rushed him in tandem with his companion.

Annoyance bubbled from Sam's guts, thick and viscous. Fine. Too much trouble to interrogate these bastards, and it wasn't as if he'd planned to let them live. Grim determination straightened his spine, and he focused his power. Two fewer sorcerers was always a desirable outcome. Drawing the opal's nascent ability into himself, he let mage fire fly from his fingers.

Pure, white light surrounded the sorcerers' fire, snuffing it out. Before shock stamped itself too deeply into the men's stark features, Sam sent power auguring into their chests, stopping their hearts. They dropped to the street like stones, and the gray bubble enclosing all of them shattered to nothingness. Sam dusted his hands together. That had been almost too easy. He whistled for his horse about the same time Cory galloped up from one direction and Tom from the other.

Both men leapt from their horses, adding mage fire to the two smoking pyres. "What the fuck?" Cory turned his dark-eyed gaze on Sam and raked a hand through his close-shorn black hair. Skintight leathers encased his tall, hard-muscled form.

"Who knows?" Sam shrugged. "They must've sensed my magic. They did say they were out for blood because I'd murdered their leader."

"Which leader?" Tom asked tight-lipped. Wrath burned hotly behind his blue eyes, and thick brown hair fell to his broad shoulders in an unruly mass. Like the others, he wore buckskin leathers, but his shaded to almost black, probably from the hours he'd spent in front of a forge crafting shoes for horses.

"I tried to get information, but they weren't very forthcoming," Sam replied. "The leader they were grousing about pretty much has to be either Alistair MacDuff or Andras, the Dark Angel. Did either of you sense anything?"

Cory shook his head. "No. Thought it odd too since I was only about a block from the wharf when I heard your distress call."

"And I was on the docks," Tom said and wrinkled his nose. "They should clean up the fish guts, not just let them rot."

"Yeah, well the town didn't smell too swift, either," Sam countered.

"It's because we're used to living on the road," Cory said.

"Sooner we finish up and get back there, the better I'll like it," Tom replied. "City living never was for me."

"Someone apparently knows we're here," Sam said. "I'm going to see if I can't locate the rest of us. Maybe we can attack as a unit and be done with things so Tom gets his wish."

He raised his mind voice and was rewarded with replies from other enforcers. After a hurried barrage of greetings, he instructed them to meet on the docks as soon as they could get there.

"Well?" Cory quirked a brow. "I'd have listened in, but I didn't want to paint a sign that screams we're here."

"Six of us are close enough to arrive soon," Sam replied. "The rest will come when they can, but I suspect it'll be all over but the crying by then." He nudged the burning bodies with a booted foot and sent more mage fire to finish them off. Sparks exploded with a loud, hissing *whoop*. The bodies cracked open, but nothing spilled out. No organs. No entrails.

"What the hell?" Sam stared at the corpses who were looking like they'd never been alive to begin with. He squeezed his eyes shut and opened them, wondering if they were playing tricks on him. Surely the sorcerers had been more than empty husks.

"Jesus!" Tom stared at the pyres.

"No point worrying about it now," Cory muttered. "Doesn't matter. Let's get our asses moving. Whatever those two were, they won't bother us—or anyone else—again."

Sam vaulted atop his horse. The others followed suit, and all of them made their way down the steep street to docks that lined San Francisco's waterfront. Cobblestones gave way to wooden planking at the bottom of the hill. Ships of all sizes were either tied up to quays or moored out in the bay. Men hurried this way and that, shouldering loads as they went. Tom had been right about the fish stench. It grew worse as they got close to the boats. It was late afternoon, and ships were returning with the day's catch, dumping their bounty on the beach and the docks.

Sam reined in his horse and dismounted, scanning for further signs of dark enchantment. Flipping the reins over the animal's head, he secured it to a hitching post. Cory and Tom did likewise. The horses stamped and laid their ears flat, not liking the noise, stench, or crowds any better than their owners did.

"I don't get it," Sam glanced from Tom to Cory. "I just looked for more evidence of Black Magick and came up dry. Surely those two I made short work of weren't the only ones."

"I don't sense dark corruption." Cory spoke slowly. "But it'd be easy enough to hide damn near anything behind all the activity down here."

"Do you think we should smoke out the witches?" Tom asked. "Sooner we rescue them, the sooner we can be gone from here."

"Not yet. It's what our enemy is expecting us to do," Sam replied. "Assuming they're here, it's why they're shrouding themselves. If it was only two dark sorcerers, the witches could've handled them."

Cory frowned. "So the absence of evil is a trap? Something to lure us into complacency?"

"That's my thought," Sam replied.

"Well, that's a bitch. They can wait us out," Tom mumbled.

"Let's settle in and postpone doing anything until the rest of us show up," Sam suggested. "We're daunting when there's an army of us, and it might make whoever's here think twice."

"Ha!" Cory chortled. "While they're *thinking twice*, maybe they'll make a mistake and we can figure out where the hell they are."

"And how many, and if they're alive or dead," Tom added sourly.

Sam gazed up and down the uneven planked street lining the waterfront. At least five hundred men were engaged in some aspect of boat maintenance or fishing. Any kind of pitched battle here would kill some of them. Collateral damage was inevitable when warfare occurred in crowded places. Far better to move the party on down the beach, well past where docks jutted into the bay.

"I agree," Cory said.

Sam glanced askance at him. "You might've waited for me to say something, rather than mining through my thoughts."

"Why? Faster this way."

"Agree with what?" Tom snapped, sounding out of sorts. "I didn't tap into your mind, so I missed whatever Cory's nattering about."

"Come on." Sam gestured. "Let's put some distance between us and all these people. It'd be a shame to kill some of them by mistake."

"Black Magick is more likely to do that than us," Tom countered, "but I'm on board with it. Besides, there's a dude in a shack down that away selling fishcakes."

Sam laughed. "You don't like how it smells, but you'll eat it."

"Damn straight, brother!" Tom laughed too.

The unmistakable feel of enforcer power pummeled him as four men rode up and jumped from their horses. "Where's the fight?" Kane asked, scratching his bearded chin. Dark red hair was braided tight against his head, and his green eyes missed very little.

"Yeah, we found the pyres up yonder." Another man jerked his chin uphill. Blond hair was chopped off unevenly, and his gray eyes twinkled with mischief. "Don't tell me we missed all the fun." He stuck out a hand. "I'm Roland. Haven't met you before, Sam, but I've heard a lot about you."

"Where are the others who were supposed to be with you?" Sam asked, sidestepping the comment about fun as he shook Roland's hand.

Pounding hooves almost drowned out his words as two more enforcers threaded through the crowded wharf, heading their way.

"Six more plus us makes nine." Cory clamped his jaws in a tight line. "Ought to be enough to give almost anyone pause."

"Yes, but where are those anyones?" Kane persisted. "None of us felt a thing."

"Now that we're all here, let's move on down the beach," Sam suggested. "Away from all these humans. We can talk more then."

"Have you sensed any more Black Magicians?" Roland pressed.

"No, but that doesn't mean they're not here," Sam replied. "There was something odd about the ones you saw burning near the top of the hill."

The other enforcers tied their horses to the hitching post, and Sam herded all of them down the beach, his senses tuned to the slightest disturbance. Nothing met his antennae but an eerie vacuum, almost as if someone had sucked everything magical out of the world. His stomach tightened, and the small hairs on the back of his neck twitched in protest.

Tom ran to catch up to them with grease-stained paper sacks that he handed around. "Something in the air doesn't feel right," he muttered around a mouthful of fried fish.

"My point exactly, brother." Sam extracted a piece of fish coated in cornmeal. "Until we know more, we wait."

~

Isla huddled with six other witches in a basement beneath one of the warehouses lining San Francisco's docks. Her hair hung in filthy strands. Grime caked beneath her nails, and she stank, but at least she was alive. Russian sorcerers—or at least sorcerers who spoke Russian—had killed four of her sisters before she'd dragged the rest of their small band to a defensible position and swathed them in layers and layers of magic.

It had been a short-term solution, but they hadn't had any choice. Not really. Only problem was they had no easy way out. If they dismantled their spell, the sorcerers would find them in a trice. If they remained where they were, eventually they'd starve to death. She was far weaker than she'd been a week ago when they'd barricaded themselves into the underground room with its dirt floor and dirt walls. Small cutouts high on two walls coincided with ground level, and provided their only source of light.

In desperation, she'd used her power stone to call Hester Thorne, a witch who'd been instrumental drawing their group into a cohesive unit. Hester promised help, but it had yet to materialize. Breath steamed through Isla's teeth as she bent forward and stirred the shallow pool she'd created from a broken pot made of crockery and water dripping down the walls. It took a while, but the water had finally grown deep enough to become a scrying instrument.

Weariness dogged her, and her vision blurred. She squeezed her eyes shut, willing them to focus next time she dragged her lids open. Thinking it might help, she pushed herself upright and walked around the six-by-ten foot room.

"What are you doing?" Kat eyed her balefully out of bloodshot blue eyes. "I was asleep." Dirty blonde hair had been braided to keep it out of the way.

"Aye, and ye'll be asleep permanently if ye're not careful," Isla shot back, the brogue from her native Scotland thicker than usual. It was one of the reasons she and Hester had bonded so tightly. Shared roots from Scotland's Highlands and islands.

"Isla! Come look at your pool!" Rowan cried. Silver hair fell about her, dragging in the dirt, but her brown eyes were lit with hope.

Isla skidded to her knees and stared at the water's surface. Nine men strutted down the rock-strewn sand fronting the ocean. Tall, rangy, hard-bodied and clad in leathers, it was obvious they were used to ruling the world. At first she thought they were a new passel of sorcerers, but she forced herself to look closer.

Not trusting her first take, she took a ragged breath. Maybe she wished for salvation from the room that was likely to become their crypt so desperately, she was imagining things, "What does it look like to you?" she asked Rowan.

The other woman turned to face her. "Help. That's what it looks like. Those men are bleeding power, and it's the good kind."

The other women skittered across the floor, jostling one another to get close to the pool so they could see.

"Be careful!" Isla cautioned. "Else ye'll tip the dish, and we might not live long enough for me to refill it."

Her heart hammered against her ribs as she took in the men. One of them in particular caught her attention and held it. Long, blond hair spilled across his shoulders, and his eyes were a bright, turquoise blue. Strong bones carved his cheekbones into bas-relief, and his jaw was square, determined. Buff colored leathers covered him, and they were skintight, leaving virtually nothing to her imagination. Broad shoulders led to deeply muscled arms and narrow hips with a high, tight ass. Long legs disappeared into boots that laced to his knees.

Her throat grew dry. Many a year had passed since she'd experienced such an immediate reaction to a man, and it confused her.

Must be because I'm half-starved.

Och aye, and ye know better, the other half of her brain inserted dryly. Whoever he was, he was one gorgeous man.

Understanding slammed into her, and she was ashamed she hadn't put two and two together immediately. "They must be the aid Hester promised." She glanced at the other women.

Rowan lurched upright. "If that's true, then we need to go outside and help them."

Isla licked her chapped lips. "They're not looking as if they need any help, but at least that way they won't have to hunt for us, and mayhap we can leave this accursed place."

"You're the one with the strongest magic," Kat pointed out. "And the only one who can project telepathy beyond the enchantment hiding us. See if they answer."

Isla exhaled sharply. It was a reasonable suggestion, but not without risk. If she was wrong, and those men were actually allied with the dark, she'd have given away their position. Opened them to a certain death. Or worse, imprisonment at the hands of evil.

"I was in your mind," Rowan said, her voice surprisingly gentle. "We're as good as dead now. I say we chance it."

"I was coming around to the same conclusion." Isla breathed deeply to center herself and drew out her pink moonstone. Before she could think things to death, and her courage failed utterly, she linked to the stone and sent her magic thrumming outward. No need to make things fancy, so she settled on the shortest phrase imaginable.

"Are ye who Hester sent?"

Depending on the answer, she'd ask for proof and take things from there.

CHAPTER 2

Sam had nearly reached a place between two boulders and a steep embankment where they could hole up and wait when *"Are ye who Hester sent?"* blasted into his mind. The other men stopped dead right along with him.

"Did you hear that?" Cory demanded.

"I figure we all did from the looks on everybody's face," Sam replied.

"Must be the witches," Kane said. "We need to answer them before they close themselves off again."

"It might be a trap," Sam growled.

"How would they know Hester's name?" Tom asked.

"Same way they knew I killed Alistair and Andras," Sam replied. He balled his hands into fists, thinking. "I am going to answer them, but I want all of you to listen in. If anyone has the ability to project a truth spell over distance, do it."

"Crap! Those sometimes don't work in the same room," Roland muttered, then added, "But I'll try."

"Yes, Hester sent us," Sam responded, waiting to see what would happen next.

"Describe her," the witch—if that's who it really was —instructed.

"Long white hair, hazel eyes, short stature—"

"Nay," the woman interrupted. *"Anyone could know those things. Where is she from? What was her husband's name? Her granddaughter's name too while ye're about it."*

Sam grinned. "It has to be the witches," he told the men. "They don't trust us any more than we trust them."

"Agreed." Cory grinned back. "Makes you kind of proud of them."

"Och aye, and I'm waiting," the witch pressed. *"But not for much longer."*

"Hester is from the Isle of Skye," Sam replied. *"Her beloved husband, Michael, died recently, and her granddaughter is Abigail. We were at Breana Giraud's outside Salt Lake City when Hester showed up a few weeks back."*

"Those were good answers," the witch replied. *"My sisters and I will join ye presently."*

"Hold." Sam used his best Coven enforcer tone, but these weren't Coven witches, and as such they weren't bound to obey him.

"Why? We can help fight if the need arises. And 'tis sure to if I'm any judge of such things." The witch sounded indignant.

"We're better than half a mile from the wharves," Tom joined the conversation. *"It would be far better for you to wait for us to move closer to you. In case evil is lying in wait."*

"Of course evil lies in wait. If it dinna, we wouldna still be here." Sarcasm dripped from her words. *"I must converse with my sisters."*

Tom doubled up a fist and punched the air. "Remind me why we agreed to this mission," he grumbled.

"Because Hester demanded it." Cory shot a meaningful look Tom's way.

"And because we're sworn to protect all witches—even the arrogant ones." Sam glanced from one man to the next as they waited. Charging back into the thick of things on the wharves wasn't ideal. If Black Magick was sequestered somewhere, waiting to challenge them, it may well mean the loss of innocent lives. On the other hand, having the witches walk out of their hiding place with no one to protect them wouldn't fly either.

"Opinions?" he asked the others.

Cory shrugged. "I say we move closer so we can shield the women. No matter what this one says—and she sounds feisty—they can't be at their best. It took us a week to get here, and that's a week when they haven't had anything to eat."

"If fighting breaks out, it won't endear us to the humans, but that can't be helped," Kane said.

"How about we use the horses?" Tom suggested.

"Say more." Sam made come along motions with one hand.

"Simple. We find out where they are and ride close in, as close as we can get. The second the witches emerge, we each grab one and gallop like mad things for this stretch of beach. If I remember right, we can skirt the town to the south and keep right on riding."

"Dark sorcerers could raise wraiths and mad wolves and block our path," Cory said.

"They could, but they won't," Roland cut in. "For one thing, no wolves—mad or otherwise—live near enough to be a threat. Wraiths, maybe, but I haven't known our enemy to utilize them in the midst of crowds of humans. I've lived in cities these past few years."

Sam narrowed his eyes. "The likeliest to bar our way would be dark mages, then?"

Roland nodded. "And they'll be furious since they already know you killed two of their ilk."

"We'll wait for ye to escort us." The witch was back.

"Good choice," Sam replied dryly. *"We'll be on horseback. Here's the plan. As soon as you surface, head for one of us. We'll do whatever we have to to get you mounted. How many are you?"*

"Seven."

"Excellent. We're nine. Look for us in a quarter of an hour." He paused, thinking. *"How'd you know we were here? Or was it just random trolling on your part?"*

"Our leader, Isla, she has the scrying gift," another voice chimed in. This one carried the lilt of Ireland, softer in tone than Isla's harsh brogue.

"Well, keep right on scrying," Cory instructed. *"Don't show yourselves before you have to."*

"Give us credit for a wee bit of sense," Isla tossed back.

"I'll give you all the credit in the world once we're safely out of this mess," Sam replied curtly. He bit off the lecture kicking around the back of his throat about following their directions to the letter. Instead he asked. *"Where are you?"*

"In the large, gray warehouse across from the two northern piers. Get moving immediately. Someone could've overheard us talking. If ye catch my meaning, lad."

"I scarcely need you to explain things to me." Sam bristled at being referred to as a *lad* on top of her other pithy instructions.

"These aren't Coven witches," Cory reminded him.

Sam snorted, wondering just how serious a power struggle they'd have on their hands once the witches were above ground. "No kidding. I don't mind Hester ordering me about, but she's a special case, given her age and rank."

He cut off communication with everyone and took off at a dead run. The other enforcers fanned out beside and behind him. If the goddess smiled on them, they'd be back on the deserted stretch of beach very soon. Once the witches were safe, he could rid himself of them—including their cantankerous leader. The one who thought he needed an explanation of why they should hurry.

Had in fact *ordered* them to hurry.

He rolled his eyes. Goddesses' teats. As if he couldn't think for himself.

His memory of geography matched Tom's. Once they had the witches in tow, they could circle far down the shoreline and cut cross-country, avoiding the town entirely. It seemed like the most prudent route, and he hoped to hell the witches wouldn't argue the point to death, if they wanted to do something else. Like return to their homes and gather their things. Even if they escaped their enemy's notice for a time, their luck wouldn't hold if they remained in the area.

Sam and the other enforcers reached the horses, mounted, and adopted a leisurely pace, moving north along the coastline. Nine armed men in leathers at a full gallop would be sure to attract the wrong kind of attention. After the women were with them, it wouldn't matter, and they could punch it.

"Must be over there." Tom jerked his chin toward a long, low gray stone building. It butted against cliffs rising from the driftwood and rock-strewn shore.

"Shit! Trouble!" Cory kneed his horse, making straight for the warehouse.

Sam felt the cold right before wraith stench wrenched his stomach into a tight knot. *Damn!* No gifts here. They'd have to fight their way out of this one. He galloped hard after Cory and vaulted from his horse's back once it reached the building. Adrenaline surged, along with the anticipation that always coursed through him before doing battle with the dark.

He hoped to hell the women had the sense to remain hidden.

The other enforcers dismounted, and the men formed two

lines. Four in front. Five behind, arranged so everyone had a clear line of fire. Wraiths surged from both sides of the warehouse. With their red-rimmed, smoke-colored eyes and blood-red claws where hands had once been, the undead could almost kill with their appearance alone. Or with their stench, reminiscent of dead things left too long under a hot sun. They sucked your soul through your mouth, and then you joined their ranks.

"Thought you said wraiths wouldn't be a problem," Cory called to Roland.

"Yeah, well, I was wrong. Fuckers." The other enforcer raised his hands, and mage fire sparked from his fingertips. The front row of wraiths folded in on themselves, vanishing in puffs of wicked-smelling gray smoke.

Sam sent power, amplified by his opal, scattering where wraiths were thickest. The first rows vanished, but more followed hard on their heels. Cory worked his circlet of pearls and Tom a chunk of turquoise to augment their magic.

"Where'd you get the power stones?" Kane asked, his green eyes shining with fascination.

"Long story. Keep killing and we can talk about it later," Sam yelled. He dealt death mindlessly, all the while hunting for whoever was driving the wraiths. They engaged in battle on their own, but coordinated groups like this meant a dark sorcerer or two lurked somewhere close.

Cory sidled closer. "We need to find their masters."

"You think?" Sam swept the area with his gaze. So far, humans had given them a wide berth. There might be some inside the warehouse, but if so they were staying put. Smart of them. So were the witches. At least they had enough sense to remain out of sight, so they wouldn't turn into one more problem.

The air currents canted. Almost as if him thinking about the witches had drawn them, a small group of women rushed from a side doorway straight toward him. The wraiths were far faster, and they surrounded the witches before they'd gotten twenty feet.

"Goddamn son of a craven bastard," Sam cursed. "Haven't those bitches ever seen wraiths before?"

"Doesn't matter." Cory raced toward one group of wraiths that had surrounded three of the women.

Sam ground his teeth together. This wasn't impossible, just harder than it had been a few moments before. He wheeled toward the other group of wraiths, focusing power to kill off the outer row as he ran. He'd have to be more careful once there weren't so many of the undead between his razor sharp, lethal magic and the witches, but for now what he was doing worked.

Tom and the others split themselves so some joined Cory and some Sam. The wraiths fell before their assault, and Sam was congratulating himself on a gambit well played, when a bolt of magic came close to clipping him.

Witch magic. Apparently the women were fighting back.

"Watch your aim," he shouted and jumped to avoid another volley of power.

Crap!

Hadn't these women ever fought as part of a group before? Annoyance quickly turned to fury as Kane yelped, batting out fire that singed his hair.

"Hold your power in abeyance," Tom bellowed at the witches.

"Sorry. We canna see through the wraiths," someone—maybe Isla—hollered back.

"Focus your magic into shielding yourselves while the rest of us finish this," Roland ordered.

Sam fisted his hands, but it got in the way of directing his magic, so he straightened his fingers fast. The women damn well better heed an enforcer's order. Or…

Or what? He asked himself caustically.

It wasn't as if he could excommunicate them from the Coven, a group they didn't belong to. Tripping over his frustration, he wiped his mind clear of everything but dousing every single wraith in mage fire. It would purify their wicked souls and ensure the dark couldn't use them again—in any capacity.

The last handful melted into shadows. They might be minions of the dark, but they weren't fools. They wanted to hang onto their undead existence, not end up toasted, crispy, and dead for good. His thoughts skittered to what he'd dispatched earlier. They hadn't looked like wraiths. Were they another variant of the undead? One he'd never come across before?

Sam whistled sharply for their horses. No one needed instructions. The small group of witches, clearly visible now the wraiths were gone, raced toward the enforcers and their mounts. Sam dragged a filthy brunette onto his stallion and positioned himself behind her.

"What are ye waiting for?" she demanded, kicking the horse viciously.

Fuck!

Just his luck to have drawn the bitchy Scott. "I'm waiting until all of us are ready to go," he said through gritted teeth. "It's not good battle practice to leave your men strung out across a field. If you dig your heels into my mount one more time, I'll slap you."

"Why, you bastard." She swung a pair of furious dark blue eyes on him, and he felt her summon power.

"Don't try it."

A blast of Black Magick snapped his head around. Three sorcerers ran toward them, black-tinged fire shooting from upraised hands. Power shimmered around them, enough to tell him these men wouldn't fall on their faces like his last two opponents.

Heh! Maybe these ones are still alive.

Sam judged the distance between them. He wanted to kill the men, but the mounted enforcers could easily outrun them, and a full on firefight might leave some humans maimed—or dead.

Last to mount, Kane was finally on his horse. He glanced Sam's way. "Ready."

"Follow me!" Sam screeched. "We're gone from here."

"What about them?" Cory pointed at the dark mages rapidly closing the distance between them. Two more had joined the initial three.

"I want their hides too, but we can outrun them. I outrank all of you, and I say we're leaving now."

Sam wheeled his horse and took off at a hard gallop back down the beach. Humans, who'd likely watched the exchange in front of the warehouse from the sidelines, cleared a path before them. Clearly, they wanted nothing to do with anything that smacked of magic. Or death.

"Why dinna we kill them?" Isla asked, her words blurred by the wind.

"To keep you and the other women safe. Humans too. It's a rare fight that doesn't yield casualties, and those men oozed power. They were far stronger than the two I killed earlier. Quiet now. There'll be time for talk once we stop."

To his surprise, she held her tongue. He urged his horse well past their original spot on the beach, leading the group away from the water and into a thick, Cypress forest. Brush grew so close together, he slowed to a walk, which was good for the horses after their reckless dash away from the warehouse.

The woman in front of him half turned. "I dinna thank ye properly, and I wish to do so now. We are most appreciative."

"Mmph." Still annoyed, Sam couldn't get past a noncommittal grunt.

"It was sinking in that we'd never get out of there alive." She kept talking, oblivious to his discomfiture. Or maybe she sensed it and didn't care. He wasn't sure which was worse.

"Hadn't you figured that out when you asked Hester for help?"

"Aye and nay. 'Twas early on in the game when I called her, long afore I'd collected enough water to fuel my scrying pool. Anyway," she went on, "once we had a way to see outside, we were waiting until we dinna sense aught of wickedness. Though it grew quiet, something still dinna feel quite right, and so we held back."

"Good instincts," he said, his tone still curt. "They laid a trap to smoke you out."

"Indeed. 'Twas why it almost dinna matter about breaking our silence once I saw ye in my pool." She prattled on, determined to tell him a story he had little interest in. "I kent that reaching out would alert the sorcerers to our location, but we were growing weaker by the day. 'Twas either take a chance, or commit our spirits to the goddess."

"And hope to hell the dark didn't find you. They can commandeer your essence even after death."

"Aye, I ken as much."

The dense trees and undergrowth suddenly opened into a clearing. A small stone hut sat off to one side, its door hanging wide open, obviously unoccupied. The clatter of water on stones told Sam a creek wasn't far. This was as good a place as any to stop and regroup.

He drew his horse to a halt and slid from its back. Before he could offer a hand to help the witch, she tossed a leg over the horse and clambered down on her own.

She cocked her head to one side. "I smell water. I'm going to bathe. Doona fash. I'll be quick about it."

He meant to let her walk away. Turning his mind to other things would've been the wise thing to do, but words slipped out before he could ride herd on his tongue. "You're Isla, right?"

The woman faced him squarely and held out a begrimed hand. "Aye. Isla McIntyre."

Sam surprised himself when he grasped her hand. "Sam Jennings. Nice to meet you."

"Och aye, and is that so? Here I was thinking ye werena over fond of me." Sending a knowing half-smile his way, she made her way behind the stone cabin toward the sound of rushing water.

The others filtered into the clearing and set about the process of settling in for a few hours. They'd put enough distance between themselves and the dark mages, they could afford a quick meal and a strategy session.

"Who's up for hunting something for supper?" Kane asked.

"Me," Roland replied.

Two of the other enforcers went with them. They'd use magic to lure and kill, so Sam figured they'd be back soon. The witches trailed after Isla, likely also intent on cleaning up after living in their own filth for many days. He scanned the ragtag group with what he hoped was a subtle enough spell they wouldn't notice. None of the women were young. All of them had emigrated from various places in the Old Country. He started to dig a little deeper, but a warning jolt from a woman with long, silver hair stopped him.

"Sure and if you're wanting to know more about us, you might just ask. My name is Rowan, and I'm second in line after Isla." The lilt of Ireland softened her words, but not her message.

"Sure and I can do that," he muttered to her departing back. Sam waited for a snappy comeback, but it didn't materialize.

He loosened his horse's saddle, removed it, and rubbed the animal down before turning him loose. The horse was bound to him with magic, so he wasn't concerned about it leaving.

As he pulled cornmeal out of his saddlebags and plucked some wild greens to go into the pot with whatever the others chased down for a meal, he thought about the woman who'd been pressed against him on the long, wild ride away from the beach. Nothing wrong with her courage. Offered a choice, she'd have stood and fought the sorcerers, never giving a thought to how badly outgunned she was. She'd need to pair with a power stone to stand a chance against any mage—evil or good.

He sucked air over his teeth. For all he knew, Isla might already have a stone. The idea—and the magic—to pair gemstones with witches and mages came from a gadget Hester had invented, and she'd lived with this group of women for years.

Sam shook his head. Isla might be courageous, but she was also annoyingly high-handed. And far too outspoken for his taste. She'd called him on his antipathy toward her, and then walked away.

Just walked away.

What did I hope she'd do?

When the answer came, he winced. His cock stiffened, pressing against his tightly laced breeches. Isla was a worthy goal. He wanted to possess her, ride that imperious attitude right out of her.

"For Christ fucking sake, stand down," he muttered out loud, on purpose to steady his resolve. "I'll make certain the witches have a safety margin, and then I'm riding back to Salt Lake to meet the Coven's wagon train."

What if they want to come with us? Join up with the Coven?

He winced again. He had to at least suggest that option. Hester would be bitterly disappointed—never mind pissed—to find out he'd neglected to offer sanctuary within the Coven to her friends, and he couldn't lie to her. She'd see through him in seconds. If he showed up without the witches, her first question would likely be why they hadn't wanted to return to Utah Territory with the enforcers.

"I'll cross that bridge when it shows up."

"Which bridge? What's all that about?" Cory made his way to where Sam stood.

"Nothing. Just muttering to myself. Let's get a cook fire going."

CHAPTER 3

*I*sla walked upstream until she found a deep pool. Though she'd put on a good face for the enforcer—gorgeous, hunk of a man that he was—she was depleted enough, she wondered if she'd be able to warm bathing water.

Och aye, and it doesna matter. Warm would be nicer, but I smell so bad, I almost canna stand myself.

She settled on a flat rock and unlaced her boots, stripping off stockings that had all but bonded to her feet. She rinsed them in water cold enough to make her fingers ache and then hung them over a nearby bush. Flexing her hands to bring feeling back into them, she started unbuttoning her clothing. She draped her cloak over a rock, following it with her woolen top, her skirt, and the thick sweater she'd been grateful for during their stint in the basement's dank chill.

The other witches filtered into the clearing. She heard them chattering before she saw them.

"Lovely pool!" Tashia trudged to a nearby clump of bushes and began to strip off her own garments, making a sour face as she got closer to her skin. "Ye gods but I reek. If I had anything else to wear," she declared, "I'd leave these things for the animals to make nests from."

"Know what ye mean." Isla walked gingerly over sharp stones and stickers, muting a yelp as a thorn pricked her foot. She hopped the last few feet to the edge of the pool and stood in shallow water. Goddess's breath but it was cold, and likely to grow even chillier as she moved deeper.

Taking a centering breath, she crouched and dropped both hands into the water, chanting softly. The ankle-deep liquid warmed fractionally.

Rowan sloshed to her side, cursing. "Christ, but that's unpleasant."

"Doona bitch. Lend your magic to help mine along." Isla cast a sidelong glance at her longtime friend.

"I'd have done so without your prodding. 'Tisn't as if I'm not wanting to be clean too." Rowan lifted a cynical silvery brow and began a Gaelic chant.

"Sorry if I'm a wee bit short-tempered. Not at my best."

"None of us are." Tashia joined them. Dark hair shot with silver reached to her knees. Narrowing her green eyes in concentration, she wove her power in with their spell.

Kat and the others trooped forward, splashing into the water. Her face wreathed in a generous smile. "Warm enough. There is a goddess after all." Shouldering past Isla, she immersed herself.

Isla laughed, surprised she still remembered how, and dove into the newly warmed water. It wasn't much more than tepid, but it was a damn sight better than its original temperature. She scooped sand off the bottom and scrubbed a week's worth of grime off herself before dunking her head and working on her hair.

Too bad she didn't have any soap. She'd bet her bottom dollar that the hard-bodied man who'd led them away from death on the wharves had a bar wrapped in his saddlebags. His type was prepared for anything.

In a moment of pure whimsy, she envisioned making her way back to him, dripping wet and naked as a newborn, to inquire about soap. The thought made her laugh louder.

"What's so funny?" Tashia asked.

"My imagination's run away with me. That and how long 'tis been since a man's laid his hands on me. No matter." Isla gathered her long hair, stood, and wrung water out of it. "Time to get ourselves back to the men and see what comes next."

"Do you suppose it's safe to return to our home?" Kat asked.

"Do ye even have to ask?" Isla sent a pointed look her way.

"But all our things…" Kat's voice trailed to nothingness.

"We'll be starting anew," Rowan said staunchly. "We've done it before."

"Doesn't make it any easier," Tashia groused. "Damn but I hate to put these filthy things back on."

"No choice about it. We haven't time to wash and dry anything beyond stockings." Isla gave the other witch a quick hug. "I have a feeling 'twill be a good, long while afore we have the luxury of clean clothes again."

Without stopping to think about it—or wish for impossible things like fresh laundry and a man's arms around her—she dressed quickly and laced her boots up over her bare feet. With her wet stockings slung over one arm, she made her way toward the scent of fires and food cooking. At least this was one crop of men who didn't expect women to wait on them.

The thought pleased her, though she wasn't sure quite why. Until Sam's chiseled features and bottomless blue eyes crept into her mind, and her heart beat a little faster. Then she understood well enough, and chided herself for foolishness.

Like as not, they'd go their separate ways soon enough.

Mayhap the men would have some way of acquiring either mounts or a wagon and team for her and her sisters. She had no way to pay for them, but she felt confident they could work something out. Hester would vouch for her making good on any incurred debts.

She didn't realize quite how far upriver she'd walked, but she was breathing hard when she got back to the clearing next to the stone hut. It might've been exertion and being half-starved, but thinking about Sam took her breath away too. And made her loins ache with wanting him.

All nine men sat in a rough circle around a fire, clearly waiting for whatever simmered in a pot to finish cooking.

Isla's stomach clenched, and she realized how hungry she was. Hurrying forward, she draped her stockings over a low hanging bush to finish drying.

"Canna we hurry things along with magic?" she asked, and bent to peer into the pot. "'Tisn't enough to feed us all." She flinched at the greed in her tone. "Not that I'm not extremely grateful for anything ye can spare," she added hastily.

Sam got to his feet and joined her. "This was the biggest pot we had," he said. "We'll cook in shifts. Reason we didn't use magic was on account of we figured you women needed to eat first, and there was no reason to hurry things along until you got here. The boys and I will brew up another batch or two once this one's gone. We've raw ingredients aplenty." He gestured to piles of skinned meat and greens sitting beneath a tree.

She stammered her way through thank yous, decided she sounded pathetic, and shut up.

"We're not feeding you to be kind," Sam informed her, his blue eyes chilly. "We have some decisions to make, and we need all of you in better shape. We may need your magic, and if I'm any judge of things, you had a hell of a time even warming bath water."

She bristled, swallowed a sharp retort, and focused on her feet, mostly to avoid staring at him. No man had any right to look as fetching as this one. "We managed well enough," she muttered and couldn't resist adding, "Ye might not be at your best had ye been hiding out."

"Been there. Done that," he informed her. "Goes with the territory. Do any of you have the healing gift?"

Isla frowned. "Aye. Rowan is quite talented in that regard. Why? Are ye injured?"

"I am." A man with dark red hair pushed to his feet. "My name is Kane. Which of your group is Rowan?"

"The one with long, silver-white hair," Sam spoke up, the corners of his mouth twitching with amusement. "She's already chastised me soundly."

"Aye, 'twould be verra like her. She'll be along soon, and I'm certain she'll help if she can. What manner of ailment?"

Kane smiled crookedly. "An old injury flared when I got tangled in your magic earlier. Because my warding was damaged, one of the sorcerers grazed me with Black Magick. From such a great distance it wasn't enough to be more than an annoyance, but I haven't been able to set things to rights with my own power. Not yet, anyway."

"I heard most of that, lad." Rowan marched to his side and let her hands hover over him. She drew her brows together and touched a spot on his ribcage. "'Tis here." At his nod, she said, "Come with me. I'm thinking this won't take long."

Isla watched them leave and then grabbed the ladle poking out of the pot, stirred, and tasted. Her mouth flooded with saliva. Holding herself back from spooning the stew into her as fast as she could proved a challenge. If she ate too quickly after her enforced fast, it would just come right back up. Besides, what was in the pot needed to be evenly distributed among them.

The other women made their way to the circle, and one of the men she didn't have a name for passed a motley collection of cups and bowls around. For a time, her entire universe narrowed to the bowl clasped between her hands. Activity unfolded around her as the men created a second potful of what turned out to be rabbit stew, urging it to cook faster with an infusion of power. She didn't hesitate when one of the men offered her more. She could always soothe her stomach with magic if it threatened to rebel.

Darkness had long since fallen when Sam got to his feet. "We've eaten and the horses are rested enough to push on. We need to talk about what comes next."

Isla stood too. Feeling suddenly awkward, she inclined her head. "I thanked ye before, but I fear we're not quite done requesting favors. Is there any way to secure transport for us?"

"You can't go home," Sam said flatly.

Isla squared her shoulders, her temper flaring. "As if we hadna figured that out for ourselves. We will need horses or a wagon and team, though. If ye canna help, we'll figure something out."

Kat, Tashia, Rowan, and the other three witches flanked her. "Aye, we'll make our own way," Rowan reiterated. "Feel free to leave, and don't waste a moment worrying about us."

"We moved west on our own," Tashia added with a touch of defiance.

Sam made a chopping motion with one hand. "Fine. You're all wonderfully capable, likely why you ended up trapped in that basement. Hester will have my hide if I don't invite you to travel back to Salt Lake with us. The Coven's relocating there, and you'd find hundreds of witches."

Isla blew out a tight breath. "Ye'll notice we left Coven-land. Some of us joined up at one time or another, but it wasna right for any of us. We canna be bound by all their rules."

"Or by enforcers—like you—ordering us about." Rowan drew herself up to her full five-foot-four-inch height.

A muscle twitched in Sam's square jaw, and Isla felt him gather the subtlest of spells. She planted herself right in front of him. "What ye stated was far more than an *invitation*, which suggests we'd have the choice to tell ye nay. Compulsion willna fix this to your liking."

His eyes flashed blue fire. "And what exactly is *my liking*, madam witch? Before you answer, know that these men—" he swept his arms wide "—and I went to a great deal of trouble, traveling hundreds of miles out of our way, to come to your assistance. I'm not fond of seeing my efforts wasted. Nor do I think it's a good idea for us to ride off and leave the lot of you here without so much as a horse to carry you to someplace farther away from San Francisco."

Isla bit her tongue, waiting. Damn, but he was gorgeous. She could almost imagine those strong, calloused hands running up and down her body. When he didn't say anything else, she quirked a brow. "Are ye quite finished?"

"No. I'm not any happier about this than you are, but the most logical course is traveling to Utah Territory with us. You can regroup there, maybe get help from the Coven."

"Mayhap not," she muttered.

"Either way," he went on doggedly. "At least I'll know I did everything in my power to make certain you're safe."

Kane strode to Sam's side and addressed the women. "We haven't seen the last of that group of dark mages. I'm sure of it. We're stronger together. Witch magic blends with mage power into something more potent than either alone."

"Oh so you liked my healing?" Rowan shot a pointed look his way.

"It was a unique use of drawing on the elements." Kane met her direct gaze. "You leverage power in a different way from Coven witches."

"Which is one of many reasons we're not Coven witches." Isla struggled for a neutral tone, but didn't quite manage it. She glanced at the angle of the moon and figured it was nearly midnight. The other women were looking at her, and she knew they'd follow her lead.

"We'll take this a step at a time." She tilted her chin upward. "I agree 'tisn't safe for us alone without horses. We'll ride with ye for a few more days on one condition."

Sam ground his jaws together. "What?"

"If my sisters and I tell ye we're striking out on our own, ye'll not make any moves—magical or otherwise—to restrict our freedom in any way."

"Agreed." Sam focused his next words on the other enforcers. "Saddle up men. We'll ride through what's left of the night."

Because she was feeling feisty, having just won what appeared to be a major concession from a man far more used to issuing orders than acceding to them, she caught his eye. "And who will we be paired up with this time? Now that there's time to choose and all?"

"Pick whomever you wish," he said with all the warmth of a cornered alley cat and stalked toward where the horses grazed, stopping to shoulder his saddle and tack on the way.

Isla gazed after him, smothering a sense of satisfaction. He might not like her, but she'd gotten under his skin.

Rowan moved to her side. "Sure and you shouldn't bait him," she said very softly.

"'Twas a reasonable question," Isla argued. "He might've wished to rotate which horses carried two."

Rowan closed a hand around her upper arm, her fingers like pincers. "I know you, Isla McIntyre. He interests you."

"What did ye do to heal Kane?" Isla changed the subject. She didn't want to be drawn into a discussion about the confusing welter of feelings Sam stirred in her.

"Simple enough. I neutralized our power that had damaged his shielding and then summoned black earth, mixed with a spot of red, to drive out two shards of Black Magick that had lodged in his aura."

"And?"

"Since when are you so intrigued by healing?"

"Since now." Isla batted irritation aside.

"I waited to make certain his own power could take over and heal everything from there. Come on. Like as not, the men are ready to leave."

"Hold." Isla pried Rowan's hand off her arm. "Do ye agree with traveling with them?"

"Sure and it's the same decision I'd have made. Tonight and for now." Rowan trotted toward the sounds of men and harnesses and the creak of saddle leather.

Isla picked up the pot and various eating utensils, scanning the area to make certain she hadn't missed anything. As she made her way to the horses, she tried to make sense of her attraction to Sam. And couldn't.

He was everything she hated in a man, and one of the reasons the Coven held zero appeal. Sam and his brothers enforced Coven rules and punished miscreant witches, among their other duties. She'd never felt comfortable putting herself in a situation where any man had power over her. Not in that way.

Why does he interest me, then?

Ye'd think I'd be running the other way as hard and as fast as I could.

"Excellent." Cory—or maybe it was Tom, since she hadn't sorted out who was whom yet—scooped the pot and dishes out of her arms. "I was on my way back for these. We're mostly mounted up. Best get moving."

"Damn it!"

"What?" The enforcer who'd collected the pot and dishes, halted.

"My stockings. They're still hanging over a bush. Back verra soon."

She left at a dead run, firing a mage light to illuminate her way. Where in the goddess's name had she left her stockings? And why hadn't she remembered them until now? Usually, she was sharper than that.

They weren't in the first three places she looked, so she stopped and forced herself to reconstruct how she'd entered the clearing. Once she did that, she found them easily and had just snapped them up when a horse and rider bore down on her.

"Get on," Sam snarled. "When I say we're leaving. It means now. Not whenever you get around to feeling like moving your behind."

"I want to ride with someone else," she said with as much dignity as she could muster.

"Too bad. They've all left. I said I'd go back to collect you. Mount up. I'm not asking a third time. I'll just move you where I want with magic."

Seething, she tucked her wet stockings into a pocket in her skirts and stuffed her foot into a stirrup. Sam had moved back onto the horse's withers to make room for her to mount. Once she was in place, he jammed his body into the saddle they shared and kneed his horse.

It took off like a shot, and she pulled magic to keep herself in the saddle. Heat from his body seared her back and thighs. Where he reached around her to hold the reins, his arms brushed the sides of her breasts. He smelled of sweat and magic, of the deepest mysteries and damp, fragrant greenery. Isla couldn't help herself. She inhaled hungrily.

He was aggravating, conceited, and a boor. But something about him touched places in her no man had ever come close to. She wanted to tame him, make him beg for the secret places of her body. The ones where she could bring him to his knees with wanting her.

Since maintaining any kind of distance sharing a saddle was impossible, she leaned into him. His body molded itself to hers, but she sensed his reluctance. And his arousal. The unmistakable bulge of an erect penis prodded her spine. No way to hide something like that. Her nipples hardened and her sex slicked with need. Years had passed since her last dalliance, and she wanted the man curved around her body. Wanted to thread her fingers into his thick, blond hair and pull his face down, so she could devour his chiseled lips.

Her fantasy unfolded, and she mentally licked her way down the stubble on his chin, to his nipples. Would they be pink or copper? Would they pucker into tight buds as she bit and nipped them? Almost as if he divined her thoughts, his cock twitched where it was trapped between their bodies.

The rhythm of the horse fed her hunger and she canted her body slightly, just enough to press her swollen nub more firmly against the saddle. Could she get away with coming and not have him notice?

She wound power about herself, but with the subtlest of strands, and she focused them on her lower body. Meantime, the rocking motion between her legs urged her higher until she didn't care about anything except coming. So what if he chalked her off as a harlot? It wasn't as if they had any kind of future together anyway.

The cock wedged against her tailbone swelled. Maybe her lust was catching, and then she stopped thinking as release ripped through her. She tried not to writhe, but it was a losing battle. At least she managed not to jam a hand between her legs.

Or cry out.

The spasms quieted, and she let go of her spell. Sam still held her between his legs with his tightly muscled arms on either side of her guiding the reins. Hard as ever, his cock prodded her spine, but it was the only evidence of his need. His chest pressed against her back, heat radiating from him.

She debated reaching between them to rub him, but it was ill conceived. There was already bad water under the bridge between them. He might let her bring him to orgasm, but he'd hate her for it afterward. Nay, if he wanted her, he had to make the first move. That he hadn't spoke of iron control.

Or mayhap I've imagined the whole thing, and he doesna want me at all.

Any woman jammed against him would make his flesh rise. 'Tis a simple reaction. Not desire.

A cold edge of reality intruded. She knew less than nothing about Sam Jennings. He might have a witchy wife back in Salt Lake City—or elsewhere. And she'd do well not to make things worse by throwing herself at his head.

CHAPTER 4

Sam felt the change in Isla's body when the stiffness vanished from her back. How could he not, with her all but sitting in his lap? She melted against him, almost as if she'd been born to fit perfectly into his arms. Her breasts firmed where the sides of his arms brushed their lush fullness, and his cock sprang to attention. He tried to subdue it with magic, but he was too late. Once he was already hard, no magic in the world could force his unruly appendage into submission.

He was having a hell of a time not cradling her breasts with his free hand. The one not gripping the reins. And an even bigger struggle not butting his hard on into her back. The laces of his breeches cut into him. Between them, the heat of her body, and the motion of the cantering horse, arousal threatened to swamp him.

He wanted the woman pressed against him with a fierceness that shocked him. She was too independent. Too outspoken. He'd usually been attracted to the more feminine types. Those who had the good sense to wait for a man to make the decisions.

Yeah, and I'm still single after all this time.

Maybe those demure types weren't as overawed by my authority as I thought.

He knew Isla was aroused, but when a climax actually threaded through her, he was so surprised, and so titillated, it took a healthy dose of magic to keep his cock from joining her in release. What? Had she thought he wouldn't notice? Magic spiraled around her as she came. Hot, sexual power that drew him in. And her wonderful scent—musk, wildflowers, and heather—intensified until he bent close to her neck, just breathing her in.

He wanted to draw the horse to a halt, drag her from the saddle, and ruck up her skirts. From there, the lush heat of her body would be his for the taking. Any woman randy enough to push herself into a climax in a strange man's arms surely wouldn't object if he took things a step or two further.

Reality drenched him in a cold blast that stayed his hand before he made an ass out of himself. No matter how fervently he wanted the woman pressed against his chest, acting on his desire was stupid. It would complicate things. They had bigger problems, like catching up to the others. He'd been using his opal-linked power to track them in the dark since they had yet to stumble across any kind of road.

Of course, he hadn't been paying much attention to anything but his raging cock for the last little while. Time to take charge of things. Something he usually did exceptionally well. He'd always prided himself on not being one of those men who let his cock lead him astray. It was how he'd climbed quickly in the enforcer ranks until he was one of their undercover agents. The upper echelon in the enforcer hierarchy. There were never more than an even dozen of them at any one time.

Best hang onto that thought, buddy, a wry inner voice inserted, but it did less than nothing to calm the desire rampaging through him.

He hadn't had a woman since the night before his best friend, Luke, got married. Come to think of it, he hadn't even had his hand in the intervening weeks, and his body had every right to bitch. His balls were overfull.

I can take care of myself later.

With a combination of will power and magic, his erection subsided a little, enough so he could think about something other than ravishing the woman nestled against him. He sent his power thrumming outward, hunting for the others, and caught a faint impression to the northeast.

How had they gotten so far ahead?

Then he felt something from the northwest. Flummoxed, he reined in the horse. It made no sense for the group to have split up, which meant the information from his mage sense was flawed somehow.

"Why are we stopping?" Isla's brogue was softer, less clipped than usual.

"Because I need to pin down where the others are."

"Och aye. And how is it ye doona know?" The caressing murmur departed abruptly, and she sounded like a bitch again.

At least it strengthened his resolve to keep his hands to himself—and deflated his cock.

He felt magic leave her in small, focused jets as she searched for the others, no doubt concentrating on her linkage to the other witches. She made a small, clucking sound of disapproval —or maybe concern—and dug in her skirts, coming up with a round, pink, translucent stone.

"'Tis curious," she said. "I feel them, and then they're gone. Let me try again—with a wee bit of help this time."

Sam stared at the gem she held between two fingers. "That's a power stone."

"Aye. What of it? They used to be much harder to come by, but Hester figured out a way to—"

"I already know about it. Save your breath."

"Ye doona have to sound so out of sorts."

It was true. He didn't, but he'd be damned if he'd apologize. "Let's sort out the current problem." He upped the ante on his gruff and grating voice tone, the one witches kowtowed to. Maybe if he sounded grumpy enough, it would dampen her complaints about him.

Or make them worse.

He levered himself over the back of the saddle and slid to the ground, leaving Isla to dismount on her own, and opened the telepathic connection all enforcers had. Created by blood, it survived damn near anything.

"Tom. Cory. Where are you?"

"The bigger question," Cory's voice sounded almost immediately, *"is where you are."*

Sam hunted for some landmark that might be memorable enough the others would remember passing it, but didn't find much. The trees were ubiquitous, as was the chopped up, rolling terrain. He sent his magic outward again, and the same impossible answer bounced back. Two groups of enforcers, miles apart from one another.

"Can you sense my energy?" he asked.

"Of course." Cory replied, followed by, *"What's wrong?"*

"I have a feeling I'm about to find out. If it's not too much trouble, could you double back here?"

"On our way." Tom's words held a bitten-off quality.

Isla tucked her stone beneath her cloak and turned to face him, her brows drawn together. She still sat atop the stallion. "I doona ken the problem. It seems evil is afoot, yet I canna sense aught. 'Tis possible we're just tired."

Sam shook his head. "That's not it. No reason we should be in any worse shape than anyone else."

"Och, I am tired, and my mind's not as nimble as usual. This must be one of those enchanted fragments that traps wickedness and perverts our power. We dinna move through it quick enough, and so it caught us unawares."

"I've never accepted those old tales as anything beyond the ramblings of superstitious country-dwellers." He avoided rolling his eyes. Was she steeped in fairy stories from her Old Country roots? Worse, did she still believe them?

"Ye shouldna discount them." Isla spoke sternly. "They're the source, the bedrock wickedness springs from. I've seen it often enough in the hills and barrows of Scotland. Even caught a glimpse of the ancient, fey spirits who craft mischief a time or two."

Her voice took on a story-telling quality. "Back in the verra beginnings of the world, 'twas always a tenuous balance between dark and bright forces. Twisted spirits set traps, places where magic dinna work quite right. Those who dinna pay close heed ended up falling into time-traps."

"Did they die?" Sam bit back more questions, wishing he could retract the one he'd just asked. No reason to dignify her fantasy world, make it seem real by pretending it existed.

"Nay, but oftentimes hundreds of years would pass afore they fought their way free. By then, the world had changed, and they no longer had a place within it. 'Twas a disaster for humans since their families were all dead and their houses fallen to ruin."

The horse stamped and whinnied. Sam sent calming energy into its mind and got back into the saddle, working his way around Isla. "I grew up in Austria," he informed her. "And I never once laid eyes on anything like a wicked spirit. Plenty of dark mages, but they started out human."

"Aye, there's the difference. These creatures, wee, misshapen beings, were never human. I heard ye call the others."

"They'll be here soon. I feel them closing. Once they get here, we'll take more care to remain in a unified group."

"We must leave here and join them." Her voice held an urgent note. "I fear if we remain, all of us will be trapped in a place where power bounces back at us, and we'll end up walking in circles."

"Why circles? Because some malevolent spirit wishes us ill?"

"'Tis exactly what I mean. Hurry. I sense my sisters. They're quite close. I led them into one trap. I'm far from anxious to mire them in yet one more."

Sam urged the stallion, who'd become increasingly restive, in the direction he sensed enforcer energy.

"Nay." She placed a hand over the one he had on the reins, and a pleasant electric sensation shot up his arm. "They're more to the left."

Sam had two choices. Alter his course to her specification or keep to his original trajectory. In truth, the two were close enough, it might not matter.

This time.

What about the next time her will tangled with his?

He funneled power through the opal, and took another reading. Sure enough, Isla's guess was closer than his. Or maybe it hadn't been a guess. Whatever energy was dicking with his power apparently didn't influence hers as much.

"I'll not say I'm sorry for helping myself to your thoughts just now." She kept her tone matter-of-fact. "I believe in the Old Ones, the gnomes, the little folk. Because I believe, they doona play me quite so false."

Sam muttered in Gaelic beneath his breath and urged the horse to move faster. He heard the others before they came into view.

"How is it ye know Gaelic?" Isla turned slightly to look at him.

"It's the language of spells. How could I not know it?" he countered, followed by, "There they are."

"Sight for sore eyes, brother," Cory cried, coming into view.

"Yes. What happened to you?" Kane asked. "Funniest thing, but we never knew you were missing until you called us through the link."

"Not so funny as all that," Isla murmured under her breath. "'Tis how they work. They wipe us out of people's memories—if the people aren't wise to their tricks."

At least the sexual tension between them had dissipated. For now.

"We found a road a little way ahead," Tom said.

"Yeah," Roland cut in. "It generally travels northeast, so I think we should chance it. Might peter out into nothing, but it's easier going than weaving through trees and bushes and hoping your horse doesn't catch his foot in a hole and go lame on you."

Sam nodded. "Good call. We'll stick with you."

"What happened?" Cory asked.

"Long story. We can talk about it later," Sam said, not wanting to launch into a whimsical tale about the little people and wicked spirits.

"Good enough for me." Cory, who was riding with Kat, turned his horse around and urged it into a fast trot.

They'd been underway for a while when Isla asked, "So who is Sam Jennings?"

"What's that supposed to mean?" he replied brusquely.

"'Tis simple enough. Tell me about yourself," she responded.

"So far I know ye're one of the Coven's enforcers, that ye're far from young. That ye were born in Austria, and that your mage power is strong."

While he was mulling over how to answer her, since he never shared anything personal with anyone, she began talking again.

"All right, 'tis shy ye are—"

"I am most assuredly not shy," he growled.

"Mayhap not. But ye are stubborn, pigheaded, and far too full of being tough and invincible for your own good."

He opened his mouth to tell her that being *tough and invincible* was what had saved her from death and that he could give a crap less about her opinions, but he closed it with a *clack* before any words escaped. Maybe her idea about doubling up with one of the other men was sound. They could switch next time they stopped.

In the meantime, he'd just have to ride things out, keep his mouth shut, and somehow avoid dragging her head around and kissing those full lips. The memory of her orgasm buffeted him, but he throttled it fast—before his body got any more ideas.

"I'll begin," she went on, apparently oblivious to his tumbling emotions. "I was born on a small island in the Outer Hebrides sometime toward the beginning of the 1500s. I'm not certain of the exact date because we dinna keep track of such things then. I was born into a family of witches, though not all of us had much in the way of power. I was one of the stronger ones, and I was quite full of myself when I was young."

"What a surprise," he muttered, but she elbowed him into silence.

"Doona be rude," she chided. "I'm telling you my life's story. Plague swept through the Highlands, and folk took ship for the Hebrides and other islands close to Scotland's coast. I was around sixteen or seventeen at the time, and I'd seen enough of the Black Death to fear it. Witch magic could prevail, but only if we caught it afore the bleeding began. Problem was oftentimes no one knew they were that ill until blood spouted from everywhere as their vessels ruptured.

"I took to the hills. Farther than I'd ever been afore to a place rumored to be a haven for the Fair Folk, the Sidhe." Isla laughed softly. "I must've taken a wrong turn somewhere because I ended up in one of those time traps. Ye know," she scolded him, "the ones ye doona believe are real."

"How'd you escape?"

"My aunt came hunting for me. She was wise to the ways of the old ones and forged a path for me to follow, but not afore I'd spent nigh onto a week running myself in circles." She paused to draw a breath. "Gave me a healthy respect for evil far older than Black Magick. And it taught me my own power wasna as invincible as I'd always believed."

Sam didn't know if it was her musical voice or her brogue, but he could've listened to her for hours. "Why'd you leave Scotland?"

She shrugged. "Same reason any of us left. Magic—and those of us who wielded it—not only fell out of favor. They hunted us, burned us, hung us, tortured us. Scotland's not a verra big place. It grew harder and harder to hide from the Inquisitors."

"But the Inquisition never reached the British Isles."

"Och aye, but it did. The ones who came after us were indistinguishable from zealots burning us in Spain, France, and Portugal."

Where her body touched his, he felt her shudder. He wanted to tighten his arms around her, reassure her he'd keep her safe— if she'd let him. Instead, he said, "That's one of the reasons the Coven hired men like me. You described us as meting out punishment. More of what we do is keep witches safe from harm. It's why we rode to your aid."

"I never joined the Coven. All I know is hearsay." She hesitated. "I apologize if my information is flawed."

Surprise rippled through him. She'd actually said she was sorry. Before he had a chance to gloat, she picked up her tale.

"'Twas 1795 on the tails of a purge when I caught ship to New York. Half of us in the Hebrides were rounded up and burned, including many in my family line. I dinna see the sense in being next. As ye know, for a while, things were better in the Colonies. So long as I kept a low profile, never mentioned my witchy roots, and helped women in childbed, humans left me alone. I had to move occasionally, to cover my longevity..."

"I can guess the rest," he cut in. "Because I lived it. You moved across the country, hoping each place would provide sanctuary. And each one did."

"Aye, but not for verra long. San Francisco was a safe haven for nigh onto fifty years, and likely would've remained so had it not been for those Russian bastards. Humankind dinna bother overmuch with us anymore. They're far more concerned with slavery and the growing discontent betwixt North and South. Black Magick's been a deeper concern these past few years. I've gone head to head with wraiths and mad wolves a time or two. Even the occasional dark sorcerer, but they're no match for a determined group of witches."

Compassion—mingled with grudging respect—filled him. Isla might be strong-minded, but she wasn't a quitter. Or a coward.

"Your turn." She nudged his arm with an elbow.

Sam took a deep breath. He'd never told anybody much about his life since signing on with the Coven when he'd had to fill out a detailed form covering everything from his birth to his family

—close as well as distant. It had taken him half a day, writing page after page, as the questions kept coming from the mages interviewing him. He'd never written so much either before or since. At one point he'd asked why he couldn't simply tell them, and they'd said each enforcer had a file, sealed with blood and illusion. His information needed to be there, along with everyone else's.

He felt grateful she wasn't pushing. Perhaps she sensed how difficult this was for him. Sam took a deep breath, ordering his thoughts.

"I was born in Austria," he began. "A few leagues outside Vienna, the youngest son of a minor noble. Since I was the fifth son, there was no hope of any land or funds from my family. Mostly fifth sons either joined the military or went into a monastery. Religion never appealed to me, so I signed on with the king's personal guard and moved to Vienna when I was sixteen. I had no inkling I commanded magic—until one day when we were out hunting. A stray arrow was headed right for the king's son.

"To this day, I have no idea how I did this without any knowledge or training, but I sensed the arrow and stopped it with magic. It burst into flames about a foot from the prince's chest."

"I'm presuming they dinna thank you." Isla's voice was soft.

"You'd be right. The event shocked me so much, I was stupid and admitted I was responsible. I'd have been far better off keeping my mouth shut."

"Och aye. What happened next?" Her question thrummed with compassion.

"What else? They dumped me in a prison cell where priests could do battle for my immortal soul."

"Ye escaped."

"You noticed." His attempt to lighten the mood fell flat.

"Aye, and I can guess the rest. Ye couldna return to your family because they'd disowned ye. Where'd ye go?"

Sam swallowed hard, grateful she was making this easier than he imagined by giving voice to parts that still bothered him. Like the letter from his father that had arrived while he was in prison.

"I experimented with my power—now that I knew I had some—in my cell. I was still the son of a nobleman, so they fed me well enough to keep my ability flowing. One night I went out the window, using magic to cushion a fall that would've killed me otherwise. I hunted down others like myself, and eventually I sailed to the Americas."

"Did ye begin in New York?"

"No. My ship was mostly Spaniards, and I ended up in Mexico. Saw a whole lot of country before I came to New York years later and signed on as an enforcer for the Coven."

"Why'd ye pick them?" Her words held genuine curiosity rather than censure.

"It's the largest organized group standing up to Black Magick. I wanted to put my talent where it could do the most good. And at least so far, it's been a solid choice. It's not like the Coven signs you up for life. I can leave anytime. Haven't wanted to." Sam stopped shy of saying it was the first time since his family disowned him that he'd found a level of respect and acceptance. He'd been with the Coven for over a hundred years, and they'd been good ones.

"How'd ye feel once ye realized ye held magic?"

"I hated it. Felt fate had dealt me the lowest of blows. I still don't understand how I ended up with power—unless my father was someone else."

"Not necessarily. Witches' power doesna always flow direct

through bloodlines. I doona suppose ye ever asked your mother about that." She twisted to glance at him.

"How? They never invited me to return home. The authorities didn't try very hard to locate me, but there was a price on my head for years."

"And how do ye feel about your power today?"

A smile tugged at his lips. "I wouldn't have it any other way. It's a part of me."

"See, telling me all that wasna so hard."

"If that's a backhanded way of saying I told you so—"

"'Tisn't. Ye're wound tighter than a watch spring."

"Takes one to know one."

Isla laughed. The warm, musical chimes of her mirth washed over him like a balm. "Look." She pointed dead ahead. "We've ridden though the night. Dawn's breaking."

"So it is." Sam snugged his arms around her. "Thanks for insisting we get to know one another."

"Och, 'twas self-serving on my part. I'm hoping we'll become friends. Ye canna be a friend to someone ye doona know."

Though Sam held silence, he was hoping the same thing. He had a feeling Isla valued her friends, and earning her trust and respect moved to the top of his list. He'd had many female associates, and the odd lover, but never a woman he counted as a friend.

Maybe that was about to change.

CHAPTER 5

Isla tugged her blanket closer. The cold from the ground seeped upward, and the blanket wasn't big enough to arrange both beneath and above herself. Morning wasn't far off, and this was always the coldest part of the night. They'd been on the road for several days and were still headed northeast. Along the way, they'd met up with a horse traders' caravan and bought enough mounts for everyone. It meant they could move faster, but she missed having the hard, rippling muscles of Sam's body curved protectively around her.

They hadn't run into any further problems, and she was beginning to hope they might reach Salt Lake City and Breana Giraud's ranch without further incident. Hoping and getting were two different things, though. It seemed too good to be true, which likely meant things would turn to shit sometime soon. At least she and the other witches had regained their full power. Everybody's clothes still needed washing, but that was the least of their worries, and she counted them fortunate to have escaped with only dirty clothes—and abandoned possessions—to complain about.

Things could've been far worse.

As they often did, her thoughts turned to Sam. He'd been far more pleasant after their shared confidences, and they chatted of this and that over meals. But she wanted him to sweep her against him. Wanted to feel the heat of his need as he wrapped his arms around her and covered her mouth with his. Instead, he treated her much as he did the other men. Like a valued companion. Had he forgotten his engorged shaft pressing into her back that first night?

'Tis my own fault. I was the one who offered up chapter and verse about being friends.

Problem was the better she got to know him, the more she wanted him in her bed. He was a decent man. Earnest, courageous, magically strong. Beyond that, she never tired of looking at him. Sometimes she felt his smoky, blue gaze trained on her when he thought she wasn't looking. It gave her hope. She'd never asked directly about a wife, but he'd never mentioned one, either. None of the men seemed to be paired up. No one ever teased anyone else about missing wives or intendeds.

Rowan, who slept beside her, rolled over. "You're awake."

"Aye, that I am." Isla kept her voice at whisper-level.

"Good, I was wanting to speak with you alone."

Isla's stomach tightened. Had something happened that Rowan was sitting on? Much more awake, and with all thoughts of Sam scattered like grains of sand in a brisk wind, she waited. Rowan couldn't be hurried when she had something to say.

"We're getting closer to the Coven," Rowan began, and then switched to telepathy. *From time to time, I catch distant flashes of their energy.*

"True enough. Why make a point of it?"

"The men have been more than kind. Tom even told me the horses they bought could remain with us."

Isla had known Rowan for nearly a hundred years, and she intuited what was bothering her. *"Ye believe we should leave off well afore we meet up with the Coven."*

"Sure and 'tis exactly what I think."

"Why?" Isla did her damnedest to divorce her reason from her longing for Sam and hear Rowan out with a clear head.

Discomfort radiated from Rowan in waves. *"I told you I left the Coven. The plain truth of things is they threw me out. I'd been warned, but I thought their rules were stupid, and I broke one too many of them."* She made a clicking sound, tongue against teeth. *"'Twas nigh onto a hundred twenty years back, but many witches have long memories. They'll not welcome me. Once that group is done with a witch, she's banished forever."*

"Mayhap things have changed."

"More likely not, and I'm not willing to deal with the unpleasantness. If you and the others want to continue, I understand. But I'm not coming with you."

"Hester would speak for ye." Isla was grasping at straws, but she loved Rowan like a mother. Their magic was strong together, and she didn't want to be separated from her. Never mind it was far from safe for the older witch to strike out on her own.

"Aye, Hester would speak for me, but I won't put her in that position." Breath rattled softly through Rowan's teeth. *"Sure and 'tis more than that. Even if they reinstated me, or accepted me on some sort of probationary status, I'm too old and too set in my ways to kowtow to some young, upstart witch keeping her eyes on me, just waiting for me to slip up so she can run and tattle."*

"Was it truly that bad?"

"For me, aye." Rowan shook her head. *"I never fully understood why 'twas harder for me than the others."*

Isla bent close and laid her mouth next to Rowan's ear. "Promise me not to do anything rash. Please. 'Tisn't a decision that must be made betwixt now and the dawn."

"But I must make it soon. You shouldn't worry about me. I was on my own for years before our group formed in Yerba Buena."

"Ye mean, afore Hester searched us out and drew us together."

"Aye. Whatever."

"Are ye willing to tell me what ye did? Why they banished you?"

"I helped a witch escape the man she was married to. She hated him and came to me, so desperate she was on the verge of ending her own life. Between the two of us, I crafted illusion that gave her a wee bit of time to catch a ship leaving with the outgoing tide."

Isla chewed her lower lip, thinking. "Surely there must've been more to it than that."

Rowan's mouth twisted into an unpleasant expression, like she'd bitten into rotten fruit. "The father was one of the first enforcers, and highly placed in Coven affairs. He considered her his property. Even worse, she was pregnant, and he wanted the child."

Isla hugged her friend. "I'm sorry. 'Twasn't fair."

"Much in this life isn't. Kat and Tashia left with me on account of they thought I'd been dealt a raw hand."

"Do ye mind if I talk with Sam about this?"

"Aye, I mind. This discussion was private. Between you and me."

"I'll honor your wishes."

"See that you do." Rowan's whisper took on sharp edges. "I

know you're fond of him, but at the end of things, he's an enforcer afore all else, and you'd do well not to forget it."

Isla searched for something to say, but Rowan shook her head. "I'm getting up. I'll start the cook fire and get something going to break our fast." She rolled to her feet and picked up her blanket, draping it around her shoulders for added warmth.

Isla watched her go. She'd often wondered what went awry between Rowan and the Coven.

And now I know.

Hester must've known, since she knew damn near everything that was Coven related. That she'd included Rowan in their small group told Isla she hadn't agreed with the other witch's treatment. If Hester believed Rowan deserved another chance, it might go a long way toward paving a new path.

Drawing her power stone from beneath her clothing, she focused her magic and called Hester. They were close enough, she scarcely needed the stone, but it did make things easier. Her conscience pricked her. Rowan hadn't exactly sworn her to secrecy, but she had said their conversation was private.

"Aye, what are ye wanting?" Hester's voice, blurry from sleep filled Isla's mind.

Isla switched to Gaelic to reply. *"How can we clear Rowan's name?"*

Hester's reply came in Gaelic far more ancient than Isla's own. *"Och aye, and I was worried that might rear its nasty head."*

"Is there aught ye can do?"

"Does she know ye're talking with me?"

A muted snort. *"Of course not. She'd never condone it."*

"I figured as much. Let me think on this. Ye'll meet up with us in three days' time, give or take."

"Maybe." Isla fisted her hands. *"She says she's leaving well afore we*

join you. If she goes, I'll go with her. I canna let her leave all alone. Not with evil about. 'Tis been strangely quiet since we fled San Francisco, but I doona trust that. Our enemies are out there waiting, biding their time."

"Doona make any decisions afore I speak with you again."

"I canna promise. It depends what Rowan does."

Silence thickened between them, but Isla sensed the other witch's energy, so she waited and watched the sky lighten along the eastern horizon. Soon everyone would be up and moving. She had to have this conversation over and done with well before that happened.

Hester's thick brogue blasted into her mind. *"I'll leave the wagon train, along with Aethelred, as soon as we can saddle horses. We should be able to intercept you by sunset."*

"Who's Aethelred? And how can ye move so quickly? I dinna figure we'd be to our destination for a good three days."

"No time, Isla. I'll answer you over dinner."

Isla's gem stopped glowing, and she knew Hester had severed their link. She couldn't help the grin that spread across her face. There was something imperious about Hester. She was old, crusty, and opinionated. And used to others jumping to her bidding. In spite of all those things, she was impossible not to like.

Och aye, should I tell Sam?

I damn near have to. The question is how I tell him. And how much.

Talking with Hester had been a gray zone. Rowan hadn't specifically forbidden her to do that, but she'd definitely said not to talk with Sam. Isla unclenched her fists, flexing her fingers. When the answer came, her grin broadened. She'd tell Sam that Hester and this Aethelred person, whoever he was, were on their way. No need for further explanations.

She and Sam often rode side by side. She'd wait until they were underway and casually let him know they'd have company by evening. The more she thought about it, the more confidence she had that she could pull it off without saying one word about Rowan and her shared confidence.

SAM FELT PLEASED when Isla pulled her mare alongside him. He always liked it when she sought him out, but he'd been very careful to be nothing but respectful toward her. Christ! It was so hard not to act on the attraction that turned his blood to white-hot lust, but he didn't want to give her cause to shun him. They'd gotten off to a rocky beginning, and he didn't want to risk something that would set off her temper—again. It seemed unlikely she had a man stashed somewhere, but she might.

He missed riding with her, but he'd been very careful to keep his cock in check. No more spontaneous erections—except when he lay in his blankets and thought about her every night. His hand had found its way to his crotch then—and more than once. He figured coming might make it easier to subdue his unruly appendage with magic the rest of the time. And he'd been right, but it didn't make him want her any less.

She smiled, and her dark blue eyes crinkled at the corners. Strands of black hair fell around her face, making him itch to smooth them out of the way—so he could run his lips down the pronounced line of her cheekbones, tasting every crevice with his tongue. The unruly appendage in question swelled inside his breeches, and he dragged his mind to something else. Fast.

"And a verra good morning," she said.

"The same to you, Isla." It was impossible not to smile back.

"I had a wee spot of news afore I woke. Hester reached out and told me she and someone named Aethelred will be joining us by late tonight."

Sam frowned. Something a shade too nonchalant flirted beneath Isla's words. "Is all well with the wagon train?"

"I believe so."

"Then why aren't she and Aethelred remaining with the rest of the group?"

"I'm sure I doona have an answer for that." Isla shrugged. "I wanted to make certain ye knew, though. So 'twasn't a surprise when they rode up."

Sam rolled questions around in his head, certain he hadn't heard everything, but equally certain Isla wouldn't be particularly forthcoming about further details. Witches could be quite close-mouthed when they chose, and no amount of prodding from an enforcer made much difference.

"What happens once we reach Salt Lake and the ranch ye told us about?" Isla continued brightly. "Surely there's not enough space there for the whole of the Coven's wagon train. Unless it's a verra big ranch."

"I expect they'll spread out through the valley where Breana and her late husband built their homestead." He answered automatically, his mind still churning as he tried to figure out the real reason Hester would alter her plans.

They rode in silence for long moments. At last, Sam made up his mind and gave voice to his thoughts. "I've known Hester Thorne for a long time. It's not like her to do anything that isn't well thought out."

"My take on her as well." Isla smiled blandly.

"There's more to this than you've told me," Sam hurried on. "I respect if there's some witchy confidence you don't wish to break..."

"Aye. That would be close to the mark." When she turned her gaze on him this time, all artifice had slipped away. "I've told ye what I can. The rest will have to wait until Hester shows up. Do ye know who Aethelred is?"

"Thank you for not lying."

Isla bristled. "I never lie. I may twist the truth a bit from time to time, but—"

"Poor choice of words on my part," Sam cut in. "I was trying to tell you I was grateful you trusted me enough to tell me that you couldn't share anything further." He inhaled sharply. "Aethelred is the mage who trained Luke. Beyond that, I don't know much."

"Who's Luke?"

"Another enforcer. He and I work closely together. He's who married Hester's granddaughter, Abigail."

A soft smile curved Isla's lips. "Och aye, that Luke. We met him and Abigail when they came to visit Hester, just afore Michael died."

Sam nodded. "After they left San Francisco, Luke and Abigail went to visit Aethelred on the eastern coast, somewhere near Boston. The old mage took over raising Luke after wraiths killed his parents and sister—and taught him magic. He'd been by himself since Luke moved away twenty years and more back. I'm not sure whose idea it was for him to relocate west, but I guess he wanted to make a new start of things."

Isla drew her dark brows together in thought. "Hester doesna throw her lot in with others easily. It says a lot that she's riding with him."

Sam opened his mouth to reply, when the unmistakable stench of rotten meat wafted close, drawn by a brisk morning breeze.

"Damn my eyes if it isna wraiths," Isla kneed her horse, clearly intent on catching up with the others strung along half a mile of trail.

Sam galloped after her and raised his mind voice to warn the other enforcers.

"Find what cover you can. Isla and I will join you. Battle formation."

"What's after you?" Cory's voice carried excitement that made Sam smile. Things had been a wee bit dull since their frantic dash away from San Francisco's shoreline.

"Wraiths." Sam shot back.

"Where there are wraiths, mad wolves are never far. Or their masters." Kane sounded pleased as well.

Sam snorted. What a bloodlusty crew enforcers were. Made a man proud to be part of a group like that. Dust rose around him as he rode hard to join the others. He caught up to Isla, pacing her, protecting her with magic.

"They're drawing closer," she called. "I was just thinking this morning that things had been a wee bit too quiet. 'Tis almost a relief they've shown themselves."

Privately, Sam agreed. He'd sensed evil at the barest edges of things for several days, but never near enough to put his finger on an exact location. "We'll be ready for them. I alerted the others." Reaching with his power, he felt the thrum of enforcer energy and angled toward it.

"Aye, I can feel where my witches are too." Isla bared her teeth and shook a fist at the wind. "Dark bastards, one and all. I willna rest until the lot of ye are well and truly dead."

Admiration filled Sam. This was one woman who wouldn't let fear get in her way. But then he already knew that about her. Dust that had nothing to do with their horses closed around them, followed by the howling of a pack of mad wolves.

Sam didn't wait for them to appear. He sent power zinging in a wide arc and was rewarded with screeches, howls, and the coppery reek of spilled blood.

A glowing nimbus surrounded Isla, and white-tinged flame flew from her fingertips. She'd drawn her power stone out and it shone with a stark inner light, suspended from a length of leather about her neck. Gaelic curses flew from her, forming spells that pushed her magic into the dead center of a river of Black Magick rolling their way.

He judged the distance between them and where the others were. They might make it to the other enforcers and witches, but it would be a close call. Power stones were new to him, but they built off each other. He focused magic through his opal, instructing it to join Isla's. Almost as if the stone understood what he needed, a shining corona flowed toward Isla's stone. Where the two met, brightness exploded just in time to meet the first line of mad wolves pelting toward them.

Mouths open, fangs gleaming in the pale midmorning sun, wolves rushed them. Hundreds converged, with wraiths mixed into the bunch. He had no idea how many he'd killed before he could see them, but he hadn't made much of a dent.

The force of his and Isla's combined magic tossed the first line of wolves into the air. With howls and screams, they plummeted directly into the snapping jaws of their snarling companions, who were more than willing to eat them.

Recognizing they'd just bought a break, Sam yelled. "Whip that horse, and run like hell. We're going to make it to where the others are. Then we'll regroup."

Her eyes on fire with bloodlust, Isla stood in her stirrups, death flashing through her raised hands. Damn but she was the most gorgeous sight he'd ever seen with her hair whipping like one of the ancient Furies. For a moment, he was afraid she'd tell him to go to hell, but she jerked her chin tersely in acknowledgment and urged her horse toward the collection of boulders and scrub oak where the others had taken cover.

CHAPTER 6

Isla reined in her magic with difficulty. Killing evil held fascination, and once she began, she wanted to keep right on slinging power until the last dark creature lay dead at her feet. The pink moonstone thrummed hotly against her chest, glowing. She assumed it played a key role urging her on. Forged by wild magic in the Old Country, the gem had been with her forever. She'd only realized its full potential once Hester perfected a gear-driven mechanism that allowed it to hold far more power.

A brazier powered by enchantment pumped steam to force a series of gears into motion. Once turning, they concentrated power into gemstones and recharged them when they grew depleted. She'd already been paired with the moonstone, but Hester's machine also linked mages or witches with gems. Not every gem worked for every magic wielder, so the system required a fine hand and a close eye.

Her horse's hooves churned beneath her, drawing her closer to the relative safety she and Sam would have in numbers. Though his stallion was faster, he rode behind her, and she felt the curtain of his power shielding her from behind. The snarls, growls, and yelps of the pack feeding on itself filled her with cold joy.

What manner of things ate their own? Nothing that deserved to live. That was certain.

She was breathing hard when they rode behind a group of enormous boulders shielding the others from sight. The land had necked into a narrow canyon, so their position would either be defensible, or turn into a trap with no exit. She'd never been here before and had no idea which it would be as she slid from her horse and slapped its rump to send it where the other animals milled about.

Magic kept the mounts from leaving, or they'd have been gone.

Sam was on the ground too, surrounded by enforcers and speaking in low, urgent tones. He turned and motioned the witches over. "Here's the plan. The men and I will shoot what we can. Our bullets are laced with silver and iron, so they'll kill anything evil. We'll switch to magic after we run out of ammo."

"And what role will we play in this plan of yours?" Isla raised a challenging brow.

"Letting us keep you safe," Kane said sternly. "It's what enforcers do. We protect witches."

"Coven witches." Rowan set her lips in a harsh line. "We're not your responsibility."

"If one of you women does something stupid, and we have to rescue you, this could become far more complicated very fast," Cory said. "Better for you to remain back here, behind the rocks. If we fuck this up totally, you can give the dark any kind of hell you want."

He grinned rakishly, and Isla wanted to slap him.

She squared her shoulders. "Ye're nine. We're seven. Ye'd

damn near double your forces if we all worked in concert. 'Tis a narrow-minded commander who ignores a chance to put every able-bodied person to work."

Sam looked away from her unflinching gaze.

She felt bad for him—trapped between how he'd always done things and pressure to rethink his strategy—but not bad enough to back down.

"Aw shit, if they want to fight so bad, let 'em," Roland snapped.

Sam clacked his jaws shut. "Move out. Witches form a band in the middle. Just stay out of the way of our bullets."

"Ye doona have to worry about that. None of us has a death wish." Isla wanted to thank him, but it could hold until later. Wolves pounded toward them, and wraith stench grew stronger, twisting her stomach with nausea.

The men raced from behind their impromptu hiding place, and the ring of gunfire filled the air. The stink of brimstone, sulfur, and ozone intensified and mingled with gunpowder. A wraith ran toward them, skirting in from the side of the boulders. Its smoke-colored eyes stabbed them with hatred.

Isla summoned a jolt of power that sliced the creature from stem to stern. Turned into a smoking ruin, it folded in on itself and vanished. She spun in a slow circle, searching for more of the abominations, but not finding any.

Rowan grabbed her arm and gestured to the other women. "Come on. No point waiting for any more of them to breach the fortress. Join our power through the stones. Let's get out there where the men are and mow our way through those Black Magick sons of bitches."

Adrenaline surged, leaving a bitter taste in Isla's mouth. Standing strong and fighting beat hiding out in that dank cellar hands down. She'd kicked herself for them getting stuck there, but at the time it never occurred to her there wouldn't be a way out.

Rowan's gem was lapis, and it flamed a deep, pure blue. Kat, Tashia, and the others stood shoulder to shoulder, stones held before them as one kindled off the next. When everyone's ignited, releasing its potential, they stepped from behind the rocks. The men had left a space for them in the middle of their formation.

Bullets sprayed from their guns, and they covered whoever was reloading their weapon. Piles of mad wolves formed on the dusty ground, but more kept coming. Like an evil overlord had loosed an endless legion against them. The once-clear day grew gloomy and ominous, and expended magic darkened the sky, blotting out the sun.

Isla began a chant to time their efforts. The other witches raised their voices to join her. Power blazed from their hands creating pure, white light that cut through wickedness. Hester had designed her machine to seek out and destroy Black Magick. Primed by its energy, the stones came very close to working independently, targeting and killing.

The wolves were thinning out, and Isla started to believe they might win this round when a wrenching, tearing sound nearly deafened her. Demons poured from a rent in the earth. She blinked, disbelieving. Surely her small band of witches wasn't important enough to send this much firepower after them. Enormous black leech-like creatures crawled out of the hole right along with the demons. They weren't moving very fast, and she figured she could ignore them.

"Whatever you do, do not crush the worms," Cory shouted in her direction. "They harbor deadly poison."

Tashia rolled her eyes. "Isn't that just great? Black Magick found a whole new weapon."

"They must not be new," Isla countered, "since the men already know about them." She ducked to avoid a blast of black flames. It missed her by scant inches, and a nearby scrub oak burst into an unnatural inferno, smoking, smoldering, and stinking of brimstone.

"Focus!" Rowan screeched. "Their numbers are limitless. Ours aren't."

Isla dragged power from what felt like an increasingly reluctant earth. Maybe they were asking too much of it, but they didn't have a choice. She mixed in more air. It would dilute their spells, but maybe their magic would last longer. Both she and Rowan were skilled water workers, but they were miles from a body of water big enough to help.

Warmth rose through her feet, and she focused it through her pink moonstone. From there, the energy joined with the other witches' and blasted their enemy. It seemed to stun the demons, but it didn't stop them.

Neither did the men's bullets.

Nearly seven feet tall, demons converged on them, their red and black scales gleaming dully. Horns graced their foreheads. Fire shot from clawed hands and small, close-set eyes. Some of the abominations had three eyes evenly spaced across their foreheads. Tails swished behind them, reminiscent of cats on the prowl.

One minute they were grappling to escape the hole that spawned them. The next they were on their feet, racing nimbly forward. Isla targeted the nearest one, focusing every shred of power at her disposal. At first she was afraid it wouldn't be enough, but she whirled in a tight circle to concentrate her efforts and loosed more darts of magic.

A rent opened in the thing's chest, spewing black ichor. She felt like cheering, but couldn't spare the energy. Rowan pummeled the thing with her particular brand of destruction, and its chest opened further, splitting from just beneath its chin to its stomach. Entrails spilled out, red and glistening.

One of the foot-long leeches scuttled forward and began eating a length of intestine. The demon shrieked at it in demonspeak, and kicked the thing, but it oozed black blood with the sharp stink of poison.

Isla never stopped hurling bolts of destruction, but she watched as contact with the leech's poison paralyzed the demon. It toppled to the ground with a *thud* she heard even over the din of battle. Too bad they couldn't harness the leeches and redirect their focus. Despite showing up with the demons, they clearly didn't hold any allegiance toward them.

Probably doona have enough brainpower to be loyal to aught but themselves, she thought grimly.

"Sam! Do any of ye hold the ability to sway animals?" she shouted.

His head snapped around. "Not me."

"I do." Roland sidled toward her, still firing his pistols at the demons. While the silver and iron didn't always kill them, at least it kept them at bay. Eventually, the men would run out of ammunition, though.

Isla leaned toward him and switched to mind speech. *"All of ye, listen up. Focus on those leeches. Propose they attack the demons. Plant ideas. Suggest the demons are easy pickings, low-hanging fruit. If each leech singles out one—just one—'twill give them food for days, mayhap weeks."*

"What makes you think they'll turn on their masters?" Sam asked.

Isla jerked her chin toward the leech cozied up in the fallen demon's intestines. *"We may have opened the thing's chest, but once we did, the leech was there in a flash, taking advantage. If the demons controlled them, 'twould never have happened."*

"Good point," Roland muttered and focused on the mass of wraiths, demons, leeches, and the occasional wolf still snarling at them. *"I count maybe twenty-five demons and over a hundred leeches. It's anyone's guess how the wolves and wraiths will react if the leeches attack."*

Isla conserved power and switched back to speaking. "Wolves will join the carnage—like as not. Plenty of leeches to do the trick—assuming it works."

"Yeah, plenty of leeches, but only if we're smart about this," Roland countered. *"We have to turn them as a herd, not one by one. How about you women? How many beyond Isla can bend animals to your will?"* A wolf lunged from the pack straight for him, but a well-timed blast from his pistol stopped it in midair, and it tumbled heavily to the ground a foot in front of them.

"Rowan, Kat, and I have that talent," Isla replied.

Roland nodded sharply. "That makes five of us since Kane shares the gift."

Isla ground her teeth together. It would remove a third of them from the battle for a short time. "What do ye think?" she asked Sam. "Can ye spare that many for a few minutes?"

He narrowed his blue eyes to slits. "Make it happen. We have to do something, and I'm fresh out of ideas, and we still haven't identified the dark sorcerers driving this charade."

"Cravens." Isla spat on the ground. "They're afraid to show themselves." She gestured to Rowan and Kat, and the three witches arranged themselves around Roland.

Kane made his way in from the far end of their line. "I heard the plan." He switched to telepathy. *"Let's use the compulsion spell but with more air and the Gaelic for Wyrms. Surely the leeches will be flattered to hear themselves likened to dragonkind."*

"And not smart enough to recognize we're manipulating them." Roland made a noise between a snort and a grunt.

Isla exchanged glances with Kat and Rowan.

"Aye," Rowan said. "Let's go."

"Agreed." Kat shoved dirty fingers through her hair to get it out of her face.

"To me," Sam raised his voice, and the other seven enforcers and four witches sidled toward him, refocusing how they blended power.

Isla didn't hesitate. With her fingers outstretched, she raised her voice to begin the incantation. Different power flowed through her as the compulsion spell gained momentum. It wasn't any easier to maintain than lethal energy, but at least it had a different feel about it. The break jolted her out of her horror at the carnage that lay around them.

She hated the dark. Wanted every single Black Magick creature deader than dead, but witches dealt in life. In healing and nurturing living creatures. To be part of ongoing bloodshed held a macabre fascination but took its toll.

The collective hum from their incantation shot forward, blanketing the field a foot above rock-studded dirt with encouragement, prompting. The demons didn't pay any attention to it. Maybe because it wasn't focused on them. Maybe because it wasn't killing anything.

An idea blossomed and Isla shouted, *"Add the wolves,"* in shielded mind speech.

A rough grin split Roland's austere features. "I should've thought of that. Doesn't take one whit more energy."

The moonstone grew hot where it nestled on her chest. So hot, the fabric beneath it began to smoke. Isla ignored it and kept funneling power into their spell. The air grew thicker with the stench of smoke and expended power. Her eyes burned. So did her lungs.

They had one chance at this. If it didn't work, none of them would have enough magic left to start over. Or if they did, their second attempt wouldn't have nearly the punch of this one, and they'd be better off switching back to killing. She eyed the leeches, crawling lazily in their direction as if they hadn't a care in the world. Certainly as if they weren't transiting a field of fallen wolves with the occasional demon. For some reason, the wolves didn't interest them. Perhaps they weren't sufficiently steeped in evil to tempt the creatures.

Roland nudged her and stopped chanting long enough to hiss, "Isn't working."

"Give it a little more," she pleaded.

"If we give it much more, none of us will have enough juice left to help when they close in to finish us off," Kane muttered.

To the left of them, Sam marshaled his small force. They worked in pairs, spelling one another. It was a wise strategy because it allowed brief spurts for everyone's power to recover. Magic burst from them, bright against the black flames churning from the demons.

Isla reached a hand to Kane and Roland. The women joined the line. Touching would augment their efforts. Heedless of running her well dry, Isla gave it everything she had.

Turn! she exhorted silently, feeling like a lightning rod as magic scoured her, picking her bones clean.

Their working reached critical mass. They couldn't maintain it for much longer. It would burn them all to cinders. Roland caught her eye and shook his head.

Movement snatched her gaze from his. The leeches twisted in one, long, sinuous wave and latched onto the demon nearest them. The few remaining wolves did the same, ending up in a wrestling match with leeches who'd chosen the same demon.

The demons bellowed in rage, spewing fire at their attackers, but the leeches glommed onto their scales, apparently boring through the tough plates with ease. Demon fire didn't harm them, but it blew the wolves to bits.

Isla panted hard, blowing air like a bellows. "Goddess be praised," she cried. "'Tis done."

Roland slapped her on the back. "Damn! I was almost certain we were doomed."

"Out of here!" Sam ordered. "Now. We bought time. Let's use it to our advantage."

Isla joined the group as they bolted for their horses, jumped astride, and galloped for all they were worth. Laying a hand over the moonstone, she thanked it. The scene playing out on the field flashed through her mind. Fell creatures at other fell creatures' throats. It was the best way to rid themselves of evil. Part of her wanted to remain, to make certain nothing walked away alive, but Sam was right to get them moving.

She hunted for his energy and spurred her mount to his side. "Where are we headed?"

He flashed a grin her way. "Brilliant plan. I had my doubts when it took so long to play out, but you've the makings of a strong tactician."

Isla snorted. "Thank ye kindly, Coven enforcer, sir. Ye dinna answer my question."

"We're moving high into the mountains. It's where we were headed anyway and where Hester will expect us to be."

Isla sucked in a thoughtful breath. She hadn't forgotten about Hester, not exactly, but it brought the problem with Rowan back front and center.

"What?" Sam quirked a brow.

"Nothing. I'm just grateful we got away. Do ye believe they'll follow us?"

"Of course, but not right away. Your compulsion spell will fade without the five of you driving it, but it'll last long enough to do a hell of a lot of damage. We never did figure out who was behind today's attack."

"Och aye, that's right. The cowards never showed themselves."

Nodding slowly, Sam squared his shoulders. "If anyone comes after us, it'll be them."

She thought about it. "Not likely. They hid behind their minions today."

"Which means they can find new minions to shield them." He hesitated and inhaled sharply, blowing the breath out. "If it's one thing I've learned in this business, it's not to get too far ahead of things. For now, we'll focus on traveling to a place I know in these mountains. It's defensible and will give us time to recharge our magic."

"With Hester and Aethelred added to our ranks, 'twill give us two more to fight."

His smile broadened. "You're beginning to sound downright feral. Sure you weren't a warrior in a previous life?"

Pleasure at the unexpected compliment warmed her cheeks. "Nay, but I've fought my share of battles. I hate dark sorcery as much as any of ye."

Something unreadable flashed behind his eyes, but was gone before she could interpret it. "Bear left at the next choice point," he instructed. "I need to check in with Kane and Roland."

Isla watched him leave. He'd been on the verge of telling her something, but had stopped himself. What was it?

Och, so now I'm a silly lass wanting more compliments?

She tossed her head in irritation. Better to focus on the problem with Rowan. It hadn't gone away. The other witch was as good as her word, and she'd said she was leaving before they got anywhere near the Coven wagon train and its occupants.

No matter how Isla felt about Sam, she'd have to go with

Rowan if she struck out on her own. Today proved how unsafe it was for any of them, even in a group of other magic wielders. By herself, Rowan would have no chance at all. Dark sorcery would label her easy plunder and move in for the kill.

Nay. If she goes, I'll have no choice but to go with her. Otherwise, how could I live with myself?

CHAPTER 7

Sam didn't really need to talk with the other enforcers, but he'd almost slithered into dangerous territory. Emotional territory. A place he shouldn't go, especially not now when he needed every single one of his faculties running at a hundred ten percent.

He'd nearly blurted out that Isla had looked like a goddess, numinous and glowing, with power cascading through her, surrounded by her long, dark hair. Her gambit with the leeches had been little shy of magnificent, so he'd focused on making sure she knew he appreciated her reasoning powers. He'd done a fair job steering clear of the rest, until toward the end of their conversation, when he almost slipped up. The mental image of her, standing with raised arms, her moonstone glowing like a beacon, pummeled him. It was a struggle not to wheel his horse around, ride back to her, and sweep her into his arms.

"What's up?" Cory glanced at Sam as he rode abreast.

"Enjoying the breather." Sam grinned.

"No kidding. Those bastards materialized out of nowhere."

Cory shook his head. "Kind of gives you pause. Not much shocks me, but they did. Usually, there's more warning than that."

Sam didn't want an instant replay. They'd kick what had happened today around once they camped for the night. "What do you think about the cave near the Sierra crest as a stopping place for tonight?"

"Plenty defensible, but it's probably still snowed in. Horses might not do very well."

They'd taken the Central Overland Trail route west to Carson City, then switched to another leading to San Francisco. Because it was well traveled, the snow had been tramped down —or pushed to the sides—through the mountainous segments.

"Crap! Hadn't considered that," Sam replied. "I've been keeping us on side roads, hoping to avoid what we just met head on. A confrontation with Black Magick."

"Didn't work very well, did it, brother?" Cory made a sound between a grunt and a groan.

"Nope." Sam sent his mage senses wide, determining where they were in juxtaposition to their route west, and drew his mount to a halt. The others gathered around him.

"Why are we stopping?" Rowan demanded. "Sure and you're not thinking we've enough distance betwixt us and our enemy."

Sam snorted. He was used to Coven witches. While they may have formulated opinions about enforcer strategies, they mostly held their tongues—until they were by themselves. "We're stopping because Cory pointed out something I should've thought about. My original plan for camping tonight is likely under a few feet of snow. These horses aren't roughshod, and they couldn't manage."

"What's your second choice?" Kane spoke up.

"Our only real choice is to return to the Central Overland Trail. It's not much more than one day's ride to the north of us. I stopped to make certain everybody knew our goal, in case anyone gets separated. Easy enough to do when there's not a track to follow."

"There's the southern route around the Sierras," Tom broke in. "That'd be snow free, but about a week longer."

"No good. Sooner we meet up with the rest of the Coven, the safer we'll be," Sam replied.

"Yeah, we may have won today's skirmish, but we haven't seen the last of those bastards," Roland grumbled.

"No, we haven't," Sam agreed. "By the way, Hester and Aethelred are joining us sometime this evening—"

"When did that plan happen?" Rowan spoke over him, but her gaze augured into Isla.

"Hester reached out to me telepathically early this morning. Told me she was riding out to meet us," Isla said. Something about her words, the rhythm or cadence or something, felt off to Sam and he focused his magic to listen more intently.

"Early this morning, you say? I'm thinking 'tis a shade too convenient," Rowan grunted. "You didn't by any chance instigate the conversation?" Her shrewd, brown eyes never left Isla's face, and Sam felt a truth spell fall between the witches.

"Hester is our friend," Isla pointed out, sounding defensive as hell. "If 'tweren't for her, we'd still be stuck in that basement on the wharf."

"You didn't answer me," Rowan persisted.

"Aye, and I'm not going to." Isla swung her attention to Sam. "We need to get going."

"Who's Aethelred?" Kane asked. "Not a name I'm familiar with."

"The mage who raised Luke Caulfield," Sam replied. "You'll remember Luke. I'm sure you've worked with him before."

Kane nodded. "That I have. Good man. Solid."

Sam glanced from Isla to Rowan. Something was amiss between the two women since they were looking daggers at one another. Or Rowan's gaze held daggers; Isla's was more pleading than angry. Whatever it was had to do with Hester, but he'd be damned if he could figure it out.

He cleared his throat. "We're moving north northeast. Compass bearing roughly twenty to thirty degrees. I want to make certain to hit the beaten track before we're fully in the mountains. We'll go through some rough terrain, but it'll get worse on the far side of Carson City. At least by then, we'll have the Central Overland beneath our hooves."

He wanted to drill down, figure out what was going on with the witches, but the group really did need to put more distance between themselves and the place they'd battled the dark. He settled his horse into an easy lope. Cory paced him on one side, Tom on the other. The other enforcers and all the witches fanned behind him. He made certain they were all on the move before he shifted his attention ahead of them.

"What do you suppose that was all about?" Cory spoke into his mind, using the enforcers' shielded telepathy.

"I have a feeling we'll find out," Tom chimed in. Even his mind voice was dour. *"Witches have hot tempers. They need us to keep them focused on the important stuff."*

"Better not even breathe that thought with this group," Sam cautioned. *"If you were to ask them, they'd tell you they were getting along just fine without us, thank you very much."*

He glanced at the angle of the sun. Somehow it had gotten to be the middle of the afternoon. In another three hours, it would be full dark. They could ride through the night on a track. Cross-country travel was harder since they'd have to power mage lights so the horses didn't stumble and end up lame. Mage lights drew magic, and were like painting a glowing arrow announcing their position.

Probably not the best of ideas, given what had already happened today.

"Do any of you know this country?" he asked the other enforcers.

"Sure do," Kane said. "There's a defensible position maybe four hours' ride from here with water for us and the horses."

"Anything closer?" Cory asked. "It'll be dark by then, and there won't be a moon until past midnight."

Kane shrugged. "We can stop most anywhere there's a creek, but this place is on top of a knoll. It has a cliff on two sides, so it's easy to defend." He drew his brows together. "I might be able to find an Indian trail leading to it. Let me work on that."

Magic flared from him, and he pulled in front of Sam, taking over the lead.

Magic pulsed from the group of witches. Sam figured they were talking with one another, but when he tried to listen in, he ran smack into impenetrable wards. Smothering wry laughter, he urged his horse after the enforcers who'd drawn ahead. He'd figure out soon enough what the hell was going on.

For now, he cleared his mind and linked to his opal, hoping it would hasten the recovery of his depleted magic. Miles clicked by under his horse's hooves. From ahead, Kane fist pumped the air, and Sam saw a faint pathway winding through rock-studded dirt. Trees grew more thickly as they moved farther east, and the sky was clouding up. The air felt heavy with the promise of rain, or maybe even a thunderstorm, but the going was easier since the horses could follow the track without constant guidance.

He didn't worry about Hester being able to find them. Their magic would draw her like a lodestone. What did concern him, though, was what she wanted. He'd bet Isla had called her, with the help of her moonstone. Whatever she'd told Hester had galvanized her into action. That Hester hadn't felt comfortable waiting the few days until they met up naturally spoke volumes.

Sam nodded to himself. He was sure he was on the right track. In Hester's mind, the summons qualified as an emergency, one she was willing to go out of her way to meet head on. Sam focused a thread of power at the group of seven witches riding in twos and threes. They weren't conversing any more, but Rowan's expression could've curdled milk.

He caught Isla's eye and motioned to her. After a rather lengthy pause, she drew her mount abreast of his. "Aye?" She lifted a dark brow, and it cut across her tanned skin in a perfect arch.

"I need to know more about why Hester is joining us."

Isla shrugged. "Ye and I, we already had this conversation. Hester is old and powerful and never takes the time to explain herself. At least not often."

Sam switched to telepathy. *"Cut the crap. I'm responsible for everyone's safety, and I can't protect you if you're not forthcoming with me."*

Isla straightened her shoulders and bridled a bit. *"Naught that should compromise us is afoot. It 'twere, I'd tell ye right enough."*

"Fine. Let me be the judge of that." He ground his teeth together in frustration.

"I've told ye all I'm about to." She narrowed her eyes, regarding him through slits. "Hester's not far. Mayhap an hour or two away. Ye'll not have long to wait to get your questions answered." With a toss of her head, she wheeled her horse, and rejoined the group of witches.

Irritation scoured his nerves. He'd asked her a direct question, and she owed him an answer, goddammit.

No, she doesn't.

She's not a Coven witch because she chose not to be one. And she doesn't owe me shit.

Something about his last thoughts banged around in his head. He went back a long way with the Coven, and he thought about the witches with Isla. Some of them must've been Coven-linked at one time or another. He'd also taken care to review all the Coven's records after he signed on as an enforcer, which meant he had access to most of their history.

Taking care to be methodical, he ran the witches' names through his memory. By the time he was done, he thought he had an answer. Rowan had been part of the Coven. So had Kat and Tashia. Rowan had been banished, but he'd be damned if he could recall exactly why. The other two had left with her.

Banishment was unusual, extreme, and the line between banishment and death a fine one. Apparently what she'd done wasn't worthy of death by mage fire, but was also serious enough for the Coven to take action.

At least I know more than I did.

He sent his power ranging wide and felt Hester closing on them. The mage riding with her was so strong, Sam's eyes widened. Despite the distance between them, he felt Aethelred's unique magical signature as strongly as if he rode next to him, not miles away. Sam smiled in spite of himself. He couldn't wait to meet the man who'd mentored Luke, and for the first time he wondered if Hester had found not only a magical partner, but a new mate. That she'd chosen Aethelred to ride with her, rather than Luke or Abigail, must mean something significant.

Isla took care to keep Tashia between herself and Rowan. After a heated exchange, she'd fessed up and told Rowan she had, indeed, called Hester. But she hadn't stopped there. She'd also said it wasn't prudent for Rowan to go off on her own, and that if loving her and wanting her to remain safe was a crime, she was guilty.

The other witch had subsided after that, but resentment bled from her. Her parting shot had been, "Hester or no, I'm still leaving come the morn."

Isla had been wise enough not to tell the other witch she'd accompany her, like it or not. She didn't want Rowan sneaking off in the middle of the night after she'd spelled everyone into a deep sleep—something she was more than capable of doing.

A distant flash of lightning was followed by thunder after a respectable amount of time. Rain splattered from a sky the color of old bruises as the day faded to night. Isla tugged the hood of her cloak over her head. Woven from boiled wool, it would do a fair job keeping her head dry.

Hester's energy drew nearer.

Isla had overheard the men discussing where they'd stop for the night. Even though she'd told Sam that Hester would meet up with them within an hour or two, in truth they'd likely cross paths about the time they made camp. Hopefully the myriad tasks would keep everyone busy enough to avoid a full-scale confrontation with Hester.

Isla had siphoned off a lot of magic coercing the leeches to their will, and she wanted food and sleep more than arguments.

And Sam. I'd like him too.

She pressed her lips into a thin line. Better if she didn't pursue either him or that line of thought. He'd been furious at her refusal to answer his query about Hester. Never mind they'd already covered that ground a few hours before.

Why would he think she'd changed her mind?

Isla swallowed a bitter snort. Sam didn't care how she felt. All he cared about was getting what he needed to accomplish the job at hand. She recognized his strategy because it was one she'd employed—and more than once. The problem boiled down to her being a witch, and him being used to their ready compliance with his directives.

Maybe leaving with Rowan wasn't such a bad idea after all. Before she got in deeper with Sam. She already liked him far more than was wise.

Yanking her thoughts away from the broad-shouldered enforcer, she made herself focus on what she'd do next. Everything she owned was in a small cabin on the outskirts of San Francisco. Clothes. Herbs. Magical accoutrements. Furniture. Books. Even a flute and a drum. Was there any way she could return to claim her property before someone else simply moved in and took everything?

Och, and I'd be better served looking forward not back.

The thought was practical, but it made her sad. She'd started over more times than she could count. It was why so many of her kind chose the Coven. It took care of them, provided men like Sam to help fight their battles.

"You're thinking about what comes next." Tashia glanced her way.

"And ye're not?" Isla countered.

"Of course I am." Tashia sounded irritated. "I don't like being pushed into things. Or walking away from better than thirty years' work."

"We'll figure something out." Isla made an effort to smooth the creases out of Tashia's annoyance.

"What's to stop them from swooping in and wrecking it all again?"

"Nothing." Isla bit on her lower lip. Tashia's words were stark, but true. And they made her heart hurt. *Them* encompassed everything from Black Magick to the Church to humans scared half to death of anything magical. "Sounds as if ye've made some decisions."

The other witch nodded. "Not completely, but I'm getting there, although I'm not ready to talk about it yet. This is the fifth time I've had to leave everything, and I'm tired of picking myself up, and heartily sick of starting over."

Isla quested about for something positive and finally said, "The years we spent with Hester were good ones."

A small smile played about Tashia's mouth. "They were, but nothing lasts." She shifted the reins to her other hand, flexing her fingers. "Don't mind me. I'm feeling sorry for myself. I'll get over it. I blew through a hell of a lot of magic, so I'm weak and weary on top of everything else. Any idea how much longer we'll be on the road? It's damn near dark."

"Not much longer, I doona think. One of the enforcers guided us onto a path. I believe it leads to where we'll camp for tonight."

Tashia rolled her shoulders, squaring them. "The going did get easier after that. I need to stay focused on right now. Looking back derails me."

Leaning close, Isla patted the other woman's shoulder. "Me too. I'm looking forward to laying eyes on Hester."

"So am I. She's such a whirlwind presence. Magic to spare, and a healthy dose of horse sense atop everything else." Tashia drew her brows together. Concern streamed from her green eyes, and she switched to shielded telepathy. *"I understand why you conferred with Hester about Rowan. We have to stay together."*

"Tell Rowan that." Isla clacked her jaw closed in frustration.

"She can be stubborn, that one. The Coven truly dealt her a rotten hand. It's why Kat and I left with her. We didn't want her to be alone, plus we were convinced the Coven did her wrong."

"Do ye believe the Coven may have changed?"

"From things I've heard over the years, yes. For one thing, enforcers work in groups and by consensus now. The one who was out for Rowan's blood made that decision all on his own."

"Aye, Rowan sketched out the bare bones of the incident, but none of the details. Did no one challenge him?"

Tashia shook her head. *"He was one of the first enforcers. The whole concept was brand new, and they were writing their own rules then. It was his woman and unborn child Rowan aided. We understood why he'd be angry, but he turned into an avenging god, hell-bent on retribution."*

Tashia hesitated long enough to draw in a breath, her nostrils flaring. *"If that bastard had his way, Rowan would've met her end in mage fire, but the Founder intervened."*

"Let's do all we can to assure Rowan doesna run off on her own."

Nodding slowly, Tashia murmured. "You know I will."

Sam rode toward them. Suspended off to one side, his mage light provided faint illumination as if he was carefully titrating the power he fed into it. Once he reached them, he extinguished it.

"We're headed to that high bluff off to the right." He pointed through the rainy gloom. "We leave the track here. Fall in and follow me. We'll make camp for the night in about ten more minutes."

Hoof beats drew toward them. Two horses, traveling fast given the darkness and the terrain. Isla sent power spinning toward the sound and felt Hester's welcoming energy.

A large, black raven materialized, cawing, "Isla, Isla."

"Aye." She gazed at the bird. "'Tis my name."

"My name. My name," the raven mimicked. Spreading her wings, she landed on Isla's shoulder digging her talons in deep.

"Hester!" Sam yelled. "Damn but it's good to see you."

The witch trotted into the circle of his mage light, riding a sorrel mare. Her long, white hair was braided in many sections, and her hazel eyes shone warmly. "The feeling's mutual, enforcer." A black woolen cloak covered her from shoulders to legs, and she shook water out of her hair before tugging its hood over her head.

A mage robed in black and sizzling with power rode by Hester's side. Wraith thin and tall, he sat ramrod straight astride a black stallion. Snapping his fingers at the bird, he said, "Mollie. Get back here. Don't bother Isla." Silvery-white hair cascaded around him, and he turned a set of penetrating dark eyes Isla's way.

"She's not a bother." Isla smiled.

The bird preened, rubbing against the side of her head. "Nice witch. Good witch."

Isla snorted. "Flattery is definitely the ticket. Mollie, is it?"

"My name, my name," the bird quorked.

"We'll catch up once we get to camp." Sam's words were edged with command.

"Aye, another who's just like my boy, Luke," Aethelred said approvingly. "Better to get out of the open. The night's alive with fell energy. Hester and I rode through enough to add a few years —not that one or two more's about to matter at this point."

"Speak for yourself, man," Hester sniped, but then she laughed and ruined the whole effect.

"Follow me." Sam wheeled his horse and led them in a zigzag path up the bluff rising before them.

Isla rode behind Aethelred, noting that he shielded Hester with his power. The smile that had begun with the bird—who still clung to her shoulder—broadened. She couldn't wait to drag Hester aside and grill her about the mage. He cared enough about her to protect her. Did she return his feelings?

Even better, had the two of them fallen in love?

Love.

She gazed at Sam's back, at the easy way he sat in the saddle, and she wanted to feel his arms around her again. Wanted the press of those chiseled lips over hers. Her resolution from earlier—the one where she'd decided she and Sam had no future—rose to taunt her, but she pushed it aside.

If Hester could find someone to care for in the wake of her husband's death, there was no reason Isla couldn't move beyond her own solitary past.

Och, and I doona know for certain about Hester.

Mayhap not, but I'll find out soon.

Isla clamped her teeth over her lower lip. Hester's love life—or lack thereof—had nothing to do with her. Not at all. Any decisions she made about Sam had to stand—or fail—on their own merits. Her horse's rear hooves slipped and slid on the uneven side hill, and she focused a beam of power to help. There'd be time to figure out what to do about Sam. For now, Rowan was her first concern.

CHAPTER 8

Sam herded everyone onto the flat area atop the bluff, and went to work moving the horses off to one side where water ran down a cliff face and into a deep pool they could drink from. The animals wouldn't have feed for tonight, but it couldn't be helped. Kane's description of the butte being an excellent, easily defensible campsite had been dead accurate. Cliffs ringed it on two sides with partial shielding on a third. Overhanging rocks provided some protection from steadily spattering rain.

"Do you think we should give them a break from their saddles?" Cory asked.

Sam shook his head. "Nah. Just loosen the girth straps. We might have to leave in a hurry."

Aethelred strode to where Sam stood and extended a hand. Sam gripped it warmly and said, "Thanks for coming with Hester." Mollie was back on the mage's shoulder, snapping her beak.

"No thanks needed." Aethelred tapped the raven's beak gently. "Two things decided me."

"I have a feeling you're about to tell me what they were." Sam grinned. Luke's mentor had a forthright quality that matched up with Hester's outspokenness.

"Indeed I am. Luke spoke on your behalf, and Hester was bound and determined to ride out. I couldn't very well let her go by herself."

"She's pretty capable, that one," Cory observed.

"It cuts both ways," Aethelred retorted. "Being overconfident doesn't necessarily work in your favor. Luke would've ridden with her. Abigail too, but this made more sense."

"More sense. More sense," the raven sagely concurred.

Sam sent a gentle tendril of power toward the bird, but it bounced back and slapped him. He'd suspected the raven was far more than she appeared, but the speed with which his power boomeranged back surprised him.

"Sorry. I meant no harm."

"You wanted to know if she's really a bird." Aethelred didn't pose it as a question.

"I suppose so." Sam grinned ruefully. "Haven't seen a familiar since I left the Old Country."

Mollie bent her head to one side, preening her shiny, black feathers.

"She's on our side and has been with me for many hundreds of years," Aethelred said. "For now, that's as much of an explanation as I'm willing to give."

Hester strode toward them and hooked a hand beneath Aethelred's elbow. "There ye are. The women and I got a blaze going, but we need something to cook beyond cornmeal."

Aethelred, who stood a foot taller than her, gazed fondly at Hester. "Sounds like a cue to get moving."

She shrugged. "Nay. Just fair warning supper willna be verra interesting unless we get something a wee bit more to add to it."

"The men will scare up some game," Sam offered, eying Hester. "Particularly if you light a fire under them."

With a squawk, Mollie pushed off Aethelred's shoulder, returning moments later with a fat, squirming mouse clutched in her beak.

Sam laughed and cupped his hands around his mouth to project his voice. "Best get cracking, boys. That bird is showing us up for a batch of lazy bums."

"Ye hunt," Hester ordered. "Aethelred and I will find something green to add to the pot." Dragging on his arm, she switched to Gaelic. Mollie stayed on the ground, munching her prize amid outraged squeaks until she broke the creature's neck.

Sharpening his magic-imbued senses, Sam loped off the plateau and down the hillside, snagging rabbits as he went. With Hester and Aethelred, they numbered eighteen—a decent number to cook for. Once he had four rabbits, he worked his way back uphill. The other enforcers were hunting too. He'd felt their magic as it snared game. If everyone caught roughly the amount he had, there'd be plenty to eat.

Raised voices met his ears.

Isla and Rowan were arguing, with the other witches chiming in. Sam slowed his pace, listening. He was almost certain the women would clam up once they knew he was close. It didn't take long to ascertain Rowan would do damn near anything to avoid a rematch with anything even remotely Coven-linked. She was bound and determined to leave—tonight if need be.

"If ye go, ye willna go alone," Isla shouted.

"Not a chance. I'll go with you too," Tashia cut in.

"Me too," Kat said. "Tashia and I have stood by your side ever since the Coven banished you, and we're not about to abandon you now."

More witch voices joined the fray. The upshot was that if

Rowan left, the other six would remain with her. They were a team, a group, and they'd stand united. No matter what.

Sam stopped dead. Isla couldn't leave. If she did, he'd probably never see her again. At the least, it would take some doing to track her down since she'd likely take care to shroud her path.

Where was Hester? Why wasn't she trying to dissuade them? And then he remembered she was off gathering greens with Aethelred.

He sent his power zinging wide, locating the witch and mage. They weren't far, so he switched direction to meet up with them.

"Nice rabbits." Hester eyed the string of bodies slung over his shoulder. "But they willna cook themselves."

Sam ignored her comments and switched to shielded speech. *"I overheard the women arguing with one another. Looks like they're planning to leave. Can you stop them?"*

"'Tis why I'm here." Hester straightened from where she'd been picking a plant Sam didn't recognize. *"Surely they willna leave tonight. We just got here, and their power is depleted."*

"I wouldn't be so sure of that."

Hester loosed a string of curses in Gaelic and shoved her armful of greenery at Aethelred. The air around her shimmered and she disappeared.

Aethelred shifted the plants into the crook of his arm. "May as well follow her. We likely have enough to feed everyone. More than enough if seven leave." He turned the full force of his shrewd gaze on Sam. "Why didn't you intervene?"

"They won't listen to me. They're not Coven witches."

"Does that mean they're immune to reason?" Aethelred drew his bushy white brows into a single line.

"I'm not sure what it means." Sam turned uphill with the mage flanking him.

"I understand why you'd be invested since you gathered a group of men to rescue them, but surely you didn't think you'd watch over them forever," Aethelred persisted.

Sam smothered a snort. "You're asking why it matters one way or the other to me."

"Yes, that's exactly what I'm wondering about." Without waiting for Sam to answer, Aethelred continued talking. "Not all of us take well to operating in groups. I ran a school for a bit of time, but Luke was the only one of my students who had enough aptitude to be worth investing more than token energy. Magic's fallen out of favor."

"I'm not sure it was ever *in favor,*" Sam grumbled.

"Eh, mayhap not. You haven't exactly answered me. My understanding is the Coven requires witches to sign some sort of blood pledge. Those who aren't willing aren't welcome. Now Hester, she was used to working in concert with a group, so she gathered the crew up yonder—" he jerked his chin toward the mesa "—after she moved west."

"Yes, yes, I know all that." Sam's worries about Isla leaving overshadowed everything. "We'd never have had a thing to do with any of these witches if they hadn't been desperate and called Hester. But that's not the point. I can't rewrite history."

They reached the lip of the plateau. Aethelred stopped walking and turned to Sam. "Being hasty is the curse of the young." He leveled his attention at Sam. "Sometimes sifting through the past is the only way to sort out how to address the present. Beyond that, those witches are long since grown. They have the right to make choices that craft their futures—without input from you. And without Hester's opinions too, but she doesn't see things that way. To her, all witches need her advice and guidance."

Sam looked away. The mage's words stung because they were spot on. "So you didn't agree with Hester coming here?"

"No, but I care about her enough to support her—even if I think she's off on a fool's errand. She sketched out what happened with Rowan. The woman has every reason to hate the Coven. No words, no matter how kindly fashioned, can change what happened to her."

"So you know why the Coven banished her." Sam kept his voice low.

Aethelred nodded. "Aye. She aided another witch. The woman was married to an enforcer who treated her quite badly. Plus, she was pregnant. Rowan made certain she got on a ship sailing for the Old Country. The enforcer was beyond incensed. If he'd had his way, he'd have killed her."

Sam mulled over the additional bits of information. Now that he had all the facts, he realized that the description of the incident written in the Coven's histories held a somewhat different slant.

"It happened a long time ago," he murmured.

"So? Bitterness has a way of growing over time," Aethelred countered, adding, "Advice is rarely welcome, but I'm going to give you some anyway. If there's a reason you care what that passel of witches does—beyond a sense of ownership on account of rescuing them—I'd figure out what it is and act on it."

Without waiting for Sam's answer, he turned and moved toward the circle of cook fires. Sam watched him go. No wonder Luke had grown into the man he was. Aethelred didn't sugarcoat anything, and he saw through to the heart of things.

Either Sam talked with Isla, told her how attracted he was to her.

Or not.

Regardless, he had to decide damned fast. Talking about

anything personal was harder than walking over broken glass. He'd rather face an army of Black Magick's minions.

Get over it.

If he did talk with Isla, what would he say? He'd been plainspoken with his last love interest in New Orleans, and look how far that had gotten him. Did women prefer more of an indirect approach?

Doesn't matter. I can't be anyone other than who I am.

With only the vaguest idea about what he'd do next, Sam set a course for the fires and dropped his string of rabbits next to Roland, who was skinning an assortment of small game.

"Thanks." Roland glanced up. "I could use a hand. These carcasses aren't going to prep themselves."

Sam hunkered next to him. "What happened to the women?"

Roland shrugged. "They're fighting about something. One of 'em wants to leave. I say good riddance. If she doesn't appreciate everything we did to haul their asses out of that pickle they landed in, to hell with her."

Sam went to work on one of the rabbits. Roland's attitude was vintage enforcer, but he could see his point. In truth, he was more interested in focusing his magic to listen to whatever was unfolding on the other side of the clearing than anything else.

"You're quiet," Roland observed.

"Just tired. Looking forward to dinner. Maybe we can hurry it up with magic."

"Maybe so. Hey! Here comes Kane. Looks like he got a small deer. Venison will really perk things up."

Isla rocked back on her heels from where she'd been hunkered in a circle with the other witches. She'd caught up with Rowan half an hour before when the other witch had draped herself in shadow and was edging toward the horses. The enforcers had all just left, presumably to hunt down dinner, so Rowan's timing was impeccable. She'd clearly been waiting for an opportunity to grab a horse and disappear.

"What do ye think ye're about?" Isla had demanded.

"You know damn good and well what I'm about," Rowan had responded. "You have no call to hold me. Let me go."

"Hester traveled a long way to help you."

Rowan had drawn back a hand, and for the barest moment Isla was certain the other witch was going to claw her—or slap her. Features flexing with bitterness, Rowan dropped her hand. "Hester's a good woman, but I'm beyond the kind of help she's thinking to provide. I want naught to do with her or the Coven."

"Things might have changed," Isla had pleaded.

"Nothing could change so much. These men—" Rowan jerked her chin upward "—they don't like it overmuch when we don't kowtow to their every command. It may be a different group of enforcers, but they're all cut from the same cloth. Nay, I'm leaving. It's been good knowing you—" Rowan turned away, but Isla clamped a hand around her upper arm.

""'Tis been good knowing me?" she'd asked, her words rising in anger. "That's all the years we've spent together mean? Why ye hell-spawned ingrate. How can ye simply walk away? Doona ye ken? We've formed our own Coven. 'Tisn't verra large, but we're all a part of something more than our individual selves. 'Tis something the rest of us value."

Rowan wrenched her arm away and took off at a dead run, swathing herself in magic.

With her choices dwindling by the second, Isla raced after her. She didn't want to use force, but Rowan had backed her into a tough spot. Tears pricked the corners of her eyes when she let a bolt of magic fly right at Rowan's back.

It brought the other witch to her knees. Uttering an outraged cry, Rowan struggled upright, screeching imprecations and hurling power of her own.

Because she couldn't talk sense into Rowan, Isla threw herself on top of her, pinning her to the ground. "Ye willna leave until we've sat as a group—with Hester since she's one of us—and hashed this out. Ye may not believe me, but ye'd regret sneaking off like a thief in the night till your dying day."

"You think I haven't considered all the ins and outs of this?"

"Not verra well, ye havena," Isla retorted.

Rowan writhed beneath her, and the commotion drew the other witches. Together, they'd latched onto Rowan and dragged her to a relatively dry spot beneath overhanging rocks. Rowan sat tucked against the cliff face with her arms wrapped around her black-clad form. The other witches formed a rough semicircle around her.

"Is there naught we can say to change your mind?" Kat asked. The corners of her eyes were pinched with pain.

"If there was, seems you'd have stumbled onto it." Rowan's tone was laced with sarcasm.

The air took on a shimmery hue, and Hester stepped out of the glowing nimbus. The sharp tang of herbs clung to her, and she crossed her arms beneath her breasts. "Ye're more trouble than a passel of newborn minxes." She focused her hazel gaze on Rowan.

Rowan rose so she faced Hester. "How could you possibly know? Was raising minxes a distant hobby of yours?" She shook her head. "Don't bother answering. 'Tis glad I am you're here, for it means we can have done with this, and then I'll be on my way."

"All on account of ye doona wish any contact with the

Coven?" Hester raised snow-white brows into twin question marks.

"Sure and you make it sound as if 'tis of little consequence. I barely escaped what the Coven considered *justice* with my life. Why would I want anything further to do with such a group?"

Hester squared her shoulders, making herself appear larger than she was. "What happened to you was wrong. That particular enforcer left the Coven not long after ye did."

"Aye. Of course. No doubt he went to track down his poor, unfortunate wife."

Hester narrowed her eyes to slits. "He dinna make it. He fell overboard and drowned."

Rowan drew back, shock stamped on her features. "Will you be saying more about that?"

"Do I have to?" Hester countered.

"Aye," Isla cut in. "I'm interested just how that could've happened since we can generally use magic to patch up most anything, including falling into the ocean."

"Come closer." Hester gestured. Once the women stood shoulder to shoulder in a tight circle, she cloaked them with magic. "Weave your power in with mine," she ordered. "This isna for enforcer ears."

Isla leaned forward, listening intently. She had a feeling Hester would shield her words, and the other witch didn't disappoint her.

"We knew what that man was," Hester began, her tone dripping venom, *"but since he put on a good front with the other men, they dinna believe us. The whole idea of developing a cadre of enforcers was brand new, and our Founder feared reprimanding the first one would cast a pall over the whole operation. Not that he wouldna have acted eventually, mind ye, but he was biding his time."*

"In the meantime," Rowan broke in, *"that enforcer's wife suffered terribly. He forced the pregnancy on her, and he beat her and bound her. Made her a prisoner in her home."*

"Och aye, and I knew all those things," Hester said. *"Many of us did, and we were hatching plans to rescue her, but ye got a jump on us all, and hustled her out of harm's way."* Rowan opened her mouth, but Hester held up a hand. *"Ye will allow me to finish."*

"If ye knew all that," Isla ignored Hester's request, *"how could ye have allowed the Coven to banish Rowan?"*

"I'm getting to that. 'Tis a crime to intervene betwixt a man and his wife. In the eyes of the law, wives are property, and the husband may do as he wishes. That enforcer dinna do aught that would cause him to run afoul of the laws of the land."

"But—" Rowan protested.

Hester cut her off with a chopping gesture. *"Hear me out. As witches we live in two worlds. Our magical one, and the world of humans. 'Tis best if we doona call attention to ourselves by running afoul of human edicts. As 'tis, humans barely tolerate us, and if we're not careful, we end up on the wrong end of a gallows—or a bonfire."*

"So ye took matters into your own hands," Isla murmured.

"'Tis exactly what we did," Hester confirmed. *"The Founder encouraged him to leave, and we made certain he'd never see land. Doona ask for the details. Suffice it to say, we surreptitiously stripped him of his magic in ways he wouldna notice afore he left, and a seaman or two ended up far richer at the far end of the voyage."*

Rowan drew her silver-gray brows into a line and creased her forehead in thought. *"While I'm glad that bastard met the end he deserved, still I'm not seeing how this changes aught betwixt myself and the Coven."*

"Some of us hunted for you." Hester glanced from Rowan to Tashia to Kat. *"But ye covered your tracks well. Before ye say aught, I fully ken just why ye did that. Ye dinna wish to be found."*

Rowan closed her teeth over her lower lip. "And I still don't. No more need to spell our words."

"I had a conversation with our Founder afore I left." Hester spoke slowly, as if she were measuring her words, making each one count. "He would like to personally offer you an apology, regardless of whether ye wish to be a part of us again."

"So that means sticking around until we meet up with the wagons," Rowan said.

"'Tis exactly what it means," Hester replied. "I lived and worked with you for many years, and I'm asking you to stay as a personal favor. No one will hold you against your will if ye wish to leave after that." She inhaled sharply. "Our war with dark forces is heating up. Our enemy gains strength from the bitterness and chaos reigning in this country. Soon, it willna be safe for any of us to be on our own."

Hester closed the distance between herself and Rowan, holding out both hands. "Please. I'll see no harm comes to you. Not at the hands of the Coven. They did you wrong. Allow them to make it up. There's little enough justice in this world."

After a pause that lasted so long, Isla was certain Rowan would refuse, she grasped Hester's outstretched hands. "You have a deal. Sure and I'll meet with the Founder. I've wanted to scratch his eyes out for many a long year. Even if I move on, and I may well, 'twill be a good thing to lay old resentments aside." She snuffled audibly. "In truth, my anger has shaped so much of who I am for so long, I want to find out what lies beneath it."

Hester folded Rowan into her arms. Before she closed her eyes, Isla saw the sheen of tears. She crossed to where the pair stood and wrapped her arms around both of them. Kat, Tashia, and the others joined them, hugging, patting, murmuring relieved words.

"Ye're a lucky woman," Hester aimed her words at Rowan.

She disentangled herself from the other witches. "And why would that be?" She arched a brow.

Hester spread her arms wide to encompass all of them. "Look at how many love you. 'Tisn't something to trifle with. Now that we have things set to rights, let's see how the men are doing with our supper."

Isla snorted. "'Twill be the goddess's own miracle if they dinna just eat it all down and go to bed."

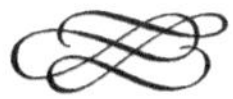

CHAPTER 9

Sam chopped, stirred, and listened—until he couldn't anymore. No matter what spell he tried, he couldn't penetrate Hester's warding. The witches clearly wanted privacy, but if the outcome meant Isla riding off into the night, he wasn't about to stand by and let that happen.

He wasn't quite sure what he could do to stop her, but he'd figure something out.

"Are you going to put that meat into the pot before it's so small we can't ever find it again?" Cory glanced pointedly at the pile of rabbit chunks Sam was cutting into smaller and smaller bits.

"Yeah. Sure." He picked up the piece of leather he'd used for a ground cloth and dumped its contents into the cookpot. "Where'd the other rabbits go?" He bent and scrubbed his hands with sandy dirt.

"Skinned and prepped them while you were focused on the witches." Cory leaned closer. "What's so all-fired important about whatever they're up to? They're witches. Always up to something. Mostly stuff we don't know shit about. Probably better we don't know everything. If we did, it would drive us crazy."

Sam shook his head, not willing to answer. Besides, what would he say? That Isla had stolen his heart in a weak moment? That his cock hardened whenever he thought about her? Cory would laugh, tell him to bed her and get it over with. Sam glanced at three other bunches of enforcers crouched around their own cook fires. Between all of them, there'd be more than enough to feed everybody.

Aethelred strode out of the darkness and dropped a clump of greens into their pot. "Last one." He dusted dirt off his hands. "Tried to split them up evenly."

"Last one, last one," Mollie chimed in.

Aethelred ruffled her dark head. "Always have to have the last word, eh?"

"Last word, last word."

Sam couldn't help himself, he laughed. "Gotta get me one of them."

Mollie clacked her beak in his direction, making what she thought of his suggestion abundantly clear.

Aethelred glanced at where the witches huddled together, nodded to himself, and said, "Best leave them to it. I'll check on the horses."

Kane strode over from a neighboring fire. "Dinner's nigh onto ready. What should we do about them?" He jerked his chin toward the women.

"Wait for them." Sam shrugged. "Eat now and save them some. I don't care." He stalked off into the darkness, intent on finding Aethelred.

Kane asked, "What's up with him?"

Sam didn't hang around to hear Cory's answer. He caught up with Aethelred in the impromptu corral. The mage was touching first one animal, then another, murmuring to them in Gaelic.

"What are you doing?" Sam asked.

"Their bellies are empty," Aethelred replied. "I'm reassuring them there'll be grazing on the morrow." He turned and faced Sam. "What can I do for you, son?"

Warmth in his words touched a place in Sam that he'd guarded for a very long time. A place he'd hidden away after his father disowned him. "Not sure you can do anything for me."

"You sought me out for a reason," Aethelred persisted.

Sam thought about it. "I suppose that's true enough." A muscle twitched in his jaw, and he unclenched it. "Is there some way to stop the witches—if they decide they want to leave tonight, that is?"

"I suspect Hester's taking care of disrupting that plan," Aethelred said. "'Tis why she came, and she's a stubborn one."

Sam swallowed a snort. "Guess you've gotten to know her."

"More to the point—and we covered this ground earlier—if there's some reason you want to keep them here, you should be talking with them, not me."

"Not exactly possible just now. They're thicker than thieves over there."

"That bothers you." It wasn't a question, and Aethelred went on talking. "You like being in control, and you have no idea what they're up to. If you've taken a fancy to one of the witches, you have to get over that. They need their own private lives in addition to whatever they choose to share with you."

Sam wasn't certain how to ask, so he just blurted, "Are you and Hester, uh, together?"

The mage's dark eyes twinkled. "We're scarcely married, but we do care about one another. Where it will lead—or if it leads anywhere—is written in the future, not the present."

"How can you not try to shape that future, though?"

A sharp sensation tracked from Sam's head to his boot soles. Magic, as Aethelred searched for something. "Why not just ask me?" he said gruffly.

"Sometimes we don't know the answers. We only think we do. Besides—" the mage cast an appraising glance his way "—this is faster. As for shaping the future, we do that every day by our actions. I suspect the women are finishing up. I felt their spell fracture a few moments ago. Run along. Follow your heart. It's in there, though you've buried it deep."

Sam opened his mouth, but Mollie flapped to him, latching onto his shoulder. "Run along. Run along," she chirped. "Good for you."

Sam eyed her, and she snapped her beak at him. "Are you coming along for the ride?" he asked.

In a flurry of feathers, she pushed off his shoulder and flew off into the night, cawing merrily.

"Sounds like she's laughing," Sam said.

"That she is, son." Aethelred made flapping motions with both hands. "Off with you. This won't get any easier with waiting."

Sam walked briskly toward the cook fires and the circle of women. They were hugging each other, so surely they'd resolved some of the unhappiness. Even though he and Aethelred hadn't said much, he felt lighter inside. Luke was lucky to have stumbled onto the mage—and Mollie—to shape and hone his power.

Yeah, could've used someone like that in my life.

Maybe, but not right after I discovered what I was, the voice of reason intruded.

He'd spent the first few years after his magic blasted through trying to run away from it, and he'd do well not to revise history.

If someone like Aethelred had shown up, the likelihood of Sam being open to what he had to teach was thin.

The women broke from their circle and headed for the cook fires, spreading themselves among the pots of food. Sam hurried toward Isla. Her face was wet from tears, but a soft smile graced her face. "Come eat with Cory and me," he invited.

"Thanks. Be happy to."

"Is everything all right? Will Rowan stay with us where she'll be safe?" Sam winced. He hadn't meant to grill Isla. Not right away.

"Och aye. 'Twas nip and tuck there, but things are settled—for now." She stopped walking and looked up at him. "How did ye know about Rowan?"

"I'm good at figuring things out. And I studied the Coven's history after they signed me on as one of their enforcers." He placed a hand under her arm. "Come eat. We can talk about everything later. You must be hungry and tired."

"Aye, I'm both. Food will be welcome. I'm glad ye dinna eat it all. The women and I figured ye might've eaten and gone to bed. 'Tis been a verra long day."

He bristled, wanted to protest that he and the other enforcers were gentlemen, that they'd never scarf down all the food and leave the women hungry, but he held his tongue. Instead, he led her to the cook fire where Cory squatted and plucked a bowl from a pile, ladling stew into it.

Isla took it from him and settled on her haunches, eating hungrily.

Cory handed Sam a second brimming bowl. "If nobody minds, I'll eat out of the pot. It's pretty much been split in thirds."

"Fine by me," Isla said around a mouthful of stew. "Thank ye. This is verra good. Been a while since we last ate."

Sam sat between her and Cory, eating methodically. He was

hungry, but he was more worried about what he'd say to Isla. If she'd even hear him out. She had no reason to. She didn't owe him anything beyond gratitude for extricating her from a bad situation.

He reached for a water skin and drank deep, handing it around. "Do we have any whiskey left?" he asked Cory.

The other enforcer grinned. "Now that you mention it, we just might. Let me take a peek." He rooted in nearby saddlebags and withdrew a flask, hefting it. "Not much, maybe a swallow apiece." Uncapping it, he drank deep and handed it to Isla.

She tipped it back and gave it to Sam. "Kill it," she said. "'Tis verra nearly gone."

He set his empty bowl down and took the flask. Her fingers brushed his, warm and electric, and he wanted to touch her forever. The liquor was all but gone. He finished it and tucked the empty flask back into the saddlebag.

Before he could let himself think too long or too hard about what might come next, he stood and extended a hand to Isla. "Want to walk with me for a bit before we turn in for the night?"

An odd look crossed her face, but maybe it was just shadows from the fire. After a pause that felt a shade too long, she nodded and took his hand, letting him help her to her feet.

The plateau wasn't large, and Sam wanted privacy, so he tucked a hand under her elbow and guided her toward where the horses milled about. "Did things go the way you wanted them to earlier?" he asked and kicked himself. He was hedging, but how did you just come out and tell someone you liked them?

"Ye know they did, on account of ye already asked me." Isla lounged against the cliff face and turned toward him. "Say what's in your mind, Sam Jennings. Ye invited me to walk with ye for a reason, what is it?"

Her lips were full, tempting. He brushed a stray curl behind her ear, loving the warmth of her, the silk of her skin beneath his fingertips. He should move his hand, but he couldn't bear to stop touching her, so he cupped the side of her face. She didn't draw away, just focused her intense deep blue gaze on him.

Words wouldn't come, so he bent his head and closed his mouth over hers.

Isla watched Sam's face, illuminated by the moon that had finally crested the horizon. Even though she'd been ready to ride with Rowan, make certain the other witch wouldn't face whatever evil chased them by herself, leaving Sam behind would've tugged at her heart. She wasn't sure quite why. It wasn't as if she knew him well.

She hadn't exactly steered clear of sex, but she'd avoided anything that smacked of encumbrances. She'd been on the move so long, a man—or worse, children—might tie her to one place. A risk she couldn't afford, judging from her headlong flight out of San Francisco. Something like the Coven might've afforded the type of protection to allow her the comforts of a relationship, but she'd never been a joiner. And Rowan's bitterness and hatred toward anything Coven-linked hadn't provided much of an argument to link her star to that group.

Sam guided her away from the group of witches and mages toward where the horses stamped restlessly. What did he want, anyway? Was it to grill her about the argument with Rowan? She hadn't offered much in the way of details, and Sam struck her as someone who liked to have everything nailed down, right to the last brass tack. Tension radiated from him. She felt it in the way his hand lay beneath her arm.

"Did things go the way you wanted them to earlier?" he

asked, and she congratulated herself for guessing right about his intentions.

"Ye know they did, on account of ye already asked me." Isla lounged against the cliff face and turned toward him. "Say what's in your mind, Sam Jennings. Ye invited me to walk with you for a reason, what is it?"

Rather than talking, though, he placed a hand over the side of her face, gentle, tender. She should tell him no, duck from beneath his touch, but warmth from his fingers seared her, wakening something primal. She longed to throw her arms around him, lose herself in his male energy.

When he kissed her, she stopped thinking and kissed him back, needing the press of his mouth on hers. Her arms crept around him, and she opened her mouth to his insistent tongue. The kiss, which began gently, accelerated fast until the only thing in the universe was the man in her arms with his mouth pressed to hers.

His heartbeat thrummed against her chest, and her nipples formed stiff peaks. Sam threaded his arms around her, caressing her back. One hand moved lower and curved around her ass, holding her tight against his stiffening cock. She squirmed in his arms wanting to be as close as she could get to his hard-muscled body. She sucked on his tongue and bit his lips, teasing, nibbling. He smelled like magic and sagebrush and something so intensely male it made her want to breathe him in and never stop.

She wanted the cock pressing into her belly too. Wanted to unlace his breeches, draw it into her hands and kneel before him, taking it into her mouth. The dark, secret place between her legs throbbed with hollowness, with need. Her breath came faster and she clutched handfuls of leather, working to push his tight-fitting clothes aside so she could touch his skin.

Sam dragged his mouth from hers. She lunged forward, not

wanting the kiss to end, but he tangled one hand in her hair, holding her head in place inches from his. "I really did want to talk with you." His words were harsh with wanting her.

"Aye, and we are talking, just not with words."

He tightened his hold on her hair. "We can have sex, but that's not what I want…"

"Och, and ye could've fooled me." She bumped her hips against his erection.

Color rose from the open neck of his leathers, turning his tanned face a lovely golden color. "I'm making a botch of this. I like you, Isla. More than I should. I'm hoping…" His voice trailed off and he tried again. "What I'm trying to say is I want us to have a future together. Something beyond us bedding one another." His sea blue eyes moved from her face to her breasts and then lower. "You're a beautiful woman."

"Aye, and ye're quite the lovely specimen yourself." Isla felt a soft smile form. "I'm all for the bedding part, but ye need to know I've never taken up with anyone."

"Never found the right man?" He quirked a blond brow.

"Far too simple." She swallowed hard, longing for the man in her arms to bury himself in her body, not jumble things up with love talk.

He brushed his mouth over hers, but then drew back. "I want you too, but this is important. Women to warm my bed aren't that hard to find. We could have a future together, Isla. Or I hope we could. Please." He cradled the side of her head. "Tell me why you don't have a husband."

She tried to look away, but something about the earnestness in his face wouldn't let her. "I told ye most of my life's story." She was hedging, but couldn't quite find the right words.

"Most, but not all," he pressed. "None of your little band have mates. Why not?"

She narrowed her eyes in thought. Where to begin? "Many reasons. We move a lot. Those years we spent in San Francisco were the longest any of us had been in one place this last hundred years or so. Humans would never accept us as partners, even though they knock down our doors quick enough whenever they need healing or animal care."

Isla sucked on her lower lip, thinking. "When we moved to the western side of the country, none of us expected to meet up with much of anyone with magic. And we were right about that. Nothing like the Coven. No haven for witches, which meant we needed to be light-footed. Able to disappear if someone targeted us, like those infernal dark mages."

"Did you plan to live out your life alone?" His voice was gentle, the question quiet.

"I don't suppose I ever thought that far ahead. We live so long, I just let the years roll by."

"Is remaining alone what you prefer," he pressed. "If it is, I need to know." He hesitated, drawing in a sharp breath. "I've been by myself because I haven't found the right woman. Once I thought I might have, but she chose someone else while I was gone. There's something special about you. An inner light that calls to me. I've fought it ever since you vaulted onto my horse in front of that San Francisco warehouse, spitting fire and power. Fiercely independent. Feisty. I wanted you then, and I want you now. Not just your body. All of you."

Isla pushed out of his embrace. It was one of the hardest things she'd ever done, but tying herself to anyone—even Sam—scared her. What if things didn't work out? Once she opened herself to loving him, he could hurt her.

"There are risks to be sure." He gazed at her. "Yes, I was inside your head. I want to know everything about you."

His words thrilled her and made her want to run hard the

other way, the contradiction so jarring she didn't know what to do with any of it. "Making love would be easy," she murmured.

He nodded. "I want more than that from you, Isla McIntyre." A wry smile turned one corner of his mouth downward. "And I'm cursing myself for being a prime fool. Most men would've taken you and not worried about anything beyond the pleasure we could offer one another."

"But ye're not most men."

"Apparently not." He ran a hand down her arm. "Think on what we talked about."

"But how would that work?" she blurted. "I'm not keen on joining the Coven, and ye work for them."

"There's no rule that says I must take a Coven witch to wife." Bending he kissed her gently. "Get some rest. I fear tomorrow will be just as long as today was. I'm going to take a good look around, and then I'll turn in myself."

Before she could say anything further, he melted into the shadowed darkness beyond the lip of the plateau. Something deep inside her wanted to call him back, but she restrained herself. Sam was a package deal. He'd made that clear enough, and she had some hard thinking to do before they talked again.

Sam made his way down the steep grade surrounding the mesa they were camped on, his magic senses on full alert. Maybe the other men had figured out a rotation system for standing guard, but he hadn't been there to hear about it. His groin throbbed, yearning for Isla's warmth. He'd done the right thing, though. Sam had slept with enough women over the years to understand relationships that began in bed rarely turned out well.

At least not for him.

Look at his friends Luke and Abigail. They'd gone through hell before Luke so much as kissed her. Taken plenty of time to delve into who the other person was, what they were made of. Sam's last relationship fell apart after he left New Orleans. The Coven had assignments for him that made staying in one place impossible. He'd promised Eve he'd be back, but she'd been married the next time he blew through town. He'd figured sex would bind her to him.

Except it hadn't.

Granted he'd been gone for a few years, but he had written. Her lack of loyalty to their pledge disheartened him, made him determined to approach women he cared about from some angle other than his achingly hard appendage.

He cupped a hand over himself. No dark power anywhere near. No reason not to take care of his arousal. His balls hurt, and he needed to sleep.

Bullshit! I want to close my eyes and picture Isla, recreate her heat, her curves, her scent.

Fingers busy with the laces holding his breeches in place, he ducked behind two scrub oak, losing himself in shadows. His cock jumped into his hand, hard, eager, desperate for release. Sam muffled a snort. He wouldn't last ten strokes, but he'd make them good ones. Tightening his grip on his shaft, he breathed in Isla's essence. It still clung to him from when she'd been in his arms, kissing him as if he was the only thing that mattered in the world.

And the look in her eyes as she'd gazed up at him. Full of the wonder at the magic they spun together. He hadn't imagined that look. She was just as smitten with him as he was with her.

Her nipples had hardened, pressing into his chest, and the sweet musk of her need fueled his lust. He stroked himself hard, knowing exactly what he needed. The firm touches that would end his torment. What would her breasts look like? They were high and firm. Would the nipples be dark or more golden? He imagined the vee between her legs, covered with dark hair, and the scorching, enchanted place deeper still.

In his mind, he entered her, felt her stretch to accommodate him, heard her cries of delight as she crested. He thrust into his hand fast and sure. Imagining her coming tipped him into his own climax. Semen burst from him, and he bit back his grunts of pleasure. Despite his nightly bouts with his hand, this latest orgasm would barely blunt the tip of his longing, but it would be enough.

For now.

Still panting, he sent wisps of mage fire to obliterate traces of his seed. If any dark mage worth his salt got hold of Sam's essence, he could do untold damage. With desire still surrounding him, whetting his appetite for more of the same, he reluctantly pushed his still hard cock into his pants and laced himself up. A chill breeze cooled his overheated body as he made his way back up the hill. At least it wasn't raining anymore, but winter's bite reminded him the warm seasons wouldn't arrive for a while yet.

He made his way to where the enforcers were scattered around two of the fires. Kane sat propped against the cliff face, and Sam crouched next to him. "Drew first watch, eh?" Sam asked.

Kane nodded. "There were enough of us, you're off the hook for tonight. You can pull two shifts tomorrow."

Chuckling, Sam mock slugged the other enforcer and hunted down blankets. Wrapping himself against the chill seeping up from the ground, he tried to relax, but his mind shuffled through possibilities like a card shark with nervous fingers. What would Isla do now that he'd declared his interest? Would she pretend he'd never said anything? That would be hard, but there wasn't much he could do about it.

Sam shut his eyes, seeking sleep. He could spell himself into slumber, but it was better if he slept naturally. After a time, the tight hold he kept on his body and mind relaxed, and he drifted into restfulness. Not exactly asleep, but not awake, either. At least his magic would replenish itself as he drifted, trying not to hope too hard for Isla to come to him. Would she act on the emotion he'd seen in her blue eyes? Or was she just as stubborn and closed off as he'd always been?

I have to let it go. She has to make this decision on her own, not with me pushing for what I want.

He turned to his other side, repositioning his guns so they'd be easy to grab if he needed them. Best thing was for him to be himself. He wouldn't hide the pleasure that welled in him whenever he caught sight of her or heard her voice. He'd said what he had to. The next move would be hers.

Meantime, he'd be well served to develop a battle plan. He had a feeling they'd need one before they met up with the wagon train. Isla's gambit with the leeches had wrought enough destruction, someone would be out for vengeance.

ISLA TOSSED and turned in her blankets. The soft snores and night sounds of the other witches surrounded her. Usually, she found them soothing, but not tonight. Hester and Aethelred slept off to one side, wrapped in one another's arms. Magic surrounded them, and Mollie stood near Aethelred's head looking like an ancient sentinel. The raven's head was tucked under one wing, but Isla had a feeling the bird wasn't truly asleep.

She was convinced the raven was an elder spirit in bird form, but it didn't matter what she was. She'd fight for them, and it was all that counted.

When Isla closed her eyes, all she saw was Sam. The resolute expression on his face when he'd told her, "I want more than that from you, Isla McIntyre." And then he'd made good on his words by not bedding her. He'd wanted her—as badly as she desired him—but he'd been strong enough to hold out for something he saw as better. Not just her body, but her heart.

Surely I'm not worth all that much.

He thinks I am.

The thought made her smile. Men had wanted her before, but only for the charms of her bed. Wives were a responsibility, expensive to provide for. Many a man never married because he couldn't afford it. She'd slept with the occasional human, but they feared her as much as they wanted her. Like she was a circus attraction that drew and repelled them at the same time.

She shook her head and flopped onto her stomach. What she really needed to think about was the two days between now and when they'd have the relative safety of the wagon train between themselves and Black Magick. She was as sure as she'd ever been about anything that they hadn't seen the last of the ones who'd cornered them today.

There were two more of them to fight—three if she counted the bird. That would help, but a concentrated demon incursion would be hard to recover from. Her trick with the leeches would only work once. Their adversary would be too smart to bring animals to the next skirmish.

Even mad wolves could turn on their masters—with the right infusion of power to coerce them. Just like they had today.

Isla's mind ran in tight, little circles as hours dragged by. Finally, her eyes felt heavy. When she closed them, she thought she might actually be able to sleep.

Tomorrow morn, she promised herself. *We'll craft a strategy afore we leave this place.*

The men were skilled fighters, one and all. Mixing and matching ideas from all of them, they'd come up with something.

Rowan lay next to her. Just as Isla was drifting off, she asked, "What did Sam want?"

Because the answer was too complicated for her tired brain to coordinate words with, she pretended to be asleep.

Rowan wasn't fooled, though, and she rolled closer. "I'm here if you need someone to listen."

Gratitude for the other witch welled. "I'm glad ye're here and not off by yourself goddess only knows where."

"Don't be telling anyone," Rowan replied, "but so am I."

Her words brought peace to Isla's spirit. Sleep claimed her soon after.

HESTER SHAKING her shoulder in the cold, gray light of a drizzly dawn brought her back to wakefulness. "Time to be up and about," Hester said before moving down the line of witches with the same message.

Isla shook herself, got to her feet, and rolled her blanket. It was still warm from her body, and she wanted to crawl back into the nest she'd made. The one where she didn't have to think about Sam. Or Black Magick. Or nasty, giant leeches.

She walked to the horses. Once she'd secured her blanket to the back of her saddle with lengths of leather, she did her best to finger comb her hair, but it was impossibly tangled. What it needed was to be unbraided, brushed out, and redone, except there wasn't time.

Sam strode to her side with a steaming cup of coffee. "Here you go." He offered it to her.

"But that's yours," she protested.

"I'll get another. Come over by the fire. We heated what was left from last night's supper to break our fast. Nothing fancy. Everyone thinks we need to get moving."

Isla glanced about. All the witches were up, attaching their blankets to their saddles exactly like she'd done. She bristled. "*Everyone* dinna include any of us."

"True enough." He smiled, and her heart did funny, little flip-flops. "You're more than welcome to share your own ideas over breakfast. We're few enough, we can't afford to overlook anything." Without waiting for her to reply, he went on. "The way we sliced and diced it, our two choices were to remain here because it's an easy location to defend, and let the wagon train come to us."

He screwed his face into a thoughtful expression. "That had a couple problems. It's out of the way for the wagons, and there's no way out for us. Dark sorcerers could effectively trap all of us here."

"What was the other choice?" she asked, enjoying the sound of his voice and his nearness.

"Riding as fast and as hard as we can for the wagon train. We won't reach them today, but we could early the next."

"Unless we're set upon again."

"There is that," he agreed. "Go eat something. We'll finalize our plans over food."

She sipped the scalding coffee—thick and bitter, just the way she liked it—and made her way to the group huddled around a fire. The warm metal cup took some of the ache from the chill morning out of her hands.

Mollie flew her way and latched onto her shoulder. "Witch. Witch," she cawed.

Laughing, Isla turned her head and met a pair of intense, avian eyes. "Bird. Bird," she retorted. "Or not."

"Not. Not." Mollie quorked.

"Enough of that." Aethelred snapped his fingers, and the raven flapped to him, perching on his shoulder. He settled his sharp-eyed gaze on Isla. "Mollie is a raven, pure and simple. You'd do well not to harbor any other thoughts. She can spy for me—for us—but not if our enemy suspects she's other than what she appears."

"Got it." Isla narrowed her eyes as she gazed at Aethelred. He was something other than a mage steeped in White Magick, but now wasn't the time to explore that. She wondered if Hester knew, then decided she almost had to. Because Isla was certain he could read her thoughts, she cleared them and set her coffee aside to dish a dollop from the cookpot into a metal mug.

The witches gathered, joining the enforcers. Once all were nearby, Sam said, "The men and I determined we should ride hard for the Central Overland Trail and the wagon train. That our best friend is speed, not stealth." His gaze swept the group. "Are we in agreement?"

"Sure and we might be better served shrouding ourselves," Rowan spoke up. "Waiting for our enemy to pass us by afore we leave. We have water here."

"Yes, but we'd have to leave to hunt," Roland pointed out.

"The other drawback with that approach," Tom cut in, "is whoever attacked us yesterday is far from stupid. They masterminded that entire battle without once revealing who they were. They know where we are. I've felt wisps of their presence ever since we got here."

"If we remain here, they'll surround the front of the bluff and trap us," Cory said after Tom stopped to take a breath.

"I see the problem." Rowan nodded. She squared her shoulders. "I didn't search for Black Magick taint last night. I was too tired, but 'tis there just as you said. Thank you for being vigilant."

Isla's eyes widened. Rowan had just thanked an enforcer.

Mayhap she really was softening her stance toward the Coven after all this time.

"As anxious as I am to leave," Sam said. "One thing's worth our time to address. How are your power stones doing? Mine could stand a shot from the gears."

"That's right. Ye brought the extra set with you." Hester smiled grimly. "This is one of those times I'm grateful ye're always prepared—for anything. All the witches have stones." She glanced at the nine enforcers. "And three of you. Sam's opal, Cory's pearls, and Tom's turquoise."

Aethelred drew out an oblong stone suspended from a chain that hung around his neck. "And then there's this one."

"Och, I dinna forget it." Hester sounded testy, but sent a fond expression skittering his way. "That one holds its power without any assistance."

Meantime, Sam had rustled in his saddlebags and was arranging five gears in descending order on a square of leather next to the fire. "What do you think?" he asked Hester. "We don't have the brazier to create steam."

"I'll power the gears," Aethelred said. "You just get the stones out so they can charge." The air around him took on a numinous glow, and magic hurtled into the clearing, so bright, clear, and pure, it stole Isla's breath. She drew her moonstone from around her neck and laid it on the leather where it was joined by all the other power stones.

Smoke rose from nowhere, prodding the gears into action. Aethelred stood still as a stone carving, hands raised with light pulsing from them. Isla tried to see the magical connection between the illumination flowing from Aethelred and the steam, but it was so convoluted, she couldn't follow it.

The stones took a charge far more quickly than she

remembered. They glowed brightly while they absorbed magic, winking out once they were full. Rather than the hours she remembered, the stones were done in just a few minutes.

Aethelred dropped his hands to his sides and said, "Six of us don't have stones. Are there any gemstones among us not paired to a mage or witch? Something in a ring, perhaps, or a brooch?"

Kat slipped a ruby ring off her finger and handed it to him. Tashia unpinned a rose quartz carving from the leather herb pouch she kept tied around her waist.

Aethelred tilted his head back, scenting the air. "Not much more time," he muttered, holding out a hand for the rose quartz. "This pairing won't be perfect—and it may not last—but for now it will be better than naught at all." He gestured for Kane and Roland to step close. At first, he handed Kane the ruby, but then shook his head and gave it to Roland.

"More suitable match for your power," he said. "Yours too." He handed the rose quartz to Kane. "Kneel in front of the gears with your stones gripped tight in your right hands," he ordered. "This won't be comfortable, but remain there until I tell you I'm done."

The men scrambled to comply.

Isla watched with interest. This was far different than how she'd paired with her pink moonstone, having selected it from an array of possibilities. She understood Aethelred was bypassing the natural order of things, forcing the stones to pair with the two enforcers. It was why he'd cautioned the pairing might not last.

Steam pulsed from the mage's outstretched hands until Kane and Roland were encased in it. Lines of strain formed on their faces, but they didn't move, even when the steam turned to flame and the flames danced around their outstretched fists holding the gemstones.

Worry carved furrows into Sam's face, but he stood still, not intervening. Isla felt tension flow from him. Clearly he didn't completely trust Aethelred and stood ready to jump in the moment he felt things turn bad.

Pride and respect rose, warming her. Sam was sure enough of himself to allow magic he didn't totally understand into his ranks. Though the men hadn't said so, it was clear he was their de facto leader.

The steam vanished as quickly as it had risen, and the clatter of gears quieted. "It's complete," Aethelred confirmed.

"We're done?" Roland grunted. Though he tried to sound invincible, his question was lined with pain.

"Yes."

"What happens next?" Kane pushed to his feet. When he opened his hand, it was blistered where the rose quartz had sat in his palm.

"Use the stone to concentrate your power while you fight," Sam said tightly. "When the time comes, I'll help."

"Me too," Cory said.

"And me." Tom nodded.

Rowan stepped forward and placed her palm over Kane's open hand. Healing energy enveloped their joined hands, and Kane grunted. "Thanks. Feels better."

Rowan turned to Roland. After an infinitesimal pause, he extended his burned fingers and she repeated her incantation.

Sam picked up the empty cookpot and scuffed dirt over the fire with a boot. Coupled with a command in Gaelic to cease burning, the flames extinguished.

"Let's move, people," he said. "Gather your things, mount up and we're gone from here." He stopped next to Rowan. "Thanks for your healing magic. Things have changed in the years since you left. There are many ways to be a Coven witch."

She opened her mouth, but before she could reply, he said, "Think on it."

Isla's blanket was already secured to her saddle. Wrapping her cloak about her, she moved briskly toward her horse. She didn't see Sam move past her, but somehow he was there, and he helped her mount.

She smiled in spite of how desperate their situation was looking. Run or be pinned down. Neither was a good choice. "Thanks, but I'm capable of getting astride by myself."

"But then I wouldn't have an excuse to touch you." He flashed her a rakish grin, before vaulting atop his stallion and leading them down the hill.

Isla ended up following Hester and Aethelred. The mage, raven atop his shoulder, had veiled his magic down to nothing. If she didn't know better, she might have believed him merely human.

Questions tumbled through her mind. What to do about Sam? Who—or what—was Aethelred? What about his bird since they were linked? More pertinently, would any of them see today's sunset? If not, none of the rest mattered.

They'd reached the flat area beneath the mesa. Clenching her jaw, she urged her horse to speed. Miles flashed by beneath her mount's hooves. No matter how she felt—or didn't feel—about the Coven, the closer they got to that group, the better off they'd be. More enforcers traveled with the wagon train, and they could ride to their assistance if need be.

Och aye, since when did I count on anyone but myself?

She shook off disgust at her weakness, but then drew herself up short. If she fell into Sam's enticing offer to explore what was between them, to let the feelings deepen and grow, she'd have to give up some of her independence.

Could she do that? Isla wasn't sure. She'd been alone for hundreds of years.

Black Magick pricked the edges of her warding just before the rotten meat stench of wraiths hit her full in the face.

CHAPTER 11

Adrenaline pounded through Sam, leaving a harsh, bitter taste in his mouth. Wraiths flowed out of the rocky ground. Where had the bastards come from? He glanced at oak-studded foothills and gauged how far they were from the Central Overland Trail. Not more than five miles. No wonder their enemy had chosen to attack here. Once they hit the trail, it would be a straight shot to the wagon train.

They'd made good time so far today, but none of that mattered. They had to mount a defense in territory that didn't provide much in the way of cover. Drawing a pistol in one, fluid movement, he drilled the nearest wraiths with silver- and lead-laced bullets. They'd be better off fighting from horseback—if it was only the enforcers. He had no idea how competent the witches were at remaining astride bucking, shying mounts. So far, their battles had been from the ground.

He glanced Isla's way. Keeping her safe was at the top of his list. She'd give him grief, but the safest place for her and the women was out of harm's way. The men could provide cover—

and keep the wraiths engaged—long enough to allow the witches to flee.

Guns still blazing, he galloped to Isla's side. Power jetted from her upraised hands as she killed whatever came within range. "Take the women," he shouted. "Ride like hell for the Overland Trail."

The gaze she shot him was laced with annoyance, tempered by compassion. "Ye wish me to be safe, but we're staying," she yelled back. "Ye need us. Dinna we prove ourselves yesterday?"

"Indeed. And then some, but I still want you far away from all this." A reluctant grin split his face. He didn't agree with her desire to stay, but her courage touched him. He wanted to say so many things. That she was beautiful and strong and he loved her independent streak. Later, if they survived, he'd make certain she knew how much he respected and valued her. How deeply he longed to protect her from every bad thing in the world…

"Doona waste your breath arguing." Her words snapped him back to the present fast. "Most ye'll get from us is we'll listen to your orders and carry them out—so long as we believe them sound."

He wanted to throttle her. Just before he claimed her mouth beneath his. "Damn, but you're one stubborn witch."

Power flared hot as she killed another wraith. "I'm listening, but not for much longer. I need to gather the women. We're sore pressed here."

Staunch words. Isla had to be scared, but she didn't let it slow her down. Sam's esteem expanded. He wished he could remain by her side, but he had a battle to oversee.

"Form a line," he barked. "Stay out of the way of each other's magic. Use your stones, and kill whatever shows up. Remain on your horse—unless it becomes unmanageable. If it does, ward it once you dismount. They'll target the mounts to strand us here."

Isla shouted to the witches in Gaelic, and they formed a ragged line. Some were obviously more comfortable than others dealing death, but nothing he could do to shore up the weaker ones. At least they all had power stones. And they knew how to use them. He hoped to hell Kane and Roland would figure out how to leverage the stones they'd paid for with pain.

The air thickened with the smells of gunpowder, wraiths, and expended magic. Where the fuck were the undead wraiths coming from? Holes in the ground opened, disgorging more by the second. He'd thought they were mere spirits of the dead, turned to evil. If so, there were a piss pot more than he'd ever imagined possible.

Hester joined the women, ordering, exhorting. Multicolored magic flared through power stones, and wraiths folded in on themselves. Enforcers wiped the creatures out in droves too. Enough were disabled from magic or bullets, the witches and enforcers should be able to ride out of there—if it weren't for the constant infusion of new wraiths. The stench of wickedness thickened, turning into a revolting miasma, and a sickly yellow hue rolled through, settling on the ground in pulsing waves.

"Fuckers won't slow down," Roland yelled.

"There's got to be an end to them," Sam cried back.

"Ha! Tell them that," Kane countered and shot two more.

Battling wraiths was unsettling because no matter how hard they fought, the bodies disappeared. Normal fights, at least you got a sense of satisfaction looking at piles of dead.

Not today.

Sam wondered where the demons were. As if he'd summoned them with his thoughts, they spilled from the same rents in the earth the wraiths had used. The enforcers and witches were already badly outnumbered, and the odds were worsening fast.

Absent a trick like the one that had saved them yesterday, Sam figured the day would end with all of them dead.

Mollie flew by in a flash of black feathers, circled, and attached herself to his shoulder. Her talons tore through leather and flesh, but her presence yanked his thoughts from the pit they'd sunk into.

Aethelred flanked him. "Of all people," the mage said, "you should know one of the ways they win is by instilling hopelessness."

"Not hopeless, practical," Sam said through gritted teeth. He ducked as a wraith closed from one side, and shot it through the heart. "There're too many of them. We'll run out of ammunition."

"If you're careful, you won't run out of magic. We have to outthink them." Fury flickered deep in Aethelred's dark eyes, turning them to molten pools of rage.

"I'm up for ideas." Sam's horse whinnied like a mad thing, crab walking to avoid a seven-foot tall coal black demon who got too close before someone filled its chest full of bullets.

"We're going to create a barrier, with them inside," Aethelred said.

Sam almost choked. "No one has that kind of power."

"I do."

"Even if you do, you'd have to stay and keep feeding magic into the spell. The second you stop, they'll escape."

"You think I don't know that?"

"What are you?" The words blew past Sam's lips before he could control them.

"It doesn't matter. Help me set the seeds for my working, then take everybody and run like mad things for the wagon train. Hester will want to stay with me. She can't. You have to bring her along with you."

"I've never known her to be especially compliant."

Aethelred cast a sidelong look at Sam. In that moment, he saw glimpses of the being Aethelred was beneath. It was so unbelievable, he focused his magic for a closer look—and ran up against an impenetrable wall.

As if nothing had happened, Aethelred said, "You're a Coven enforcer, son. Hester's a witch. She has to obey you. It's part of the blood oath she took. And part of yours."

"I'll do my damnedest." A million unknowns bombarded Sam. He couldn't believe what he thought he'd just sensed beneath Aethelred's robes.

Mollie tightened her talons, ripping through flesh. "Your damnedest better be good enough." Her beak snapped right next to his ear.

Sam twisted to eye the bird. "You're not sounding much like a bird anymore."

"Bird. Not bird. Bird. Not bird." Cawing, she flapped back to Aethelred.

Sam could've sworn the raven was laughing at him.

The mage—or whatever he was—shot a glance Sam's way. "Are you coming? I can do this alone, but it will go faster with two of us."

"Lead out." Sam closed his roiling mind to everything but galloping after Aethelred. They dropped magical magnets at the four compass points. Once they were in place, the mage raced back to the two lines where everyone fought.

Sam's eyes were gritty and stung from smoke. Wraith reek clung to everything. Spilled entrails from dying demons added to the disgusting brew until his stomach threatened to rebel and he swallowed back bile.

To make certain everyone heard him, Sam used telepathy. *"We're leaving. Come with me. Don't look back. Ride as hard as you can."*

"How?" Isla demanded. *"They'll never just let us ride out of here."*

"They will because I'll be holding them," Aethelred broke in.

"Ye canna remain by yourself." Hester nosed her horse to his side.

"I can and I will."

Though Sam was listening hard, he didn't hear anymore, no doubt because Aethelred didn't want him—or anyone else—to know what passed between him and Hester.

The mage bent close and kissed Hester's cheek. Tears glistened in her eyes, but she squared her shoulders. "I am not leaving you here alone," she said out loud.

"Yes, you will." Sam aimed his words at her. "As a Coven enforcer, I order you to follow us when we ride out of here."

Hester turned stricken hazel eyes his way. "Ye wouldna."

"Yes, I would. And I am. Aethelred can take care of himself. He'll find you when this is over."

Sam wasn't at all certain his words were accurate. No matter how powerful Aethelred was, holding the barrier in place may well prove his death sentence.

Unless he was immortal. In that case, all bets were off.

"Ready?" he eyed the mage.

"Never readier." Something wild and fey danced behind the mage's gaze. It was clear he hated Black Magick with everything in him and welcomed the confrontation he'd invited.

"Cory!" Sam gestured to the other man.

"Brother."

"At my word, lead everyone out of here."

"Will do." The other enforcer nodded his understanding.

Sam wheeled his horse, waiting for the thunderous clap that would signal Aethelred kindling his spell. "Don't let your mounts throw you. Use magic if you have to, but remain in the saddle. It's going to get very loud, and the horses won't like it," he shouted just before strident, discordant sound blasted him from all sides and blue-white lightning blanketed the field. It homed in on demons and wraiths alike. Whenever one tried to flee, it vaporized in poofs of wicked smelling gore.

"Go!" Sam shrieked, waiting to make certain everyone followed Cory in a jumble of hooves churning up sod.

"Are you sure?" Sam eyed Aethelred, with Mollie on his shoulder.

"Of course I'm sure. I'm going to enjoy the hell out of this. Keep your guard up. This isn't all of them, but if you kill whatever shows up in front of you, you should be able to keep moving."

"I could remain here. Help you," Sam persisted.

"Don't you understand?" The mage morphed into what Sam thought he'd seen earlier. "They can't hurt me." Blond hair flowed to Aethelred's waist, and his black robe turned a shade of silver that amplified the day's light. Eyes that had been dark turned a pure, cerulean blue.

"Goddess's breath! You're Gwydion, aren't you?"

"I'll never tell. Now move!"

An unseen whip snapped, and Sam's horse took off after the others.

He laughed, filled with wonder at what he'd just seen. If Danu could show up to help Breana, why the hell couldn't the other gods materialize at will? Except this one had raised Luke. No wonder his friend's magic was so potent. He'd been taught by the best. Gwydion was not only the master enchanter in the Celtic pantheon, but the warrior magician, father of all battle tactics. Not only that, he was Arianrhod's brother.

"Keep my secret, or I'll be forced to erase your memories," rang in his mind as he thought about Arianrhod, virgin huntress and

mistress of Caer Sidi, where she looked after the moon and the tides.

"No need for that. I'll hold my tongue."

Sam caught up to the group handily, but remained in the rear guard position. Who was the raven? Could she possibly be Fintan Mac Bóchra? The sex was wrong, but Fintan had lived out his life as a hawk, though Sam couldn't recall the rest of the myth.

"How could ye do that to Hester?" Isla demanded, dropping back to ride next to him. Rage flickered around her, turning the air a reddish hue.

"Because Aethelred wanted it that way." He longed to say more, to share his wonder about what he'd just seen. Words sat just behind his teeth. Words to reassure Isla the mage couldn't die, and this way Hester would remain safer. But he'd promised to remain silent, and a vow to a god—or to anyone—had to be honored. He quested about for something to add that would make him look less like an insensitive oaf.

Isla didn't give him an opportunity. "I was considering your offer, but not anymore. Ye canna treat females as if they doona have free will." Nostrils flaring with anger, she kneed her horse until she caught up to Tashia and Hester.

A cold, dead place opened within Sam, but he shuttered it fast. Isla had sounded as if she were truly lost to him. Forever. He shook himself and straightened his spine. For now, his only job was leading the group to the relative safety of the wagon train. He'd try to patch things up with Isla later. Duty had been his mistress all the years since he'd grown up.

Maybe she was the only mistress he'd ever have.

～

Isla couldn't believe it when Sam ordered Hester away from the man she clearly cared deeply for. If Hester wished to remain with Aethelred, it should be her choice. Not Sam's. All the warm feelings that had been growing within her uprooted savagely, making her heart hurt on their way out.

Sam wasn't any different from the enforcer who'd made Rowan's life hell, and she'd do well to remember it.

Her horse shied, its eyes rolling wildly, and a pack of mad wolves launched themselves out of increasingly thick timber. Tongues lolled. Jaws snapped. Isla reached into their minds and planted the suggestion they turn on one another. Because she focused the thought through her moonstone, the pack didn't hesitate, but fell on one another, snarling, snapping, dealing deathblows that severed their thick neck vessels.

Blood spattered her as she raced past the brawling pack.

"Nice work!" Hester shouted.

"Thanks. How are ye?"

"Och, and I'm over being mad at Sam. He did what he thought was right. Aethelred told me I couldna remain, that I'd see things that would change the feelings betwixt him and me forever more."

Isla frowned. "What exactly does that mean?"

Hester shrugged. "I'm not certain, but I've come to trust him." She turned the brunt of her hazel gaze on Isla. "Ye've never been married, but there are times when ye do whatever your husband desires—without asking too many questions."

"What if what ye want is different?" Isla demanded, still annoyed Hester's wishes had been thwarted.

"If ye'd always have your own way about everything..." Hester hesitated. "Better to remain as ye are. Being two means sometimes listening to another perspective—even if it sticks going down."

Another gaggle of wolves pounced. One flung itself at Isla, and she was thrown out of the saddle and ended up on the ground grappling with the thing. Hot stinking breath seared her, and its jaws hovered inches from her neck when she loosed a bolt of magic to stop its heart. Hissing with annoyance, she scrambled upright, hunting for others that could do damage.

Her horse was long gone. The wolf had totally spooked it. Another wolf rushed her. Followed by a companion. Both were dirty black with amber eyes burning like coals. She sent magic into one's mind, suggesting it attack the other.

It ignored the idea and kept coming right for her.

What the hell? Why wasn't it bowing to her will? Had Black Magick come up with some sort of antidote? The other wolves had torn into one another. What was wrong with this one?

Isla gathered power, focused it through her moonstone, and finished off one of the wolves as it sprang at her throat. The thing exploded, showering her with bits of bone, ichor, and gristle. At least it got the other wolf's attention, and it altered its reckless path toward her long enough to snap up mouthfuls of the other wolf's remains.

Hester doubled back, but Sam bore down on Isla, waving Hester off. Before Isla could protest, he scooped her off the ground and swung her into the saddle in front of him. A blast from one of his six-guns finished off the wolf snacking on its companion.

"This is why I ride in back," he informed her. "We'll catch up to your horse. He didn't get far."

"What if I'd rather walk?"

"Not your choice. Right now you're my responsibility."

She wanted to scream at him that she was no one's responsibility except her own, but what was the point? He held her firmly, an arm wrapped around her middle. His scent, and the feel of his firmly muscled chest against her back reminded her of their headlong flight out of San Francisco. It was how they'd begun. With her riding in front of him. She made a grab for her anger and outrage at him ordering Hester about, but it scampered away.

Without indignation to anchor her, Isla was lost. She fought against it, but the bald truth was she wanted Sam's warmth, enjoyed the hell out of his arm pressing into her side, holding her tight to make certain she remained in the saddle.

"Did you get hurt when you fell?" His deep voice rumbled near her ear.

"Bruised, but I'll live."

"Good. I wouldn't have it any other way." He paused a beat. "I'm not asking you to understand, but I know exactly how Aethelred feels about Hester. Because I feel the same way about you. I'd move heaven and earth if it meant keeping you out of harm's way. Here's your horse."

Snaking out the arm that wasn't around her, he grabbed its trailing reins and brought both horses to a halt. He held her a moment longer than absolutely necessary, and helped her switch to her own mount, a move they finessed without her having to get down and remount.

"Catch up to the group," he instructed. "I'll be right behind you. Now and always if you'll have me."

Isla kneed her horse, urging it forward. The Central Overland Trail loomed before her and she turned her horse hard right following dust the others were kicking up. Despite her harsh words, Sam still cared about her. His reassurance that he'd be there—no matter what—gave her a solid respect for him. He had principles. It was why he hadn't slept with her. How could she appreciate those principles in one circumstance and dun him for them in another?

He was still Sam, guided by what he was convinced was the right thing to do.

Hester's words filled her mind.

If ye'd always have your own way about everything, better to remain as ye are. Being two means sometimes listening to another perspective—even if it sticks going down.

Isla swallowed hard. Being prickly and stubborn had always been one of her downfalls. She'd never taken well to direction—from anyone. It was one of the reasons the Coven never held any attraction for her.

Och aye, and at least I know myself.

Does it mean I'm destined to be alone forever?

Hester had obviously gotten past her unhappiness about being pried from Aethelred's side. If she could forgive Sam and Aethelred, so could Isla. But did she want to?

Sometimes Sam felt strongly enough about something to force his will onto others. Like he had with Hester. Other times, he backed down. Right after the wraiths appeared, he'd ordered her to take the women and leave. She'd argued, and he'd acquiesced.

Isla turned things over in her mind. It was a whole lot like arguments she'd had with other witches over the years. Sometimes she dug in her heels, and others she came to appreciate the other woman's opinion and backed down.

Why would it be any different with a man?

Feeling like a fool, an idiot finally recognizing something obvious to the rest of the world, she closed off her overactive brain. They'd made the Overland Trail, and the going was far easier than it had been, but they were far from safe.

Maybe none of them would ever be safe again. The sheer numbers in the Coven's wagon train might dissuade the dark, but they'd never go away.

We will beat them. We have to.

Isla clung to those thoughts. They buoyed her as she sent her power ranging wide, seeking the next thing lying in wait for them. Sam's energy pulsed from behind her, and she welcomed it. Maybe she was too stubborn and set in her ways to join her life to anyone's, but she was going to give it a try.

If she read his signals right, and he'd still have her. She wouldn't blame him if he decided she was too temperamental, too much trouble.

Och, and I canna tell him aught. Not yet.

That discussion would take time, something they'd have precious little of until they caught up with the Coven and everyone had divested themselves of wagons and teams.

CHAPTER 12

Sam herded the group forward. Mad wolves darted from behind trees and boulders from time to time, but not in enough numbers to force them to quit moving. They'd long since slowed from a full out gallop to alternating loping with trotting. Even so, they'd have to stop soon. The horses were tiring and needed water and a break.

The day had moved past its zenith. The sky still spit freezing rain, and the higher they'd gotten, the more sleet-like it became until ice crystals spattered down, stinging his face. They'd traversed a pass about half an hour before. It had grown a little warmer as they descended, but bursts of hail followed them.

No more wraiths—or demons or wolves—barred their path, and for the first time, Sam allowed himself to believe they might make the wagon train without having to stop and take a stand. He sent his power ranging wide, seeking Black Magick's taint. When he didn't find anything, he did it again, just to make certain. A creek burbled ahead, disappearing into timber growing thickly along its banks.

"Stop at the water." He projected his mind voice to Kane and

Tom who rode in the lead. The enforcers had been trading off who led the group since it required a continuous infusion of power to make certain they weren't riding straight into a trap.

Sam slowed his horse and sent telepathy skittering far ahead. *"Luke?"*

"I'm here. Are you all right?"

How to answer that? *Yeah we're fine because the man who raised you mutated into one of the Celtic gods.* Sam shut that line of thought down damned fast—before Luke could intuit anything.

"Sam?" Luke's mind voice was edged with concern. *"Do you need help?"*

"Nope. We're good at the moment. Just crested the highest pass, so I figure we're closing on Salt Lake. You?"

"We're only about two or three hours from Breana's place. Soon as we see everyone settled, me and Joshua and Chris can grab fresh horses from her pasture and head out to meet you. How's Aethelred?"

Sam smothered a snort. *"Fine. He's fine. About meeting us. You don't have to—"*

"Spoken like a true Coven enforcer. Meanest, toughest hombre this side of the Pecos. See you soon, brother."

Before Sam could protest, tell Luke to stay put, the other man severed their connection. Sam wondered how Aethelred was doing, but when he focused his magic that way, hoping to communicate, no one answered. He hoped to hell what he'd told Luke was accurate. Someone was bound to tell him about his mentor remaining behind to face a horde of demons and wraiths all by himself.

Luke wouldn't take that well. Particularly if Aethelred was nowhere to be found.

Sam clamped his jaws into a tight line and slid from his horse, leading it to the creek and encouraging it to drink, but not too fast or too much right at first. The enforcers milled in a tight group, the witches in another. Everyone chattered in Gaelic, their spirits higher than they'd been since the previous day's skirmish.

Savage protectiveness filled him. These were his people. They'd been through hell, beset from all sides. They were hungry and they had to be tired, but they were able to find pleasure in simply being off their horses for a little while.

Not being under attack helps too, a dour inner voice chimed in.

Still concerned about what he'd told Luke, he joined the witches. "Heard from Aethelred?" he asked Hester.

She turned a bright smile his way. "Now that ye mention it, I just did. He trounced the sorry lot of them, and he and Mollie should join us within the hour."

Breath whooshed from Sam. He covered it by clearing his throat. "Excellent. We'll stay here until he catches up. We'll have other company soon too. Enforcers from the wagon train are headed our way, or they will be. We may not see them until early tomorrow, though."

"How many more?" Kat asked. She raked her hands through her blond hair and shook her head. "I'm doing the best I can, but I wasn't cut out to be a warrior."

"Me either." A corner of Rowan's mouth twisted downward. "I'd rather put a body back together any day than tear one up."

"Three." Sam answered Kat's question.

"Who?" Hester asked.

"Luke, Joshua, and Chris." Sam shrugged. "I tried to tell Luke not to come, but you know how he is. He insisted, then ran off where I couldn't argue him out of it."

Cory strode to Sam's side. "Do we have time to cook something?"

"Yeah, but make it fast. I want to be moving again as soon as Aethelred catches up to us, which should be in about an hour."

Cory furled his brows. "You've heard from him then?"

"I did," Hester spoke up.

"Did he tell you anything about what happened?" Cory asked.

"Nay. Only that our enemy is vanquished—for now." Hester's smile developed a definitely feral aspect, her lips thinning over bared teeth.

"Excellent. Now there's a story I want to hear—once he's back here. Meanwhile, the men and I will work on food." Cory loped to Tom's side and gestured for two others to join them.

Sam glanced sidelong at Isla. She'd actually been looking at him, but she busied herself with digging in one of the saddlebags she'd removed from her horse. He wanted to talk with her, clear the air between them. At the very least, he was champing at the bit to know if she'd been serious about slamming the door on a possible future together.

Or if she'd just been reacting and had cooled off.

He couldn't talk with her while she was surrounded by witches, so he took a chance and walked to where she crouched in the shadow of a tree. "You busy?" He kept his tone neutral.

"Why would ye ask?" Isla didn't look up.

"Greens would go well to add to the cookpot. Some of the men are hunting small game to cook us a meal. I'm going after onions or watercress or maybe leftover berries, and I could use an extra set of hands."

Even though her head was angled away from him, he saw color rise to one cheek. She didn't say anything for so long, his worst fears raced in from every quadrant. She truly was done with him, her harsh words far more than momentary ire.

"Sorry to have bothered you," he mumbled and turned away intent on putting some distance between himself and the woman he was falling in love with. Why in the goddess's name couldn't he pick women who appreciated him for who he was? Who wanted a life with him? Was he so damaged from his years by himself that no woman would tolerate him for more than a roll beneath her sheets?

He was twenty feet away and moving fast when he felt her energy close from behind him. "Sam," she called. "Bide a bit. Sorry I was a mite slow to answer. I'd be glad to help ye gather greens for a meal. 'Tis the least I can do."

The sound of his name rolling off her tongue in her lovely brogue sliced through his defenses. He could listen to her say his name forever. Even if nothing else happened between them, that alone made him happy.

He turned and watched her walk toward him, body rolling from side to side with her defined stride. No one had ever trained her that women were supposed to move demurely, but he was glad of it. Isla was her own person. She'd say what was in her mind, and maybe knowing her thoughts would make him a better man.

She caught his gaze with her forthright one and pointed to where the creek flattened out. "Just down from that small cascade, we should find something. The horses have already discovered it."

He followed the direction of her extended finger. The horses had indeed made their way to greenery decorating the edges of the creek. "We'd better hurry," he observed. "Or there won't be anything left."

She laughed and the crystal bell sound of it warmed him. "Mayhap we should call them off. Redirect them further downstream."

"Nah. Better if they stay close. Easier to round them up if we have to leave in a hurry."

She frowned, drawing her dark brows together. "Does it

seem odd to you that our enemy has thinned out since we left Aethelred?"

Sam helped her down a steep slope slippery with moss and walked beyond where the horses grazed. The short answer to her question was it didn't seem odd. Once the dark mages who were after them discovered they faced a Celtic god, it had probably knocked a rather hefty hole in their confidence and forced a hasty regroup.

Isla knelt and began plucking long green stalks he didn't recognize. "Ye dinna answer me," she said.

"I wasn't sure how to. On one hand, yes it seems odd, but I've had experiences like this many times." He was hedging, but he had to protect Aethelred's secret.

"What kind of experiences?"

She handed him stalks, interest plain on her face. Gods, but she was beautiful with her high cheekbones and square chin. Her eyes darkened to midnight blue in the pale afternoon light.

"Where dark sorcerers vanished after they'd been at my throat so long I could taste their vileness even while I slept." Laying the plant he couldn't identify aside, he tugged bunches of wild onions from the creek's shore and piled them atop Isla's greens.

"I suspect they'll attack again. Do ye concur?"

Sam shrugged. "I have no idea, but that wasn't what I wanted to talk with you about. We could've stayed much closer to the group if all we were going to do was speculate about Black Magick." Without taking too much time to craft flowery words, he dove right in. "Are you still angry with me about Hester?"

She narrowed her eyes in thought. "No. Not really."

"Thank all the gods for that." Hope spurted through him, layered with an optimism he'd all but squelched.

Sam wanted to say so much more, but his tongue tangled on

the words, so he knelt next to Isla and wrapped her in his arms. Relief beat a steady tattoo through him as he cradled her against his body, reveling in how she felt in his arms. "I can't be other than who I am, and a big part of that is I protect what's dear to me." He smoothed hair away from her face.

"That's what Aethelred was doing with Hester. Protecting her." Isla's voice was muffled against his chest.

"Exactly. He told me I might have to pull rank. Order her to leave, but I understood full well why he wanted her somewhere safer than that field crawling with wraiths and demons."

"I ken that now too." She pulled away and cupped the side of his face in a calloused hand. "I have a temper. Sometimes it runs away with me."

He wrapped a hand around the back of her neck and ran his fingers down the side of her face. "I care what happens to us. When you told me you had no use for me, it cut deep."

"Och aye." She shut her eyes for a moment. When she opened them, she said, "'Tisn't pretty, but ye'd hurt my friend, so I wanted to hurt ye back. I'm sorry. I havena had much experience with men."

"It doesn't matter. None of it does so long as you haven't shut me out of your life." He brushed his lips over hers wanting to kiss her. His cock pressed against the laces of his breeches, hungry for far more than kisses, but they couldn't make love with Black Magick set to pounce.

Even if he didn't sense any dark taint nearby, wraiths had a nasty habit of materializing out of everywhere and nowhere. He couldn't maintain vigilance and bed the woman in his arms. No matter how much he wanted to.

"Jennings!" We need those greens now," Cory called.

Sam chuckled. "We're forever destined to put duty first."

"I ken that too. More than ye might think." Isla kissed him softly, letting her lips linger atop his, and then pushed to her feet.

He joined her, filling his arms with what they'd gathered. "Thank you."

"For what?" She quirked a dark brow.

"Giving me another chance."

Isla shook her head. "'Tisn't quite right," she murmured. "What I did was give myself a chance as well. Hester said a few things that sank in. We've both been by ourselves for a long time, ye and I. If we're to alter that, 'twill require adjustments on both sides."

"Good thing one of us has a practical streak." He helped her up the same steep section where her feet had slipped going down.

Isla snorted. "Practical could be your middle name. Ye live to seek out problems and fix them."

"Seems you're not under any illusions about me."

"Ye'd best not harbor any about me, either."

They reached the two cookpots bubbling over fires and divided the greens between them. There wouldn't be more than a spoonful or two of stew apiece, but it was something to tide them over.

"Who's sitting watch?" Sam asked Cory.

"Kane and Roland. They're up on that rise yonder." Cory jerked his chin to the north.

Sam nodded and drew Isla off to the side, switching to telepathy. *"No illusions, sweetheart. I like strong women. Women who know who they are and what they want."*

Color stained her cheeks, but she held his gaze. *"That's the sweetest thing anyone's ever said to me."*

He wanted to say a whole lot more. To tell her he dreamed about running his hands through the silk of her hair and feeling it tumble through his fingers. If she got tired of him talking about her hair, he could switch to her eyes that reminded him of a tempestuous sea. Or her golden skin stretched over stark bone structure that made her look like an old world deity. Or her breasts. Though he hadn't seen them, he was certain they'd be so perfect they could make warring armies lay down their weapons to worship her beauty.

Her mouth curved into the softest of smiles that made the corners of her eyes crinkle with delight.

"Are you inside my mind, sweetheart?"

She nodded. *"Aye, that I am and loving every minute of the flattery, laddie."*

"It's not flattery—"

Mollie winged her way between them, digging into the same shoulder she'd shredded earlier. "Mage man. Mage man," she cawed.

Isla stroked the raven's feathered head. "I'm so glad ye're safe."

"Safe. Safe," the bird agreed sagely.

Sam turned his head, hunting for Aethelred. The mage stood in the midst of the group of witches with Hester wrapped in his arms. His hair was white again and his robes dark. He must've felt Sam's gaze because he glanced up and nodded slightly.

Sam understood and smoothed his thoughts until they were filled with nothing but Isla. The gods danced to a fiddler only they could hear. Aethelred had lived among men for at least the last fifty years, maybe longer. He had his reasons. Sam might find out what they were, but he probably wouldn't. And it didn't matter. The god had thrown in his lot fighting for their side.

Maybe disgust with Black Magick, fear for what might happen if it continued unchecked, had filtered far higher than Sam ever imagined.

Isla followed the line of Sam's gaze. Compassion spilled from her eyes. "I'm happy for Hester. She may have accepted not standing by Aethelred's side to fight, but it dinna mean she wasna worried about him."

"I'm happy for both of them."

Mollie laid her beak next to his cheek, leaving it there for a moment before she launched herself off his shoulder. Rather than returning to Aethelred, she dove into a nearby bush, emerging with a squealing vole clamped in her beak.

"Wonder how our supper's doing?" Isla laughed warmly.

"Probably done enough." He laced his fingers with hers. "Promise me something."

Her face turned solemn. "If I can."

"Don't push me away when you're angry." He hurried on. "I expect both of us will lose our tempers from time to time. I'd rather have you scream at me than walk away."

"Not running away when I'm angry." She bit her lower lip. "'Tis a long-standing pattern. It willna be easy for me to alter it. Is there aught else?"

"To talk things through until we understand one another. We won't always agree, but I'll try my hardest to respect your viewpoint."

"Sometimes I'm too angry to talk." She looked down, long dark lashes grazing her cheeks.

"I'm a patient man. I can wait until the words find you."

Isla closed her arms around him for a quick, hard hug. The others were moving toward the cook fires intent on splitting supper amongst them. When she let go, she murmured, "Ye're a good man, Sam Jennings."

"And you're quite a woman."

Isla rolled her eyes and laughed. "Let's see if ye're still singing that particular tune six months from now."

"I will be."

"Ye're sounding damn sure. How could ye be?"

"Because your energy's a good match to mine. Beyond that your soul kindled something in mine the moment I met you."

"But I'm outspoken and volatile and opinionated."

"Yup." He swatted her bottom and they covered the distance to the fire pits. "You may not see yourself as perfect, but you're the perfect woman for me."

"What if I doona join the Coven?"

"I don't care. That's your choice."

Hester handed Sam a metal mug. "Short rations," she said succinctly. "Share what's there." Focusing her gaze on Isla, she smiled knowingly. "Listened for once, did ye?"

"Ye might say that."

Both witches laughed heartily before Isla took the mug from Sam and spooned stew into her mouth.

The meal was over in scant minutes, and everyone pitched in to break camp. Sam picked his usual rear guard position. He liked keeping an eye on everyone, and the end of the line was the best choice for that.

They'd been on the road for half an hour, and the sun was tracking toward the western horizon when Aethelred maneuvered his horse next to Sam's. For once, Mollie circled overhead.

Sam angled his head, glancing at the mage. "What happened back there?"

"About what you'd think. I remained until the abominations stopped flowing out of the ground. Once everything was dead— or obliterated—I left."

Sam nodded and held silence. Aethelred wanted something.

"Indeed I do." The mage smiled, but there wasn't any warmth in it. "Open your mind to me and listen."

Rain began falling in earnest once they set out again, but it had finally stopped. Isla tossed her hood back. It would be dark soon, and maybe her hair might dry a bit before the day ended. Maybe. Bitter cold closed in once they lost the sun, and she shivered, drawing her cloak closer about her. Their route skirted the base of a major mountain range to the north, but it was easy enough to follow. It wasn't the way she'd traversed the country when she went to its western coast. Back then, she'd followed a series of Indian tracks interspersed by cross-country sections. It had taken months with many stops before she finally arrived at the Pacific Ocean.

That was years ago, though, and the country was growing fast. She bet well-constructed wagon roads would offer easy access to every corner before much longer. The railroad would likely expand as well—just as soon as they laid tracks for their engines and cars. Would there be a place for magic wielders when all was said and done? She remembered why she'd fled the Old Country, and concern for the future of her kind filled her with dread.

As they'd done off and on through the afternoon, her thoughts turned to Sam. She would've dropped back to join him, but Aethelred rode beside him and magic flowed between them. Probably nothing she should interrupt.

Excitement alternated with sheer terror that she'd opened herself to Sam as much as she had. They'd actually had a conversation about how to build something lasting between them. Would she be able to hold up her end? Or would sharing her innermost hopes and fears prove too much for her?

Her mouth twisted wryly. If she could face off against wraiths and mad wolves, surely she could let down her guard enough to allow a man to love her. And to love him back. All of him, without wanting to change him into something else. Likely someone she wouldn't care about nearly as well.

Quite aside from her tumultuous emotions, Isla ached to hold Sam, to feel his arms around her, cradling her as if she was the most precious thing in the world. The memory of his mouth on hers made her yearn for more. He kissed as if he had all the time in the world to savor every nuance of her lips and tongue. What would that mouth feel like sucking on her breasts? Or better still, teasing the dark, secret place much lower that throbbed with wanting him?

She wriggled forward, nesting her crotch against the horse's warmth, rising through her saddle. She'd come this way that first night sharing Sam's horse, and the memory made her want him with a desperation verging on obsession. Their shared kisses, the feel of his acres of muscles pressed tight against her, his erection snugged against her spine combined to stoke her lust. She rocked forward, pressing her nub against the saddle and let the motion of the horse do the rest as she spun a fantasy of loving Sam.

She imagined his hands running the length of her body. Of

him suckling her breasts and stroking fingers into the hot tightness between her legs. What would his cock look like? She had a pretty good idea from feeling its length and girth press into her, but she wanted to wrap her hands around it, tease it with her tongue, and feel it spasm when he came.

Her nipples hardened and she added a small jolt of power to drive herself over the edge. Orgasm crested through her, and she wrapped herself in magic long enough for the spasms to subside. She let her breathing return to normal before loosing her spell. Maybe tonight, assuming they stopped sometime before the dawn, she could find her way to where he slept. Even if he was too shy to bed her in close proximity to so many others, just sleeping with his arms wrapped around her would be heaven. To have him close enough to inhale his scent would be enough —for now.

She laughed, loving the fine edge that filled her with longing. Loving the possibilities Sam opened in her life.

"I could use a good joke." Hester brought her horse alongside.

"I was just thinking about Sam and feeling hopeful."

Hester looked askance at her, but she was smiling. "Weddings seem to be in the air here of late. Will I be performing another?"

Isla felt her cheeks warm and she shrugged. "I have no idea. We haven't gotten that far yet."

"Far enough to be considering something close, though?"

"Aye, far enough for that." Isla tossed a fond smile Hester's way. "We havena had much of a chance to catch up, but 'tis good to see ye again. I missed ye when ye left San Francisco."

"Aye, and I missed all of you as well. Remember when we were growing up in the Old Country and families remained close together?"

"Of course I remember, but the world is changing. 'Tis what I was thinking on a while afore ye rode up."

"What'd ye come up with?" Hester furled her white brows.

"Och aye. Nothing good, I fear. At first, I thought this country was big enough for everybody, but I'm no longer certain of that. The empty places are filling up fast."

"Exactly." Hester clacked her jaws shut.

"Exactly what?" Isla prodded.

"We need something like the Coven. 'Twas why I gathered our small band together after Michael and I moved. At the first, ye'll recall Abby was with us, but then she returned to New York."

"Of course I remember. In terms of the Coven, I can see arguments on both sides," Isla replied. "We're less visible when we're not in a group of any kind."

"And more vulnerable to Black Magick." Hester narrowed her eyes. "I doona hold the gift of foreseeing, but dark sorcery has grown far more aggressive of late. I fear they mean to strike fast, hard, and constantly till none of us remain."

"That's always been their goal," Isla retorted.

"True enough, but mayhap now they finally have enough recruits to seize the upper hand. And enough negative energy from the hostility betwixt North and South to fuel their efforts."

"What a horrible thought. Do ye really feel 'tis that hopeless?"

Hester shrugged. "I doona know. But they've been far harder to deal with since I set out for Breana's place. 'Tis been but a short span of time, and I've spent most of it embroiled in one battle or another."

"Mayhap 'twasn't mere coincidence the women and I were set upon in San Francisco." A shudder tracked down Isla's back as she rolled the implications around in her mind. "Here I was thinking 'twas an isolated incident."

"Nay. 'Twasn't. I'm certain of that. When ye called on me for assistance, we were between battles. To be candid, it curdled my blood for it meant what I'd been living and breathing was widespread."

Isla inhaled raggedly. "What can we do?"

Hester squared her shoulders. "One thing is certain. Running willna fix things. Those days are over." She sucked in an audible breath. "In a backhanded way, Don Giraud did us a favor—"

"Stop a minute. Who's he?"

"Och aye, ye wouldna know. He was one of the Coven leaders, a witch turned by Black Magick, except he hid his new allegiance. I'm certain 'twas part of a bigger plan to sow sabotage from within."

"Was this Giraud man that canny then?"

Hester shook her head. "Nay. He was merely an instrument. If there was a master plan to destroy the Coven, 'twas crafted by the Dark Angel."

Breath gathered around a narrow place in Isla's throat as fear gripped her. "Then why the hell are we meeting up with the Coven if they've been turned by evil?"

"I'm doing a botch of a job explaining this." Hester held up a hand. "Don and the Dark Angel are both dead. Don's wife is married to Joshua now, one of our enforcers and a good man. He, Sam, and a few others are who killed Andras, the Dark Angel."

Isla reminded herself to breathe deep. She needed to know more and if she sank into hopelessness fueled by terror, she wouldn't listen well. "So how did this Giraud blackguard do you a favor?"

"By highlighting that the Coven wasn't immune to being infiltrated by evil. He and his daughter were the only ones, but ye can be certain the Founder assessed every single witch and mage traveling west with the wagon train."

"Were there those who dinna come west?"

"Aye. Quite a goodly number. Many said they dinna wish to travel so far, but it also got them out from under scrutiny at the hands of the Founder."

Isla wanted to know more about who this Founder person was, but that wasn't central to where she suspected Hester was going. "Say more," she urged.

"The group that will gather on Breana's lands is solid, trustworthy. There'll never be a better time to mount a war against Black Magick."

"What if we lose?" Isla clapped the hand not holding onto the reins over her mouth. "Och aye. I dinna mean to give voice to that."

Hester shot a pointed look her way. "Nay, but 'tis what we're all thinking. Better to give it our best effort than have them pick us off one by one over the next few years, though. We stand a better chance this way."

"We're the only thing standing betwixt this world surviving or failing." Isla spoke slowly, measuring her words. "If bright magic dies out, and black is all that remains, humankind will fade. They willna be able to stand afore the tide of evil."

"True enough. But wickedness will feed on them as long as there's a man, woman, or child left standing."

"Doona forget the animals." Isla clucked, making a disgusted noise. "The dark loves turning them to their nefarious purposes." She inhaled deep and did it again. "We canna fail. Too much depends on our magic to balance out evil."

"Aethelred and I have spoken on this. He agrees with what ye just said."

Isla jerked her chin behind them. "He's been closeted with Sam for a long time. Do ye suppose they're talking about this same thing?"

Hester nodded, her expression sad and resolute. "Aye, I'd bank on it."

SAM WAITED while Aethelred shrouded them in his particular brand of power. No wonder it felt different, impervious to incursion from Black Magick. Time passed before the mage was satisfied.

"It's done," he said at length. "We can speak normally without fear of being overheard."

Sam cracked half a grin. "Why do I have a feeling it will be mostly you talking and me listening?"

Aethelred nodded sagely. "Maybe you've the gift of foreseeing, but more likely you understand the way of things and are curious as the devil why I'm here."

"That did occur to me."

"I must admit I'm grateful you're not peppering me with endless questions."

Sam shrugged. "You wouldn't answer them anyway, so what's the point?"

"I'm going to tell you part of a story, but—" he caught Sam's gaze and held it "—you can't ever tell anyone. If you do, you'll never be able to speak again."

"What? Will my tongue fall out?"

"Something like that." Aethelred narrowed his eyes to slits. "If you'd rather not hear anything and would prefer to launch straight into plans I'd like to trigger—and your part in them— now's the time to speak up."

Sam looked away. He was curious, but was knowledge worth the price if he slipped up? "Isla is often inside my head," he pointed out.

"So? You understand how to segregate thoughts and lock them away."

"Yes, I can do that." Sam blew out a breath. "Yeah, I want to know why you're here and not hanging around with the other gods in the Old Country—assuming that's where most of them still are."

"We're not bound by geography like mortals."

"Which means?" Sam began to make a come along motion with one hand, but stopped before his fingers could curve into their get-on-with-it position. Urging a god to say anything felt like courting disaster.

"We're anywhere and everywhere. Problem is, no one believes in us anymore."

"We do." Sam frowned. "Witches and mages. Probably the other side as well."

"It's not enough, and we could do without any attention at all from the dark side of things." Aethelred's nostrils flared. "Mortals used to worship us, leave offerings. We replenished part of our power from their prayers and adoration."

"Does that mean your powers have grown weak?" Sam winced. "Forget I asked that."

"Weaker, yes. I left the others quite a while back to see if I couldn't rustle up a few shrines in the American Colonies, before they turned into the States."

Sam thought back to when he'd first shown up in Mexico and his journeys crisscrossing the country over the years. "Didn't have any luck, did you?"

Aethelred laughed, but it held a sour note. "Not much. Meantime, I found I rather liked masquerading as a mage. I married, but picked badly. The woman was terrified once she found out I commanded even the small amount of power needed to kindle a candle. I was careful not to have children.

Half-divine toddlers would've posed a problem. Once Hagan left me, I faded out of sight for a few years. When I surfaced again, I started a school to train those who showed aptitude to become witches or mages, so we could add to our cadre of practitioners."

Sam leaned toward Aethelred, fascinated. "That was when Luke found you."

"Indeed. Actually, we found one another. And not a day too soon, but you already know much of that story. By then, I'd seen enough and heard enough of Black Magick's insidious behind the scenes machinations to understand what a threat they were becoming." He clamped his jaw into a harsh line. "I tried to convince some of the other gods we had to help. If we didn't, I feared it would be the death knell for humankind."

"Did they listen?" The question tore out of Sam.

"To a certain extent, but not the way I wanted them to. Many were still angry because of the way humans spurned us in favor of other deities."

"Can we win this war without their help?"

Aethelred nodded knowingly. "You see through to the heart of problems. Just like my Luke. It's what makes you good warriors."

"You didn't answer me."

"Because I don't exactly know. Maybe. I was surprised how little it took to vanquish that field of wraiths and demons." Aethelred drew his brows into a thoughtful line. "The problem is more because their numbers appear to be limitless than because they're hard to get rid of. Rather than engaging them time and time again, we need to find a way to close off their worlds from our own once and for all."

Sam looked away, considering Aethelred's words. "If we did that, there'd still be dark sorcerers. If they didn't have access to their minions, though, they'd become more of an annoyance than an outright threat."

"Your assessment mirrors my own." Aethelred shook his hair over his shoulders. Half out of its braids, shiny white strands trailed down his back. "While I traveled with the wagon train, I spent a fair amount of time talking with the others, assessing how willing they'd be to wage a full out war against Black Magick."

"I bet most of them said they would."

"You'd be right about that." Aethelred caught and held Sam's gaze. "The Founder knows what I am. I didn't tell him. He guessed as he watched me moving from one group to another asking questions. That one is old and very strong. The Coven is fortunate to have him as their leader."

"I always thought so. What would it take to seal evil's various borderworlds permanently?"

"Another good question. I'm working to recruit Arawn to our side. The paths of the dead are open to any world, no matter who controls it. He designed things that way because spirits come from both sides of the fence, and he worried what would become of wickedness if he didn't allow them access to his realm."

"If they couldn't cross over—" Sam frowned "—then they'd remain on this side of Arawn's jurisdiction, wreaking untold havoc in death, just like they did when they were alive."

"That sums it up nicely."

"Maybe so, but it doesn't provide a solution. I'm guessing we can't barricade wraiths and the rest of them into their borderworlds without help from the god of the dead. They'd just slither from wherever we corralled them into Arawn's realm and escape from there."

"Arawn does have safeguards in place to keep his shades from fleeing."

"Pfft." Sam remembered himself. "Sorry. Didn't mean to be rude, but Hester and Breana paid a visit to the paths of the dead and freed a whole bunch of them."

"She told me. And I made a side trip for the specific purpose of alerting Arawn. It may have opened his eyes to how vulnerable his system is if he's not there every single minute to oversee it."

Sam sucked air through his teeth. What chance did someone like him have of convincing a Celtic god of anything? If anyone could get through to Arawn, it was Aethelred. Sam tried to call the man riding next to him Gwydion in his mind, but choked over the god's real name every single time. Probably just as well.

"What happens next?"

"We'll meet up with the wagon train tomorrow evening. Next day at the latest," Aethelred replied. "As soon as we can after that, I want to hold a war powwow. Within the group, we command enough magic to seal the gates and keep the wraiths and demons contained. It will be a tricky maneuver, though, requiring exact timing. If we don't do exactly the same thing at the same time, focused on separate portals into their worlds, we'll end up with hundreds—mayhap thousands—of fell creatures in full attack mode."

"Will Arawn do what he has to to ensure they can't use the paths of the dead as an escape hatch?"

"He's my next stop, once you and I are done. My conversation with him isn't finished."

"Is the Founder in agreement?"

Aethelred nodded. "I've said what I needed to. Be ready once we join the wagon train and I convene everyone."

"Ready for what?"

"Why to sort out any who have the least doubt about what we're doing. I already told you how delicate this is. We can't afford to include anyone who doesn't believe with their entire being that we've embarked on the right—the only—course of action open to us."

Sam felt the casting shift and change around them. "Hold."

Aethelred's magic froze in place. "What?"

Sam's stomach tightened, but he forged ahead anyway. "This is none of my affair, but I care about Hester. I've known her for a very long time. Will you ever tell her…anything?"

The mage's dark eyes glittered dangerously, displaying the god beneath. "You overstep yourself, mortal. Suffice it to say, I care about her too, and I'll make certain no harm befalls her."

The air splintered into a blast of magic so bright, Sam shut his eyes. When he opened them, he rode alone.

CHAPTER 14

Dark had long since fallen when Sam began hunting for a decent campsite for the evening. Though they lacked moonlight in the cloud-ridden sky, the track was easy enough to follow. Mad wolves had continued to attack, singly and in small groups, but never enough of them to actually stop for. Whoever saw them first killed them with bullets or magic, and everyone rode on.

He hadn't seen Aethelred for hours, but wasn't worried about him returning. Sam spied a sidetrack. A cursory exploration led him to a glade half a mile from the Central Overland Trail. After determining it was as close to perfect a camp as they were likely to find, he raised his mind voice and called everyone to join him. Water burbled through a meadow, and grass would provide grazing for the horses. It was sparse, winter grass, but the animals would welcome any feed at this point.

While he waited for everyone, he dismounted and loosened his horse's girth strap. "Tomorrow," he promised the stallion. "I'll get this saddle off you and keep it off for a while."

The animal whickered near his ear, and Sam bent to pull a

choice clump of grass, holding in it the flat of his hand for the horse. Mollie plummeted out of the skies and attached herself to his shoulder.

Sam winced. "Damn, but those talons of yours are deadly. My shoulder will never be the same. Does this mean Aethelred's nearby?" He cast a sidelong glance at the raven.

"Didn't go with him." The bird cawed raucously, then in a burst of something that felt like whimsy added, "With him. With him."

Sam snorted. "That's more like it."

Hoof beats told him the others would arrive very soon. Likely why Mollie had reverted to repeating things. Cory, Tom, and Kane rode in front with the witches sandwiched between them and the other five enforcers.

Kane slid out of his saddle. "About time," he groused. "Much more riding and I'd be permanently fused to the horse."

"Split up." Sam ignored Kane's complaint. "We need fires, meat, and greens. I'll take care of the horses to free everyone up."

Unlike the carefree chatting from their last stop, everyone hurried to work on some aspect of setting up the camp or getting supper going. They had to be tired. Sam sure was, but they'd set two hour watches through the night. He built a perimeter with magic and sealed the horses inside where they could graze and drink their fill. Moving among them, he scratched ears and stroked noses, encouraging them, letting them know they were appreciated as he released their girth straps to let them breathe a bit.

Mollie had taken up permanent residence on his shoulder, but at least she'd relaxed her death grip on his bruised shoulder muscles. "If you want dinner," he told her, "you'll have to scare something up."

"Dinner. Dinner," she quorked, back in full raven mode. Launching herself off his shoulder, she flew off squawking.

Sam took advantage of being alone for a moment to draw power from the earth and fill his depleted places. He had a feeling there'd be no rest for several days, between riding, evading dark sorcery, and putting Aethelred's plan into action.

What the hell was Arawn thinking? He had to shutter the paths of the dead so evil spirits couldn't find their way in from their perverted, twisted borderworlds—and thence back to Earth.

Ducking beneath his magical enclosure, he left the horses to what he hoped would be a peaceful night and headed toward the fragrant smell of wood smoke rising from several fires. Small groups hunkered around four fires and the smell of food cooking made his mouth flood with saliva. Rations were often short on the road. Magic went a long way toward keeping hunger at bay, but it would be good to have a hot meal to fill his stomach.

Isla detached herself from a group with Cory, Kane, and Hester. "There ye are." She smiled warmly. "I was about to see if ye needed help settling the horses."

Sam's chest swelled with joy. She was happy to see him. It shone from her like a beacon. Even though they'd talked earlier, the validation of her bright smile lent his heart wings. He opened his arms, and she walked into them, closing hers about him. He splayed his hands across her back, just holding her, enjoying the feel of her against his body. Desire buffeted him, but he focused on the simple pleasure of her next to him.

"Hey you two lovebirds," Cory called. "We need more firewood."

Isla laughed softly. "I'd left to gather some when I saw ye— and got sidetracked."

He kissed the top of her head and let her go. "We'll get twice as much together." Taking her hand, he walked into the forest and bent to pick up deadfall and twigs. Isla did the same.

"What happened to Aethelred?" she asked. "One minute he was with ye, and then there was this unholy blast of magic, and he was gone." She shook her head, barely visible against the dark of the night. "I've never seen the like of his level of magic. Fair takes the breath right out of a person."

"Know what you mean." Sam glanced at the bundles of wood they'd gathered. "This is likely enough to cook one meal."

They made their way back to Cory and alternated stacking wood beneath the fire until it blazed bright. Sam glanced inside the pot, gratified to see enough stew to feed all four of them. "Rabbit?" he asked.

"With marmot and a mouse or two." Cory shrugged. "Beggars can't be choosers."

Sam glanced at Hester. She'd been uncharacteristically quiet. Before he could ask if everything was all right, she turned and hustled back toward the main road, moving fast. He started after her, but Isla made a grab for him.

"'Tis likely Aethelred returning." She kept her voice low, pitched mainly for him.

"You don't know. Not for sure," he said. "I don't want her out there by herself."

"Then we'll both go." She matched his stride.

Sam wanted to send her back to the safety of the cook fires. Instead, he laced his fingers with hers and summoned power so he'd have it ready, if something other than the mage had drawn Hester away from the others.

"Good idea." Isla extricated her hand and he felt her kindle power of her own. Different from his, but complementary. Witch power was a good adjunct to his; it was why the addition of enforcers had strengthened the Coven's magical talents.

A flash of blue-white light and the unique feel of Aethelred's gift drew Sam to a halt. He sheathed his power, grateful he didn't have to use it. Mollie streaking past, a blur of black feathers, confirmed his impression.

"Feeling better?" Isla asked, but there wasn't any sarcasm or I-told-you-so lurking beneath her question.

"Yes." He took her hand again. "Let's give them a bit of privacy."

She leaned into him. "Here I was hoping we might find a private spot of our own—but after we've eaten. That stew pot smelled awfully good."

Hester and Aethelred walked toward them with Mollie perched on the mage's shoulder chittering at him. Hester's face was wreathed in smiles. Sam tried to read something from Aethelred's expression, but couldn't. He'd have to wait to find out if Arawn was going to help them. Even absent compliance from the other god, Sam had a hunch Aethelred would come up with something else.

"Smells like supper." Aethelred smiled, nodding hello to Sam and Isla.

"Aye, we'll feed you and then both of us need our rest." Hester's trademark brusqueness was back in force. "Come along now. Food's ready." Tugging on Aethelred's arm, she trooped past.

Sam smothered a grin, waiting until they were out of easy earshot. "No matter how much you want to," he spoke into Isla's ear, "don't mother me. It won't go down well."

Isla chuckled. "Och aye, she is who she is, and naught will change that, but I dinna raise bairns, so my mothering skills are a wee bit lacking."

"Thank the gods for small favors."

"Nay. I'd rather thank them for ye." She stood on tiptoe and kissed him softly before starting back toward the fires.

Sam's heart cracked wide open. He wanted to swing her into his arms, kiss her until both of them were breathless with desire, and then divest her of her clothes slowly. One piece at a time with his mage light close to hand, so he could see every delectable inch of her as he uncovered it. Once her breasts were bare, he'd—

"Later." A cascade of silvery laughter followed that one word. "I'll hold ye to it, though."

He wrapped an arm around her waist. "Stay out of my head, woman."

"Why? I learn so much by listening in."

ISLA LAID her blanket next to Sam's and hoped he wouldn't draw first watch. Wanting him burned so bright within her, she was almost reduced to nothing but cinders. The thought made her smile, and she lay down to wait for him. He was meeting with the enforcers as they decided who'd take which watch.

Dinner hadn't taken long. Nor had passing various flasks around before they ran dry. Cory, or maybe it was Tom, had joked they were overdue for a resupply stop. Hester and Aethelred had disappeared as soon as they were done eating. No matter how diligently Isla searched with her magic, she couldn't sense either one, and she thought again about Aethelred's power.

What manner of being was he? Could he possibly be one of the first mages? She'd heard stories of them when she was growing up back in the Old Country, but according to legend they'd all passed to other worlds long before her birth.

Sam's unique magic moved close, and she forgot about everything but him. He sat next to her and bent to unlace his boots. "We have a couple hours," he said as he tugged off his boots. "The guys took pity on me, said I wouldn't be worth a tinker's damn because all I'd be thinking about was you."

"Were they right?" Isla moved her hands over his leather-clad torso before working to undo the laces holding his shirt in place.

"And then some, but it'll take a damn sight longer than two hours to drive you from my mind. Two lifetimes wouldn't be enough." He twisted, placing a hand on her shoulder and pushing her onto her back. Pale illumination flickered from his mage light, suspended off to one side. "You're so lovely. I could look at you forever."

Isla let her gaze play over his stark cheekbones—lined with several days' stubble—his square chin, and his high forehead. Blond brows cut a line across it, and his blue eyes, blazing with twin fires, promised passion akin to her own.

"Nay. Ye're the lovely one. Such a beautiful man. Ye remind me of the fey creatures that used to dance with us of a midsummer night on the Highland moors. Part spirit, part human, they held a beauty that's never left me."

"We have something in common then." His eyes burned all the way to her soul. "Because I'll never leave you, either."

Lowering himself, he gathered her into his arms and slashed his mouth down on hers, tangling his hands in her hair to hold her head steady. She kissed him back with a ferocity to match his own, and tangled her tongue with his. He bit her lower lip, sucking on it and she bit back, stringing kisses up and down his whiskery cheeks. Reaching behind him, she splayed her hands across his broad shoulders, enjoying the spread of muscles that flexed beneath her touch.

Her breath quickened as she shaped her body to fit the hard

planes of his. He moved a hand from her head down her back until it curved around her butt and snugged her against the hardness jutting into her belly. Sam groaned, making a decidedly male sound. His lips found hers again, and his scent—magic mingled with evergreens—rose around them.

She wanted to hold him forever, but she wanted to see the body jammed against hers too. Wanted to explore every part of him. Her hips thrust against his erection with a mind of their own. Just when she was considering pulling her skirts up and out of the way and unlacing her underthings, he broke away from their kiss, breathing hard.

"I want to make love with you, not find the fastest way into your body." Sam rolled far enough away to begin undoing the fastenings holding her jacket in place.

She reached for the leather thongs at the neckline of his shirt. Unlacing them the rest of the way didn't give her purchase to remove the tight-fitting garment, so she slid her hands beneath warm leather to the skin beneath. "Take it off. I canna."

"I propose a trade." He'd tugged her jacket half off.

"What kind of trade?" She licked dry lips, only too aware of the hot, slick place beating like a second heart between her legs.

He knelt on the blankets and drew her upright until she knelt facing him. "Better." He finished getting her jacket off and unbuttoned her blouse, pushing it off her shoulders to bare her chemise. A smile split his face. "Women. You wear more layers of clothes."

"'Tis to keep our virtue intact," she informed him with a sly grin. "But I've never been the virtuous type, which is why ye willna have to fight your way past stays atop my shimmy."

Isla gripped the edges of his shirt and drew it over his head, tossing it into their bedding pile. Her gaze was riveted to his naked chest and arms. Blond hair grew thickly around his nipples and scattered like motes of gold across his upper chest. Slabs of muscle shaped his shoulders and arms, and a hard, flat stomach trailed into the waistband of his breeches. The unmistakable outline of his cock was fully visible now that his shirt was out of the way. She ran her hands down his body, delighted in the hot silk of his skin.

Meantime, he tugged the chemise over her head, gazing at her breasts like a starving man sitting down to a long overdue meal. Reaching forward, he filled his hands with them, rubbing her nipples to hard peaks. She moaned, muffling the sound with magic in case she totally lost control of herself and shrieked her delight to the skies.

Sensation spilled through her, shooting from her distended nipples to her crotch. Liquid dribbled onto her thighs, and she dropped a hand to curve around his erection. He pushed into her hand, and his cock bucked hungrily.

"This shouldna be so difficult. Ye've turned my brain to mush. I have to think how to unlace your breeks." Finally, after undoing what felt like knots, she moved the leather aside and drew his ridged flesh into her hand, exploring him from tip to base, where a mat of golden curls grew.

He fastened his mouth to hers before moving it lower to capture a nipple. His hands were busy with the buttons of her skirt, and it pooled around her knees. Isla leaned toward him and wrapped her other arm around him without releasing his cock. He felt so incredible in her hand, she couldn't bear to break contact.

Sam let go of her breasts long enough to scoop her into his arms and lay her on her back. He knelt between her legs, erection jutting from his body, letting the heat of his gaze play over her.

She reached for him, but he shook his head. "Let me enjoy

you. If you touch me much more, I'll spend, and I'm not ready to do that yet."

Bending, he cupped a hand over each breast, rubbing her nipples and stringing kisses down her belly, lower and lower until his mouth hovered over the center of her pleasure. She threaded her hands into his hair and bucked her hips upward, trying for contact, but he just breathed on her, directing thin threads of magic to hold her body at a fever pitch.

Minutes ticked past before he snaked out his tongue and teased the tip of her. He repeated the movement before settling his mouth around her and sucking. The rhythm and cadence of his magic changed. This time it urged her to tumble into ecstasy.

Isla didn't need much prodding. Orgasm spooled deep in her belly, spilling through her in a cascade of sensation and magic. Sam didn't let her off the hook, though. He kept on suckling her and feeding magic into her until a second peak followed the first. Only after her spasms subsided, did he let go.

Making a very satisfied male sound, he moved up her body, kissing as he went until he lay full length atop her and closed his mouth over hers. The taste of herself on him, all salt and musk, heated her blood as if she hadn't just spent—twice.

Isla groaned, writhing against the erection pushing for entrance between her spread legs. "Roll over," she panted. "My turn to love you."

He wrapped her in arms and legs and flipped them to where she sat astride him. Isla knelt over him, watching his face in the glow from his mage light as she grasped his cock and ever so slowly lowered herself onto it. He was big, and he stretched her, touching places no one else ever had.

Gripping her hips, he held her in place for long moments flexing his cock deep inside her. Power spilled from him, mixed with pure, unbridled lust. He smiled lazily, and it made him so profanely beautiful, she couldn't tear her gaze from his.

Strong hands moved her hips, slowly at first, then faster as he plumbed her depths, taking her measure as woman and lover. Arousal built again, but she ceded control to him, let him direct how hard, how deep, how fast they moved. It was a new experience for her. She'd always kept the upper hand before.

Golden flecks danced around his pupils. "Soon," he promised and his cock swelled inside her.

Her climax began in her soul, spreading outward in pools of multihued light. She felt him release right after her, juddering hard, as his fingers tightened around her body. Surrounded by heat, magic, and lust, he drew her down until she rested in the curve of his arms against his chest, cock still buried in her body.

He kissed her face, her cheeks, her hair, murmuring in Gaelic, his voice low, musical. Isla knew she cared about him, but what just happened deepened her feelings.

"Och aye, but I'm falling in love with you," she murmured, "and it scares the stuffing right out of me."

Sam turned them onto their sides and slipped from her body. "I'll never hurt you, sweetheart." He kissed her again, sweet and lingering, before he tucked the blankets around her and gathered his garments to dress.

"Time for ye to go already?"

He nodded. "Yes, but this will be the sweetest watch I've ever taken because I know what's waiting for me at the end of it."

"Quite the silver-tongued devil, laddie."

"Only for you. Get some sleep. I'll be back before you know it."

CHAPTER 15

It was nearing sunset the next day. Another three hours, more or less, would bring them to Breana's and the wagon train, so Sam decided they should push on. It didn't make much sense to spend another night on the trail if they didn't have to. Besides, the thought of an entire night next to Isla in a real bed was quite an incentive. They'd made love twice more before the dawn. Each time better than the last as they got to know one another's bodies. His groin ached from all the activity, but it was such a sweet sensation, he longed for more of the same.

"What do you think, brother?" Luke dropped back to Sam's rear guard position. He, Chris, and Joshua had met up with the group just past noon.

"We keep going," Sam said, snapping his attention away from the hours of loving Isla and his cock that was swelling again, making the sore places worse.

"Does it strike you things have been a mite too quiet? I feel dark sorcery, but it's elusive, like it's coming from a long way away. When I try to track it down, it vanishes entirely." Luke drew his dark brows into a frown.

"Yeah. Same here, but there's not much I can do about it. Did you float that concern past Aethelred?"

Luke snorted laughter. "I did indeed, and he was just as inscrutable as when I was growing into my magic. Getting a straight answer out of him is a trick and a half sometimes."

Sam had tried to get the mage alone since he'd returned from his meeting with the god of the dead, but without success. It was obvious Aethelred wasn't going to say anything until he absolutely had to. Maybe not even then. Sam had also been trying to figure out how Aethelred was going to marshal the Coven into following his direction without revealing himself, but he hadn't come up with much.

Having the Founder in on the secret would help, but in the end witches and mages weren't all that cooperative if they didn't agree with something. Which was likely why Aethelred had assigned him to keep a close eye on everyone and figure out whose heart wasn't fully engaged in the plan he had yet to flesh out.

Luke reached across and poked him, following it up with a knowing look. "You seem distracted. Don't blame you, though. I recall what it was like when Abigail and I were brand new. She was almost all I could think about. It's one of the goddess's own miracles I wasn't killed the day after we first got together."

Sam made a dismissive grunting sound. "It was a miracle any of us survived. That was one hell of a battle. I wasn't sure we were going to win until Alistair and Don were both doused in mage fire."

"Yup. Even then, events ran far too close for comfort. Particularly with Alistair. The way he latched onto Chris' essence for a free ride back from certain death chilled me—and not much does."

"You and me both, brother. I had no idea dark mages could even do that."

"We know now. To tap a far more pleasant vein, I'm happy for you." Luke tossed a rare smile Sam's way. "My life's a hell of a lot better for having Abigail as a part of it. You'll see once you and Isla put in some time together."

"Think I already do. She's really something. Want to let everyone know we're going to keep riding?"

"I suspect they figured that one out, but I will. Say, you'll have me stand as your best man, right? Just like I did for you."

Warmth and caring for the man riding next to him filled Sam. Luke was the closest thing he had to a real brother. They were both undercover enforcers. Part of an elite special group who handled the delicate assignments where the Coven didn't want their hand quite so visible. They'd worked together for a long time, and he trusted Luke more than anyone else. Luke felt the same. When Abigail had been possessed by darkness, and the only realistic choice was to kill her, Luke had hunted Sam down to help him figure out another way.

"I'm waiting," Luke pressed.

"We haven't gotten as far as weddings yet," Sam replied. "But when we do, you'll be the first to know."

"Those were the right words." Luke's green eyes glittered playfully through loose strands of coal black hair blowing in the wind.

"What if I hadn't said them?"

"I'd have shown up at your wedding anyway and taken my rightful place by your side." Luke chortled. "You can't escape your destiny, brother." Laughing harder, he rode up the line, stopping long enough next to each group to let everyone know they were going to keep right on riding.

They'd pulled off the trail to water and rest the horses around three. Sam didn't think they'd need another break.

Isla dropped back to ride next to him. "Ye're grinning like a verra satisfied cat. What happened?"

"More happy than anything else. Last night would be enough to make any man smile."

"Thank ye kindly. Ye make my heart glad too, but 'tisn't why I sought ye out. Rowan's getting more and more nervous," she confided.

Sam transferred his reins to the other hand. He'd assumed that problem was solved. "But we're so close to the wagon train —" he began.

"'Tis exactly why she's on tenterhooks," Isla broke in.

He switched to problem solving mode. "What are you most worried about?"

"That she may break and make a run for it even now."

Sam clamped his jaws together. As if they didn't have enough problems. "Have you talked with Hester?"

Isla nodded. "Aye, and she's with Rowan now, smoothing things over. Or trying to. Rowan believes we may be past the worst of dark sorcerers chasing us down. Things have been so quiet, I'm certain she's convinced she can go off on her own without undue risk. No more than anyone would face in unsettled country."

"But things aren't quiet. I've caught glimpses of Black Magick off and on. It's just it goes away so fast, if you weren't paying attention, you'd miss it."

"Aye, and I tried to tell her the same, but she dinna listen."

Sam sucked in a thoughtful breath. "There's a reason you're

telling me. Is it something beyond being worried about her safety?"

Isla nodded, her expression somber. "Aye. If she goes, I'll go with her. I canna let her run off by herself." Something on his face made her hold up a hand. "Nay. Hear me out. 'Tisn't an easy decision. I'd much rather remain with ye, but she and I have been the closest of friends for many a long year. I canna desert her."

Sam felt as if a mule had kicked him square in the chest. He wanted to bind Isla with magic, keep her by his side, but it wasn't a choice. Not really. She had to remain with him because she wanted to, not because he forced her.

He steadied his tumbling emotions and asked, "What will that mean for us?"

Isla blew out a tense breath. "Once I get us settled in a safe place, I'll write and let ye know where we ended up." She licked her lips, and he sensed her nervousness. "If ye havena changed your mind by then, we could pick things back up."

"Not going to happen."

"Och, and if last night meant so little, ye're not willing to bide a bit and wait for me, then—" She gathered her reins, preparing to urge her horse forward.

"You misunderstood." His voice was harsher than he'd meant it to be, and she looked as if he'd slapped her. "Please. Isla. Don't leave just yet. What I meant by *it's not going to happen* was that there's no way in hell I'm letting you ride off with Rowan into a countryside riddled with evil."

"Appreciate the thought." She spoke stiffly. "But ye doona own me."

"I know that. But I'm falling in love with you. I care what happens to you. If you leave with Rowan, I'll come with you."

Her eyes widened in disbelief. "But ye work for the Coven. Surely they'd never sanction—"

"Easier to ask forgiveness later than permission up front. I can sort things out with them if I have to. I'm afraid you're stuck with me, Isla McIntyre. Unless you tell me you don't want me—that you don't care about me—I'll stick to your side worse than any saddle burr."

The corners of her mouth twitched into a smile. "Ye're the most aggravating man, Sam Jennings."

"Why thank you." He tipped his hat her way.

Isla burst out laughing. "'Tisn't much that's verra funny, but it still feels good to laugh."

"Promise me you won't leave without telling me. That you'll find me to ride with you."

Isla nodded, and her expression turned serious. "Aye. That I will." She hesitated. "Even if Rowan makes it to the Coven and has that sit down with the Founder, there are no guarantees she'll remain with the group."

"How about if we cross that milepost when we get there? Luke's wife, Abigail, is quite talented as a healer. It's possible she and Rowan will get on famously."

"They already know one another." Isla nodded. "And they did enjoy swapping herbs and healing lore when Abby visited Hester in San Francisco just afore Michael died."

Sam thought about his next words, but decided now was as good a time as any for them. "The thing about the Coven is each person comes to it for somewhat different reasons. It's not as if all the witches and mages are cut from the same cloth. We're not."

Isla angled her head to one side. "Is what ye're saying that there's a place for anyone magical within it?"

"There is. Almost all of what I've done as an enforcer has been dealing with Black Magick, dark sorcery, and the odd Coven member like Breana's first husband, who'd been turned by evil. Despite rumors to the contrary, enforcers don't spy on witches." He rolled his eyes. "Goddess's breath, they'd eat us for breakfast."

"Yet ye have the power to order a witch to your will."

"And I've exercised it exactly three times in a hundred years."

"I see." Isla nodded. "And better than I did. I'm going back to Rowan to make certain she hasna snuck off when I wasna looking."

"She hasn't. I feel her energy."

"As do I, but her power's strong, and she's cagey enough to create the illusion she's still here when she's not. Doona fear—" Isla cast a sad-eyed glance his way "—if she's gone, I'll come for ye afore I leave."

"And then *we'll* go after her."

"Thank ye."

"No thanks needed, sweetheart."

Sam watched her ride up the line and disappear around a bend in the road. What if she hadn't told him about Rowan? What if she'd just left?

Stand down. None of that happened. She cared enough to find me.

Sam closed his jaws into a tight line. Rowan might feel jittery about meeting up with the Coven, but it couldn't happen soon enough to suit him. He wanted to punt Aethelred's bold plan to get them out from under demon and wraith incursions into action. For that, he needed to concentrate, not have his magic splintered along multiple competing priorities.

Almost as if the mage sensed he was thinking about him, Aethelred wheeled his horse into place next to Sam. "Yes?" Sam met the mage's dark-eyed gaze. Mollie rode in her customary place on his shoulder.

"That problem we discussed. It's been taken care of."

"Good to know. Can I ask for details?" Sam cleared his throat.

"You can, but it won't do you any good."

Sam tamped down half a smile. "Yeah. Luke said you can be pretty close-mouthed."

"Close mouth. Close mouth," Mollie mimicked.

"Oh he did, did he?" Aethelred chuckled.

"On a slightly different note," Sam pressed on. "I've been catching glimpses of Black Magick since yesterday afternoon, but when I focus on it, it scampers away. Then I don't feel it again for a while."

"What's your interpretation?" Aethelred raised one snow-white brow.

"They're massing. Waiting for something before they attack." He narrowed his eyes to slits. "If I was a betting man, I'd lay money they hit us before we get to the rest of the Coven." Sam shrugged. "But I've been feeling that way for days now, and nothing's happened."

"We're strung out along half a mile of trail," the mage pointed out. "Bring everyone close together. Within sight of one another."

"What do you know that I don't?" Sam stared at Aethelred, trying to see into his mind.

"When I tell you to do something, I expect you to do it, not ask questions."

Sam clacked his jaws together and switched to shielded telepathy. *You can't have it both ways. Either you're a god. Or you're one of us. You can't pull rank when you feel like it and order me around. I'm not Luke, a scared kid you rescued when his magic threatened to swamp him.*

Aethelred tossed back his head and laughed long and loud. When he got done snuffling and snorting, he said, "Funny thing, but I can't order him about, either. He never tolerated it—even when he was that *scared kid I rescued.*"

The mage's smile faded fast. "Do what I told you, or I will. It's why I'm here next to you and not riding closer to Hester. We're running out of time."

Sam kneed his horse, calling to everyone as he caught up with them and instructing them to circle back to Aethelred and Mollie. When he caught sight of Hester, Rowan, and Isla riding in a tight row, he breathed a sigh of relief. He trusted Isla to keep her word, but seeing her was like a balm. It reminded him there was more in his life than being an enforcer for the Coven.

Kane and Roland came into view at the head of the line. "Circle back," he called. "Trouble."

The two enforcers wheeled their horses and loped to Sam. "Yeah. I've been feeling dark taint more and more," Roland said. "Almost called us to a halt, but Kane thought we were better off moving. Closer we get to the rest of the Coven, the easier they can get to us if things turn to shit."

Sam spurred his horse to where the group had reformed in a tight formation, riding three abreast in six rows. He gestured to Kane and Roland to fall into the rear guard position with him. Luke, Aethelred, and Cory were in the front row—at least for now—followed by Chris, Tom, and Joshua. The witches came after, with more enforcers behind them.

"What's up?" Kane asked.

"I don't have anything firm, beyond sensing the stink of Black Magick," Sam said. "It's been getting worse, though. Not fast, but it's like they're planning something. We were too spread out to mount a defense."

"Thing I couldn't figure out," Roland said, "was why we haven't been riding bunched up like this all along."

Sam winced. "Touché. It would've been better, but at least we didn't pay a price for my negligence." He didn't mention that with thirteen men and eight witches, maintaining any kind of formation over the kind of roads they'd been traveling would've been challenging.

Light leeched out of the day as they rode, and another hour ticked past. They switched out who rode in front, and Sam's sense of foreboding grew. Hints of dark power jabbed him with greater and greater frequency, and he made his way to where Luke rode. "I think we should hunt for a place to fight from. It's always better if we can pick than if we get railroaded into something from wherever they attack us."

Luke's forehead creased in thought. "Shit. We're close enough to Breana's, I recognize the terrain."

"It doesn't matter. We'll never make it."

"Strike out for that hilltop." Aethelred, who'd been riding next to Luke, extended an arm.

As if it was a done deal, Mollie took wing and flew fast and sure for the ridgeline above them.

"Does that mean you agree with Sam?" Luke trained green eyes on his mentor.

Aethelred nodded slowly. "That's exactly what it means. We're close enough to the Coven, let's put out a call for them to ride out and meet us. I have a feeling we'll need every witch and mage who heeds our summons."

"What about your other plan?" Sam asked him.

"We'll see if we can't weave it in." Aethelred wheeled his horse and galloped after Mollie.

"What other plan?" Luke asked, looking mystified. "I know Aethelred is hard to read more often than not, but did he foresee this or something?"

Sam trod a careful path, telling enough of the truth so Luke wouldn't ask any more questions. "He had an idea to involve the Coven in closing off the portals wraiths and demons use. I actually don't know much beyond that. He'd planned to get everyone together once we got to Breana's and flesh things out better. About all I know is it was delicate and required careful timing."

"Yeah, and a whole cauldron full of power." Luke rolled his eyes. "Let's get everyone headed uphill."

Sam moved among the witches, directing them. Isla cast a worried glance his way. He wanted to reassure her, but the hard truth was he feared things would get ugly fast. She needed to be on her guard. Goddess only knew what surprises the dark sorcerers had in store for them.

He rode by her side on the way to the bluff where everyone was gathering. "Do you know anything about the sorcerers who targeted you in San Francisco?"

"Verra little."

"Did they say why they wanted you?"

"Och aye." She made a bitter face. "That they did. They wished to drain us, capture our magic somehow and use it to strengthen their own. 'Tis what they did with the witches afore they turned to their will."

"I thought they killed them."

"Aye, so did we at first, but 'twasn't so. They became servants of the dark. I know, for I saw women who'd been my friends skulking about, bleeding Black Magick's taint."

Isla's words set off alarms. There was no way for a living mage—dark or bright—to feed off another's power. They could hide themselves within another like Alistair had done with Chris, but they couldn't remain long. Their presence would kill their host, and then they had to leave.

None of that was true for the dead, however. They craved the warmth of living beings, fed off it, and turned them into fiends just like themselves. Was this a new breed of wraith? One that looked like a man, rather than a monster? With a deep sense of foreboding, Sam recalled the empty husks he'd dispatched above San Francisco's wharves.

"Are you certain they were alive?" he asked.

Sudden understanding transfixed her expression into one of horror. "Nay, and that might explain a lot. We've been doing far more running than thinking since ye rescued us."

They crested the rise, and Sam was gratified to find a large, flat area with excellent visibility from all sides. Not much of anywhere to hide, but at least they'd see their enemy approaching.

He projected his mind voice toward the Founder. *"Send reinforcements."*

The words were no sooner out when a ripping, tearing sound nearly deafened him and the earth split open along both sides of the hill, disgorging wraiths and demons.

"Hold on, son. We'll be there as soon as we can." If the Founder's words hadn't been in telepathy, Sam never would've heard them as a cacophony rose around him. Maddened by the noise, his horse bucked and reared. Sam leapt from his back with instructions to the stallion to not get himself killed.

Running on adrenaline and fury, Sam pelted toward Isla and the witches the second his feet connected with the ground. Determination to protect them no matter what ran hot, filling him with steadfast resolve.

CHAPTER 16

Isla watched dark gateways form as the earth split open. Recognition slapped her hard, and fear turned her guts into a roiling mass of sharp knives. She couldn't tear her eyes from the scene before her. Convinced it was impossible—a twist of fate—she kept right on staring. Wraiths and demons plunged through, spitting Black Magick at everything close enough to target. Her horse became just as uncontrollable as all the others, so she jumped off and said a quick prayer it would survive.

Och aye, it canna be.

Yet 'tis.

She bit through her lower lip, tasting blood. The broken places in the earth mirrored a vision she'd had when she wasn't much more than a girl. Back then on the Isle of Skye, the older witches had reassured her it was only a bad dream. That there weren't enough wraiths and demons in the world for her foretelling to be prophetic.

"Mayhap not then," she gritted out through tightly clenched teeth, "but the world has changed." She'd never forgotten those hours wrapped in terror. And here they were, risen from some abysmal subterranean chasm, for her to relive. Except they weren't a dream this time.

"What'd you say?" Kat screeched.

"Naught to be concerned with. Join your power with mine. We'll fight until we win."

"Or until there're none of us left," Tashia countered dourly.

"None of that!" Rowan tossed her head. "Sure and we'll be believing in a good outcome. Remember. They conquer by instilling hopelessness."

Isla focused on Tashia for a scant moment. Had darkness taken root? Was she a weak link in their chain? The other witch locked gazes with her, her green eyes pinched with worry at their corners. "I'm fine," she snapped, clearly having intuited Isla's thoughts.

Hester stalked into their midst. "If ye're thinking ye have time for idle chatter, think again. Form two lines back to back. Kill whatever gets close enough. Use your stones like I taught you. Doona waste magic."

Wraiths boiled over the edges of the mesa with demons in their wake, pushing them on. The stench was so unbearable, Isla's eyes watered and her stomach clenched, threatening to rebel.

Sulfur. Brimstone. Dead things. Rot.

Heedless of the part of her that wanted to shriek and pull her cloak over her head, blocking out the abominations racing their way, Isla felt for her link to the earth, finding it easily. It steadied her. When she raised her hands to call power, it leapt to obey as if everything strong, bright, and good in the world knew their days were numbered. Her pink moonstone took on the inner glow that meant it welcomed evil's challenge.

Hester began the incantation to control the dead, send them

back beneath ground. Isla stared at her. Had she lost her mind? That casting had never worked for wraiths, and she suspected demons would be impervious to it as well.

Before she could ask Hester what the hell she was doing, Sam bolted to their ragged lines, gun in hand. "Pay attention. There are holes in your wards—between them too. They're uneven. Make a barrier those bastards can't get through." Taking aim, he mowed a sea of silver and lead through half a dozen wraiths. They folded in on themselves in a cloud of vile-smelling greasy smoke.

Luke and Aethelred joined them, power flaring from their raised hands.

Wraiths circled, surrounding the mesa's perimeter. Their red-rimmed, smoky eyes bled fury, promised certain destruction. Isla tried to look away, but couldn't. No matter what she did, it wouldn't be enough. She was only one against many. Too puny to make a difference. She may as well kill herself, save everyone else the trouble...

Her hand snaked toward a knife hanging from a sheath at her belt when she recognized the insidious feel of dark mind control and yanked her fingers back.

"Nay. I willna listen. Not now. Not ever."

She spit the words into the crash of sound around them. No one but her could hear them, but that was enough. Wraiths roared as they attacked, and demons screeched in their own evil language. Thank all the gods she couldn't understand the devil's tongue. She felt certain they'd exhort her to walk right into their waiting arms, adding a solid jot of compulsion to their commands.

Goddesses' teats. She'd come within a hairsbreadth of plunging her dagger into her own breast. If she'd actually closed her hand around its handle, she'd have been lost. She tried to remember how her childhood nightmare had ended, but it eluded her, and this was scarcely a place she could concentrate on anything beyond staying alive.

Magic burbled around the men. They sent power and bullets auguring into one wraith after the next, but it didn't make a dent in their numbers. More surrounded them now than before, and still more streamed from the open places in the earth.

Was there no end to them?

Doona think about it. Kill what's in front of me.

Demons urged the wraiths forward with harsh commands and magical whips dripping with dark power. Isla had seen red and black scaled devils before, but a new variant with dirty gray scales and glowing red eyes joined their ranks. As she watched, it seemed they commanded the others. Fire spewed from their mouths and clawed hands, and their forked tails swung wildly. Cloven hooves scratched deep divots in the ground.

A wraith squealed and dove atop Tashia. Heedless of Sam pumping bullets into it, the thing closed its mouth over hers, intent on pulling her soul from her body. The look of desolation and hopelessness in her green eyes kindled blind fury in Isla. She threw herself on the wraith's back, driving magic into it. One lethal blast after another as she wrapped her hands around its neck to cut off its air.

"It's already dead," Sam shouted, but she didn't lessen the pressure of her fingers. The feel of its flesh—slimy and cold—repulsed her. As she squeezed, skin sloughed off in disgusting layers, and her fingers plunged into cold, gooey gunk beneath. The stink of the thing intensified, and bile splashed the back of her throat.

"Roll off it. I have this," Aethelred shouted.

She tried to let go, but her hands were mired in the goo of the wraith's dead tissue. Sam closed his hands over hers and dragged her to the side. White light pulsed from Aethelred's hands, and the wraith vaporized into motes of black-edged fire.

Tashia scrambled to her feet, eyes wild with fear, but at least she was still fighting back. Isla gathered herself and poured magic into a ward. Once it was solid, she latched onto Tashia's, making it stronger too.

"Thanks." Tashia was breathing hard. "I was sure I was lost."

"Mage fire would've solved that problem," Sam growled. "But I'd rather have you alive. We're badly outnumbered."

Tashia quirked a silvery brow. "So glad you told me. I hadn't noticed."

That she could still engage in grim humor lightened Isla's bleak mood, instilled hope.

Sam twisted out of the way of a bolt of Black Magick, sending mage fire to wipe out a trio of black demons. "Take that you bastards," he yelled and followed it with more mage fire.

Isla's lungs burned from wraith stench and her eyes ached, but none of that mattered. She'd been embroiled in battles before, but this was one that wouldn't end until they were dead —or the demons and wraiths somehow vanquished.

The end of her childhood dream that had eluded her earlier flashed into her mind of its own accord now that she wasn't trying to force it. She laughed. The sound bitter and fey.

No way in hell would a man in a shining robe rescue them. Believing in divine intervention was the purview of children and fools. She spared a glance Sam's way. His expression was harsh, resolute, and when she dug deeper she saw determination. Men like him faced whatever threatened them. If he was afraid, he'd found a way to bury it so deep, he didn't have to acknowledge it.

Not me. I'm scared to my bones.

The worst of it wasn't that they'd all probably be dead before the next day broke, but that she'd finally found a man to love, and they'd never have a chance to get to know each other. Let alone raise bairns or grow old enjoying one another.

Isla pulled herself together, pushed the bleakness that had dogged her earlier aside. She had to remain present, in this moment. It was the only chance she had. Mouthing a quick prayer to the goddess to keep them safe, she focused her magic outward, sending wraith after wraith—and the occasional demon—to god only knew where. Maybe they bounced right back. It might explain why there were so many of them.

On the far side of her, Hester uttered a harsh cry. Isla turned in time to see her fall, a red stain spreading across her back from a spear that had run her through.

Aethelred bellowed his ire and sent a blast of lightning to kill the demon who'd given up on magic and sent a spear Hester's way. Not just any old spear. One spelled to penetrate her wards.

Isla fell to her knees next to the other witch. "Protect us!" she screamed at Sam, and laid her hands over either side of the spear. It throbbed with wickedness and raised blisters on both her palms, but she didn't let go.

Rowan joined her. "We have to get it out. It's bewitched with Black Magick."

"Aye, but how?" Isla turned Hester onto her side. The front of the spear protruded through her breastbone with wicked notches on its tip. They couldn't pull it out from behind, it would rip her to shreds.

"Like this."

Rowan split the shaft with magic, breaking off its end. Where her bright magic contacted the spelled length of hardened wood, sparks flew. Isla's hair and clothes smoldered, but she pushed power after Rowan's working. The spear kept trying to fix itself, the broken end floating toward the rest of the shaft.

Luke kicked it out of the way and incinerated it in mage fire, muttering. "Take that you son of a bitch."

"What next?" Isla kept her hands on Hester, sustaining life in her body by force of will.

"Hold her," Rowan exhorted, and pushed the spear through. A torrent of blood followed in its wake, and Rowan chanted frantically, calling magic to staunch the flow.

Tears spilled from Isla's eyes. Hester was as good as dead. No way would she survive with such a lethal wound. Isla wanted to encourage her soul to cross to where it could find peace, but that would tangle with Rowan's magic.

A burst of light so bright it drove her lids shut was followed by a man robed in silver, with long, blond hair gathering Hester close against him. Isla blinked hard, wondering if she'd been killed and moved beyond the veil herself.

The god from her dream was here, so real he glowed. Damn, if he wasn't sitting right next to her, holding Hester and chanting in an arcane form of Gaelic she hadn't heard since she was a child. The world seemed to slow around them. Even the constant din of wraith and demon shrieks faded.

The river of blood stopped immediately. Hester's skin healed, became whole again, until no evidence of the spear wound remained. She stirred in the god's arms. "I'm fine. I'll be fine. Let go of me and save everybody else since ye're far more than any of us ever guessed."

"Feisty witch. Stay put." A sharp whistle brought the raven, except it turned into a red-haired man with a silver bow and golden arrows, dressed in old-fashioned, embroidered leather clothing and knee-high deerskin boots.

"I'll watch over her," the man assured the god, his dark eyes liquid with concern.

"See that you do." Glittering blue eyes incinerated whichever of the enemy they focused on as the god rose to his feet. He raised his hands. Blue-white lightning and white fire flashed from them, and the legions marching against them backed away.

Isla's dream had ended here, so she had no idea what would come next. Which god was this? And why had he saved Hester?

"Arawn!" he bellowed. "Show yourself, man. I could use a spot of help."

A black-rimmed gateway formed, and a tall, thin man robed in black from head to toe stepped through. Dark hair swirled to his waist, and intense dark eyes took in the tableau. "This is ridiculous," he muttered in Gaelic.

The other god shot an annoyed look Arawn's way. "You didn't believe me. Here's the evidence."

Behind them, a row of black-edged fire took shape, pushed forward by a dozen dark sorcerers. Isla stared at them. Some were the ones who'd chivied them in San Francisco. The ones she'd assumed were commanding some arcane power from the Far East.

"Look out!" she cried.

"At least we finally get to see who's behind all this," Sam muttered from behind her.

Arawn, god of the dead, turned slowly, lazily, as if he had all the time in the world and surveyed the sorcerers. "Ha! Found you." He wove his hands in an intricate pattern, and the earth opened beneath half of them, swallowing them whole. The rest of the group kept right on coming, though.

Fire jetted from their outstretched hands. "Some of us found a way to circumvent your commands." One of the sorcerers grinned, displaying a mouthful of blackened teeth.

The air temperature plummeted, and Isla's teeth began to chatter.

"Keep yourself safe," Sam told her. "I love you. We're going to end this once and for all."

"Wait."

He crouched next to her. "Yes, darling. What is it? Are you hurt?"

"Nay. Not hurt. Ye doona seem surprised—by any of this."

"I'm not, but I can't talk about it now. The sorcerers were evil men when they lived, but they escaped the paths of the dead to do even more harm." He grinned crookedly. "Convenient being dead. Just like wraiths. We can't kill them. At least demons can die." Sam shook his head. "I'm rambling. The men need me."

"How can I protect Hester until she's stronger?"

"Just worry about yourself and the other witches. Whatever Mollie turned into will watch over Hester."

Isla sucked breath through her teeth. "Aye, but who is he? And who's the god that brought Hester back from the far side of the veil? For that fact—" Isla gazed through the murk, smoke, and grit flying through the air "—what happened to Aethelred? I'd have thought he'd be by Hester's side."

Her eyes grew wide and she choked back disbelief. "Och aye, 'tisn't possible, but they're one and the same. They must be."

Sam gave her a quick, hard hug and deflected black-edged lightning that struck inches away. "Stop thinking. Fight. I'll watch over you as best I can."

"Sam!" Luke shrieked. "Over here, brother."

"Soon. This will all be over soon." Sam tipped her chin, sending his blue gaze auguring into her. "Keep yourself safe. No heroics."

"I canna promise. If another of us is gravely wounded, I—"

"Sam!" Luke sounded frantic.

"No heroics," he repeated and bolted to his feet, streaking for the sound of Luke's voice.

Hester screeched for the witches to gather around her. The man was arguing. "I gave my word I'd keep you safe."

"Fine. Fight next to me then, but ye'll not be my nursemaid. Not when my kinfolk are dying."

Isla raced to Hester's side, raised her hands to concentrate her power through the moonstone, and dispatched a group of wraiths creeping up from behind them.

Arawn and the other god—whoever Aethelred had turned into—were having a hell of a time with the dead mages. The men evaded everything including blue-white fire. Part of them would incinerate, but they'd simply pull off whatever appendage was burning, and a new one grew to take its place.

"Behind us. Demons! Look sharp!" Rowan shouted, lethal magic spewing from her upraised hands.

"Aye, indeed," Hester cried as she knocked two to their knees, their guts spilling onto the ground. "We'll kill what we can. Let Arawn and Gwydion handle the bastards who escaped the halls of the dead."

Gwydion. So that's who he is.

In spite of herself, Isla grinned broadly. With the warrior magician on their side, they couldn't help but win this battle.

Doona get cocky, an inner voice cautioned. *He may be a god, but he canna be everywhere. 'Tis up to us to watch out for ourselves.*

CHAPTER 17

"*D*o you have any idea what the hell just happened?" Luke hissed at Sam after Aethelred took it upon himself to don his god form and heal Hester.

"Yes and no." Sam answered carefully.

"Let's focus on the *yes* part. Who'd Aethelred turn into?"

"Can't talk about it, brother. Later."

"What do you mean, can't talk about it?"

Sam leveled his gaze at Luke. "It means I'm not going to say anything else. That information has to come from Aethelred."

He left Luke muttering and killing wraiths and hurried to Isla's side where he hunkered next to her, grateful beyond words she was alive. He'd done his best to shield her, but she'd been vulnerable when she aided Rowan's efforts to coax Hester back from death.

He tipped her chin, sending his blue gaze auguring into her. "Keep yourself safe. No heroics."

"I canna promise. If another of us is gravely wounded, I—"

"Sam!" Luke sounded frantic.

"No heroics," he told Isla, hoping she was listening, and bolted to his feet, streaking toward the sound of Luke's voice.

He joined the other enforcer and wove power in with his. The wraiths were finally thinning out, but six more demons leapt through one of the dark portals. One of them incinerated in a blast of mage fire, but the other five headed right for them.

"We've got to close those gateways," Sam growled.

"Easier said than done," Luke grunted. "We can't fight and free up enough power to blow the portals right back to Hell."

Off to one side, the god of the dead's face twisted into a snarl as he faced off against the dark mages. "Abominations. What's dead shall remain that way."

"It would appear you're wrong," one of the sorcerers said and sent a blast of flame auguring toward Arawn. A corner of his robe caught fire, and he focused a stream of magic to extinguish it, cursing all the while.

Sam wanted to see what happened next, but he couldn't remove his attention from the rows of dark creatures that wanted them dead.

"About those gateways," Luke muttered. Power blasted from his upraised hands, mowing through wraiths, but more rose behind them.

"I hadn't forgotten. Bet someone might have a workaround for us. Hold down the fort. I'll be back in a few."

After a terse nod from Luke, Sam bolted to Aethelred's side. "Are there enough of us to seal those bastards away for good?" He peered through the murk. "What happened to the dark sorcerers and Arawn?"

Aethelred grinned savagely. "My kinsman finally got angry and herded them through a gateway he constructed—one they couldn't escape from. They won't bother us anymore, but it cuts both ways. We won't have Arawn's help, either. He'll be too busy barricading the fugitives into something they'll never be able to defeat."

"Without him, do we command enough power to chase the demons and wraiths back where they came from—and hold them there?" Sam repeated a variation of his question.

Hissing breath scalded Sam as Aethelred bent close. "We're going to have to find enough. No choice in the matter. This mesa is sealed with magic. Even if the Coven sends help, they won't be able to get through to us." Aethelred's voice was grim. "Call the enforcers over here. Witches too. Except Hester. Leave her to finish healing."

"Hester's fighting."

"What?" Aethelred tossed a hand skyward. "I told her—"

"That's the thing about witches," Sam broke in. "They do what they think best. It's a rare witch who lets what any man thinks—even someone like you—influence her overmuch."

"What about Fintan? Didn't he convince her to remain behind wards?"

"If that's who Mollie really is, no. He is fighting, though. Right next to Hester, if it makes you feel better."

"Not particularly." Aethelred bared his teeth in annoyance.

Not wanting to deal with the god's ire, Sam raised his mind voice in summons, and everyone streamed toward them.

Luke skidded to a halt and planted himself right in front of Aethelred. "Who in the hell are you?"

"The man who raised you, and that's all you'll get for now."

"I deserve an explanation."

Aethelred sent a sidelong glance Luke's way. "Then make certain you live through what comes next."

Aethelred erected a hasty barrier around them and passed out assignments, along with an incantation he made them repeat, minus the magic to ignite its power.

"We're here." The Founder's voice battered Aethelred's warding. *"But we can't get through. The hill's shrouded in wards."*

"Keep trying," Sam told him. More firepower was always better than less.

"You've got your instructions," Aethelred cried. "Find your stations and wait for my signal. The moment I say, loose your power. Focus it through power stones if you have them."

Luke was still looking at his old mentor as if he didn't believe his eyes. Sam didn't blame him, but they'd have time later to dissect everything. He hoped. He swept Isla into a fast, hard hug and they headed for where Aethelred told them to stand. The god had taken advantage of their magic's natural affinities and instructed them to stand witch alternating with mage.

Sam gathered magic, letting it build in intensity, and waited for Aethelred's signal. His opal pulsed, excited to join the fray.

"I love you," Isla called across the space between them. "Figured I'd best tell ye, in case things doona go well for us."

He flashed a crooked smile her way. "Love you too, sweetheart. Everything will be fine. You'll see."

Cocky words. Sam narrowed his eyes to slits, concentrating. They'd only have one chance to get this right. Not only would the spell drag every undead thing back to Arawn's kingdom, it would seal them there forever.

Maybe.

Possibly.

If he believed Aethelred.

Sam inhaled raggedly. He could see demons not resurfacing, but wraiths? They'd never made it as far as Hell. They were spirits of the dead who'd refused to leave Earth, and they had a nasty habit of making more just like them.

A white whirlwind started at ground level and spun, turning

into a maelstrom, twisting faster and faster. Bits of dirt and small stones flew through the air, smarting when they connected.

"Now!" Aethelred's command rose from the ground, reverberating from all sides. "Now. Give it all you've got."

Sam voiced the incantation, hearing it rise all around him. The earth rocked and roiled beneath his feet. He fell to his knees, but never stopped chanting, pouring every shred of magic he could lay hold of into his opal and the working. Things flashed at the edges of his vision, but he didn't pay attention to any of them. The spell was almost cast. One last line, shouted at fever pitch, and they'd be done.

Thunder crashed overhead, lightning forked—one flare after the next—white mingling with red and black. He'd never channeled so much power. It raced through him from his boot soles to the top of his head and back again, making every cell quiver. The opal glowed so hotly, smoke rose from his leathers along with the acrid stench of his own flesh burning.

The thrum of voices died away. Sam tried to see if they'd been successful, but a thick, dark cloud obscured his vision, followed by a sensation of falling.

"Got you!" a red-scaled demon chortled. "And now that you're mine, I don't have to squander power."

Something hard, hot, and tight closed around one of Sam's ankles. Talons. He wrenched hard against them, tried to kick the demon in the face with his other foot, but the thing just laughed at him.

"You motherfucker!" Sam screeched. Being dragged into Hell along with the wraiths, demons, and sorcerers hadn't been on the menu.

"Sweet praise. Keep it coming. I might just let you be one of my special pets."

"Why'd you pick me?"

"No reason other than you were closest. We'll need leverage to negotiate a way out of here once Arawn, fucking bastard that he is, throws away the key."

"Lucky me, huh? Somehow I never fancied myself hostage material." Sam hissed venom, but the demon either didn't hear or didn't care.

"You'll do as well as any of the others. Like I said, don't flatter yourself. You were nearest when the spell snared me."

They continued to fall headlong down a black-as-pitch shaft. Sam jackknifed his body, forcing himself alongside the demon, who hadn't shown any inclination to let go. He was positioned head to foot with it and battered a fist into where the thing's balls should be.

The demon laughed harder. "I'm dead. You can't hurt me." He tightened his hold on Sam's ankle until he felt the bones grind together. "Now you, on the other hand, are still very much alive. Give me too much trouble, mage, and I'll make you long for death."

Sam gritted his teeth against the pain. Would his power still work here? No reason why not, except he ran the risk of blowing the portal to smithereens, which would make getting back to Earth damned difficult. He'd be lost in the airless void between worlds until his magic failed.

No! Can't let that happen. I have to get back to Isla.

The stench of a charnel pit rose and Sam's gorge along with it. He'd been to borderworlds before, but never into Hell. His eyes watered and his nose burned. Ripe, rotten smells from decaying flesh surrounded them.

"Ah." The demon made a snuffling sound. "Home. Wonderful, isn't it?"

"I'd prefer apples, cinnamon, and piecrust."

"Nothing like that down here. Shut up. So long as you brought up preferences, I prefer my servants silent."

Sam made up his mind and crafted a finely timed plan. He'd wait until the halls of Hell appeared, and then he'd blast the demon with mage fire. Once the son of a bitch was well on the way to incinerating, he'd use the shaft they'd descended through to return to Earth. Or build a new one. So long as he wasn't between worlds, anything was possible.

Their descent slowed, and Sam readied his power. It wasn't as strong here, but he'd been prepared for that. Something about the other worlds muted it, and he planned accordingly.

The shaft opened into an enormous cave. Sam used his proximity to the demon to his advantage and shoved mage fire into the thing with everything he had. The hold on his ankle evaporated, and the demon screeched in pain and outrage. They hit the floor, but Sam kept his power flowing, incinerating the demon who'd tried to capture him.

"Guess being dead doesn't insulate you from everything," Sam snarled and upped the ante on his spell. Mage fire bloomed bright. It was one flame that wouldn't burn him, so Sam didn't spare power as he made certain his fire consumed the demon. He rolled to his feet, still chanting.

The god of the dead strolled over. "I can take it from here." He grinned, his stark face taking on an even gaunter aspect. "Good work, mage. One less for me to ride herd on." His grin broadened. "Actually, this is a damn good idea. Here I was feeling sorry for myself since I figured I'd be stuck here babysitting these pieces of shit. If I thin the herd, my life will become much easier."

Sam sucked air hard. "Mind if I return to my side of things?"

Arawn glanced Sam's way as if he'd already forgotten him

and waved a dismissive hand. "Not at all. Go. Give my best to Gwydion. Tell him to drop by once in a while."

Sam reached deep. He was tired, but not too tired to escape the halls of the dead. Pushing bright magic through every pore, he leapt for the shaft, feeling air currents propel him upward. The tunnel was still thick with Black Magick's taint, and he used the opal to dispel it.

Longing for Isla, for clean air and bright sunlight filled him. The upward trip took longer than the descent, but finally the dark shell around him cracked open, and he was back on the mesa, on his knees and sucking air like a winded racehorse.

Isla threw herself at him from one side, driving him to the ground. "There ye are," she crowed and hugged him hard. "I told Aethelred, or Gwydion, or whoever the hell he is, ye'd been snared, but it took a wee bit afore he believed me." She raced on before he could say anything. "Ye missed the part about anchoring yourself to something in this world so the spell wouldna sweep ye away with it."

Sam twisted and wrapped his arms around her. "I didn't miss that part. A demon decided he wanted me for a house pet. I've gotten tangled up in my own bungling a time or two, but today wasn't one of them. You're sounding suspiciously like a nagging wife, sweetheart."

"I'll nag all I want if it means keeping ye safe." She kissed him firmly.

Sam lost himself in the kiss, but not for long. Dragging his lips from hers, he asked, "Did we lose anyone? How's Hester? Is Aethelred himself again? How about Mollie?"

Hoof beats thundered toward them. Sam lurched to his feet and pulled Isla to hers. "Must be the Coven," he said just before a hundred horses powered onto the plateau, filling the air with churning dust.

The Founder's energy burned like a beacon, and Sam headed toward it with an arm firmly wrapped about Isla's waist.

Aethelred, back in his mage guise, reached the Founder before Sam. Mollie was perched on his shoulder, quorking for all she was worth, her Fintan form discarded. At least that answered two of Sam's questions.

"All is well," Aethelred said, meeting the Founder's dark gaze. "We can leave now."

The Founder set his jaw in a tight line. Dressed in his usual black robe, he sat his horse ramrod straight. Silver hair was braided tight against his head and fell past his waist. "It was the oddest thing," he said. "This mesa was shrouded in impenetrable magic for the longest time, but then it shattered and was gone all in the span of a heartbeat. Wasn't anything we did to defeat it. We'd all but given up and were waiting for things to alter, so we could ride to your assistance."

Aethelred shrugged. "Magic is like that. Unpredictable."

"I expect to hear more about what happened up here," the Founder persisted.

Sam erased half a grin from his face. The Founder wasn't going to accept some vague platitude and go away happy. Not when he knew who Aethelred really was.

"Later. For now let's get everyone to Breana's ranch."

Hester walked to Aethelred's side and threaded an arm around his waist, leaning into him. "Aye, Breana's is a most excellent idea. My stone is tapped out, and so am I."

"Your horses were milling about near where we waited at the bottom of the hill," the Founder said.

"Excellent news." Aethelred nodded. "Means we won't have to chase them down."

"And that most of them are still alive," Hester added.

Sam walked down off the mesa, picking his way through

sagebrush and scrub oak, never loosening his hold on Isla. She seemed content to walk by his side and accepted his help once they located their mounts.

"Today closed a circle for me," she said once they'd headed their horses after the rest of the Coven, leading the way to Breana's.

"How so?" Sam asked.

"I dreamed what happened today when I was ten years old. Dreamed being set upon by evil and about the god who rescued us."

"Is prophecy one of your gifts?"

She sent a lopsided smile his way. "I never thought so. Not until today." She closed her teeth over her bottom lip thoughtfully. "None of what happened up there on the mesa seems real. The god of the dead. The other god. Mollie turning into a man. I've always believed in the power of magic, in the numinous, but today we witnessed something extraordinary."

Sam had no idea what Aethelred would do next. Would he find a way to wipe out everyone's memory of what he truly was? What about Hester? Would knowing change things between them?

"Ye're quiet," Isla murmured.

"It's a lot to take in. I'm grateful we're all safe. After Hester took that spear through her chest, I was certain we'd sustain heavy losses. Not at all sure we'd get out of there alive, if you want the truth of things."

"Do ye believe they're truly gone?" Isla asked after a long silence.

Sam shrugged. "I don't know. Maybe for a while. Evil has a way of showing back up, though. I'm not brimming over with confidence that we can ever dust our palms together and walk away."

He didn't bother to add his thoughts about wraiths from earlier. About how they'd never been quarantined in Hell, and that wasn't likely to happen now, either. Particularly in light of the god of the dead, who was already feeling put upon having to ride herd on demons.

The fence posts lining Breana's property came into view and Sam pointed. "That track leads to the ranch. I want to find a quiet corner, hole up with you, and never surface."

"Let me see." She touched two fingers to her forehead miming a fortuneteller. "My guess is we'll get dragged into food and talk and strong spirits. That'll be two silver pieces, sir."

"Everything I have is yours." Sam laughed. "I fear you're right, but we have to find a quiet corner sometime, so I can kiss you and tell you how much you mean to me."

"Only kiss me, is it?" Her blue eyes glittered playfully, but he saw through to how weary she was. Fierce protectiveness filled him. He wanted to find her a bed and stand guard at the door, so no one would bother her.

"Yup. Until I draw us both a bath. I'm not fit company for a woman's bed until I clean up." He reined his horse to a stop in front of the barn that sat fifty yards past Breana's front door, dismounted, and reached out his arms. Isla slid into them and helped him unsaddle the horses. After a rubdown, Sam turned them loose in the stream-fed pasture behind the barn.

He linked an arm through Isla's and drew her to some upturned log ends where he sat heavily. She perched on his lap and put her arms around him. "I'm so glad ye dinna end up in Arawn's halls for any longer than ye did. Not that we couldna have gotten ye back, but..."

"Hush." He kissed her forehead. "Isla. Darling. This isn't fancy, and I'm not down on one knee, but will you be my wife?

I'll care for you for the rest of my days, and beyond if you'll have me."

Her eyes widened just before they filled with tears. "Aye. And the sooner the better." She grinned and swiped at her wet cheeks. "It may well be the only way ye and I get a moment alone."

Sam laughed long and low before he bent his head and kissed her.

CHAPTER 18

*I*sla picked her way down the back stairs of Breana's house on her way to the kitchen. She'd bathed in the upstairs tub, and the women had found clean clothes for her from their various trunks and dressers. A dark red skirt fell just above her ankles, its owner clearly shorter than Isla. A cream colored sweater and a red knitted scarf made her feel almost like a new woman. Her feet were bare because she craved contact with the earth. Plus, it would take a day for her stockings, that she'd finally washed with lye soap and water, to dry.

Sitting outside the barn, Sam had kissed her until all she wanted was to drag him inside and divest him of his trousers, but other witches and mages trooping through convinced her they should wait until they could find time to themselves. Not because she was shy about sex. Because she didn't want to be disturbed. The brief taste she'd had of Sam's body whetted her appetite for more.

Lots more.

Besides, he was right about them both needing to clean up.

The roomy ranch house was crowded with witches and

mages. Because she wasn't part of the Coven, she didn't know very many of them. A peek into the kitchen convinced her she was starving, but so many women were lined up at the stove and counters cooking, they scarcely needed help from her to hurry supper along. As a stopgap for her hunger, she snatched a hot biscuit off a plate and nodded to Hester, who stirred an enormous cauldron sitting atop the woodstove.

A woman with long, blonde hair and merry blue eyes detached herself from the group working on several cakes and strode forward, hand extended. "I'm Breana," she said. "Welcome to my home."

Isla grasped her outstretched hand with the one not holding the biscuit. "Thank ye kindly for your hospitality."

"One of the enforcers who rode with Luke to offer aid before you got here was my husband, Joshua."

Isla catalogued names and faces. "Red hair?"

Breana smiled broadly. "Yes. That's the one. He said you and the other witches were beyond brave. Hester said the same." Her grip tightened. "I'm proud of you. You're a credit to our heritage."

Heat swept from Isla's chest to the top of her head, and she figured she turned bright red. Her throat thickened with unexpected emotion. She didn't know quite what she'd expected from Coven witches, but acceptance wasn't anywhere on the list.

"Why thank ye verra much." She'd planned to leave the kitchen, get out of everyone's way, but Breana made her feel welcome.

"Is there aught I can do to help?"

Breana rolled her eyes and let go of Isla's hand. "We have cooks aplenty at this point."

"How about if ye hunt down the Founder and find out what

he has planned for the rest of tonight?" Hester suggested brightly.

"Me?" Isla squeaked. "I'm not exactly one of his flock."

"He's scarcely a pastor." Hester's tone was dry. She balanced her spoon on the edge of the cauldron. "It's pushing midnight. Most of the rest of us would just as soon eat and find our beds, but if I know him—and I do—he has other plans. Find out what they are and come on back to tell us."

"Here." A tall, hazel-eyed redhead stepped forward and shoved a glass bottle that smelled of spirits her way. "I'm Abigail, Luke's wife. We met when—"

"Of course I remember. Ye're Hester's kin." Isla set down the biscuit. She took the bottle, then set it down as well so she could open her arms and hug Abigail. "Good to see ye."

"Not as good as it is to see you." Abigail hugged her firmly, let go, and pushed the bottle back her way. "We've all been worried half to death about you ever since Hester intercepted your distress call."

"We're hoping you'll join forces with us." Breana spoke up. "There's strength in numbers, and—"

Hester made a chopping motion with one hand. "Not now. She just got here. Give her—and the other witches—a span of breathing room."

"Sorry." Breana glanced down. "I didn't mean anything by it beyond a warm welcome."

"'Tis fine. No offense taken." Isla tilted the bottle, enjoying the burn of the whiskey as it slithered down her throat. "I'm guessing ye think I'll need fortifications afore hunting down this Founder person of yours?" She shrugged. "I met him, and he seemed nice enough."

"Last I heard, he was meeting with Rowan," Abigail said, "but that was an hour ago, so he's like as not done."

A fist constricted around Isla's heart. Maybe she should've kept an eye on her friend instead of bathing and washing her hair. "Has anyone seen Rowan since?" She chewed on her lower lip and glanced from one woman to the next.

The kitchen door banged open, and Rowan stood framed in it for long moments. "Sure and I heard my name."

Isla hurried to her and yanked her into a hug. "Ye willna leave without telling me. Just so we're clear about that."

"And since when did ye become my mum?" Rowan shook wet silver hair behind her shoulders. She pried the whiskey out of Isla's hand and drank deep.

"Never. Just your friend." Isla blinked back tears of relief. Nothing would mar tonight quite like Rowan slinking off into the night. It might be a safer night because of what they'd done atop the mesa, but still, it wasn't a time to be alone.

Abigail strode to Rowan. "I'd love it if you'd sit with me for a bit. Hester told me what you did after she took a spear through the chest. I want to hear more about it, know what incantation you used."

"Of course." Rowan glanced around the room crowded with various foodstuffs. "Could we bring a plate of something with us? I haven't had enough to eat in days. Weeks if you count the time we spent hiding in that basement."

Isla snorted. "Aye. I dinna cater much in the way of provisions for us."

Rowan stepped close and kissed her cheek. "'Twas on account of ye were preoccupied keeping us alive."

"Of course we can bring something with us." Abigail snatched a plate from a cupboard and piled biscuits and cheese on it.

"The Founder." Hester sent a pointed look Isla's way.

"On my way." Isla took another swallow of whiskey and walked out of the kitchen and into a hallway that led to the front door. Open doors on either side of the hall revealed a dining room, a library, a sitting room, and two small parlors.

Out on the front porch, she sent her power ranging wide and smiled. Enforcers had gathered in the creek. From the hoots, hollers, and laughter, they were cleaning up—and drinking. Witches—hundreds of them—spread in all directions from sleeping children to couples locked in tight embraces. Most were in the wagons they'd traveled cross-country in, but some had laid bedrolls out on the ground. The night was beautiful. Cold, clear, with half a moon hovering just above the horizon and a sky shot through with stars.

The pulse of Aethelred's distinctive energy came from one of the wagons. When she homed in on it, she located the Founder as well and intuited the men must be talking. Should she disturb them?

Mayhap. Just for a moment or two.

Though she hadn't asked Rowan, the fact the other witch hadn't bolted into the night meant the Founder had been gentle with her. Perhaps he'd even apologized. Isla wouldn't pry. Rowan would tell her in her own time—if she wanted her to know.

Isla made her way to the coal black wagon thrumming with power. No doubt, the men sensed her as she moved closer, but no one came out to greet her. She cleared her throat and called, "Hester wants to know how to plan for what remains of tonight."

The Founder thrust the canvas at the rear of the wagon aside and jumped down, followed by Aethelred. "She does, eh?" the Founder asked.

"How's our supper coming along?" Aethelred asked, his dark eyes twinkling in the glow from his mage light. "I stopped by the kitchen earlier, but it was such a bastion of femininity they threw me out."

A winged shape flew straight at them and latched itself to

Aethelred's shoulder. "Dinner. Dinner," Mollie quorked, rubbing her beak against the side of the mage's face.

"Haven't you been hunting?" he asked. The raven didn't answer, just fluffed her feathers around her.

Isla glanced about. No one was near enough to overhear unless they focused magic, but she lowered her voice just the same. "Will ye be staying then?" she asked Aethelred.

"Why wouldn't I? I came west with the wagons to settle here."

Heat suffused her face for the second time in the last half hour. "I meant now that people know…" Her voice trailed off, but she tried again. "About, well ye know. And then there's Mollie."

"Me. Me." The raven piped up.

Isla started to laugh. "Pretty hard to believe ye ever turned into aught," she murmured.

The Founder drew her aside and spoke into her mind. *"The only ones beyond myself who will remember anything are you, Sam, Luke, and Hester."*

"Why us? I understand ye and Hester, but why the rest of us?"

"Luke is too canny." Aethelred cut in. *"I can't erase his memories, not easily anyway. Since I'm the one who taught him, he'd sense my magic and know I was up to something. Since Sam and Luke are worse than an old married couple and can't keep secrets from one another— not for long, anyway—it meant including him. And now that I think on it, likely Luke's wife as well."*

"Since you'll be Sam's wife soon enough, you ended up part of things." The Founder smiled at her. Isla was certain he didn't smile often. It didn't look natural on his face.

"There will be periods when Hester and I leave—for months at a time when I return to Inverlochy Castle and the Old Country," Aethelred went on. *"Other than that, not much will change."*

"Change. Change," the raven cawed.

Isla ruffled her feathers. "I'll never see ye in quite the same light again, *Mollie.*"

She focused on the Founder. "What shall I tell Hester?"

"That we'll gather in front of the house to eat as soon as supper is ready. I'll address the group, but not for long. It's late."

Luke strode to where they stood and eyed Aethelred speculatively. "I managed to survive, which means you owe me a long-overdue conversation. I tried to pry information out of Sam, but he can be surprisingly close-mouthed. What'd you do? Tell him you'd turn him into a toad?"

Aethelred laughed. "Hardly. I may have threatened his manhood, though."

"Uh-uh. Not on my watch." Isla shook a finger his way. "I have a vested interest in that part of him, as do my future children."

"What's the world coming to?" Aethelred addressed the raven. "No respect from anyone."

Mollie left him and flew to Luke. "Fool. Fool," she cawed sagely.

Luke snorted. "This fool wants information." He leveled his green eyes on Aethelred, waiting. His freshly washed dark hair dripped water, darkening his leather shirt.

The mage blew out sharp breath. "You're worse than a saddle burr. Come on. Walk with me."

Isla trotted back toward the house, intent on relaying the Founder's message to the women cooking in the kitchen.

Tashia, Kat, and the rest of the witches she'd led into the San Francisco basement ran lightly to her from a wagon they'd borrowed. It had served as a supply wagon on the trip west, and now it held bedding for the group.

"Isla! Wait for us," Kat called.

Winding their arms around one another, they trooped into

the house. Isla's heart was glad. She'd been so certain her decision in San Francisco would mean the deaths of women she'd lived and worked with for years. Women she'd come to love and appreciate.

"I canna tell ye how grateful I am we're all here. Alive and together," Isla murmured.

"Beats the alternative," Tashia said dryly.

Isla stopped in the front hall and drew them into a cozy parlor, pushing the door shut behind them. "So long as we're all together, what would ye think about remaining here, with the Coven?"

"Rowan needs to be part of this conversation," Kat said.

"Aye," another witch chimed in. "We're seven. 'Tis a power number, and whatever one does, we all should."

"I'm fairly certain Rowan would be willing to remain." Isla spoke slowly. "She met with the Founder and dinna run off screaming into the night."

"Seems like a good enough omen," Tashia agreed. "For me. I'm good with remaining."

"Yes," Kat said. "Me as well. Plus, there are men here. Men with power who aren't married." She spread her arms expansively. "Why all of us might find husbands. Not just Isla here."

Her face grew warm. "'Tisn't as if I'm married yet."

"No, but you will be. And damned soon if Hester has her way about it. She's already talking about the wedding." Tashia grinned.

"Maybe she should talk with me about it." Isla bristled.

The door to the parlor flew open, and Hester strode in. "I will. I'm verra good at eavesdropping. Now what did the Founder say? Supper's done, and I need to know what to do with it."

"We're eating on the front porch and in the yard in front of the house. He'll talk, but keep it short," Isla replied.

"Short will be the goddess's own miracle for that one," Hester muttered and stomped back the way she'd come, calling out directions to the witches in the kitchen.

Rowan came in through the open door, shutting it firmly. "I eavesdrop too, and I figure the lot of you are determining our future. Do I get a vote?"

"Of course." Isla folded her hands in front of her, waiting. Maybe she'd read Rowan wrong. Perhaps the other witch still harbored enough bitterness, she'd never be comfortable remaining with the Coven.

"Thanks for not pushing," Rowan said softly and moved her gaze from one woman to the next. "I love you all dearly. You're my sisters. My family. I'm content to remain with the Coven if it's what the rest of you want."

"Mayhap, we'll take it a few months at a time," Isla said. "We can assess how things are going. How we feel, and if we wish to remain."

Rowan broke into a smile. "I heard all that husband talk. A year from now half of you will be settled in with lads of your own." She shrugged. "You never know, I just might find my own magic man. Sure and 'tis been a lonely enough life."

Someone knocked at the parlor door. When Isla sent her magic outward and found Sam on the other side, joy surged.

"Come in," she called.

He pushed the door open and walked through. "Are you sure?" he asked. "I'm not interrupting something important?"

"Nay. The important stuff is done." Isla walked to him and slipped her hand under his arm. "Ye're my *important stuff* right now."

Hester trotted down the hall, a dish of food in hand. "Get into the kitchen and carry something out here," she ordered. "Hurry, afore everything grows stone cold."

"So much for a romantic interlude." Sam laughed and they walked toward the kitchen to do Hester's bidding.

"'Twill keep for later," Isla said. "Once food and the Founder's words are done."

"Yeah. I heard he was going to talk." Sam lowered his mouth to her ear. "Let's hope he's not as longwinded as usual."

"Funny. Hester said the same thing."

They settled in a corner of the porch, leaning into each other as they ate hungrily. Though it looked as if there was enough food to feed a small army, it disappeared quickly. Once her belly was full, Isla's eyes fluttered closed and she half-dozed against Sam's shoulder.

The Founder jumped onto a wagon bed and stood facing them. "I promise I'll be brief."

His voice shook her back to full consciousness, and she focused on the straight-backed man in front of them all. He oozed power, almost as much as Aethelred.

"Those of you who know me probably doubt those words—the ones about keeping things brief—so let's see if I can't convince you otherwise." He narrowed his eyes and gazed around the crowded yard.

"I had my doubts about moving west, but today dispelled them. Fortune made certain we were in the right place at the right time to vanquish evil. Though we may have the odd wraith and human turned to darkness cross our path, I truly believe today was a turning point for our kind. Humans still won't trust us, but we may well be mostly done fighting dark sorcerers who want to wipe us out."

He waited until the cheers and applause subsided before

continuing. "The States will be at war very soon. It's better for us to be on this side of the country where the battles have far less chance of touching our lives. I want all of you to carve out homesteads. Figure out how to farm if it's a skill you've forgotten.

"Help each other. By the time the acrimony between North and South settles, we should have established a firm toehold in this valley."

"What about Black Magick's ability to feed on chaos and discontent, turn it to their advantage?" someone asked.

"It may happen." The Founder set his jaw in a resolute line. "If we haven't dealt them as grievous a blow as I expect, we'll develop a strategy to beat them down again."

"Will we remain here?" Another witch spoke up.

The Founder nodded. "I've looked into the future, and I believe we'll be here for a very long time." He clapped his hands together. "Told you I'd be brief. That's all I wanted to say. At least for now. Get a good night's sleep. Tomorrow we'll start figuring out how to carve up plots of land. When we go into Salt Lake City, I'd like to have things tacked down so we can claim homestead rights."

He jumped down from the wagon and strode into the night before anyone could ask him anything else.

The hum of voices rose and fell. Sam wrapped an arm around her. "I asked Breana if I could use one of the bedrooms inside. When she said yes, I made it up for us."

Isla laced her fingers with his. "Ye should've gotten me. I would've—"

"Ssht. It's little enough." He got to his feet and pulled her into his arms.

She clung to him. Desire spilled through her, pushing her exhaustion aside. "Show me where we'll be."

"You're sure you don't want more dinner? A walk in the moonlight? A visit with—?"

She swatted his arm. "Nay. Ye're what I want. If ye doona show me where our bed is, I might embarrass us both and take ye right here in the corner of the porch."

"If I didn't want to be alone with you so much I can taste it, I might take you up on that. I want to see you naked, though, not grapple beneath your skirts." He threaded a hand under her arm and led her inside.

"Grapple away," a nearby male witch urged. "We love public sex."

"Watch your tongue, man. She'll be my wife."

"All the better to grapple with," the witch insisted.

Isla shut the door behind them and walked up the stairs on Sam's arm. Her mouth was dry, and her heart hammered in her chest. Soon. Very soon. They'd be locked in each other's arms, and she couldn't wait.

CHAPTER 19

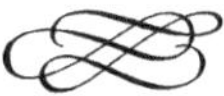

Sam breathed in Isla's scent. Wildflowers, heather, and a sweet, musky, magical female tang. "You smell like the moors." He nestled his cheek against her damp hair.

"And ye smell like forests and mysteries and magic."

They passed the top step, and Sam led her down the hall to the bedroom he'd chosen for them. In a corner, it butted under the house's eaves. He sent a small jot of power to push the door open so he wouldn't have to take his hands off Isla. The fire he'd laid in the hearth crackled merrily, and candles sat in pools of fragrant wax casting shadows as they flickered. The moon was just visible through the window.

"Oooh, 'tis wonderful." She walked into the bedroom next to him. Angling a foot, she kicked the door shut.

He noticed her bare feet and worried she might be cold. "What happened to your shoes?"

"Do they matter?" She moved so she faced him and wrapped her arms around his neck.

"No. All that matters is you and me." He gazed down at her, taking in her long, dark hair and deep blue eyes. The carved lines

231

of cheekbones and chin. Her high, arched brows. "I could look at you forever. You're so beautiful, I can't believe you're mine."

She cupped the side of his face in one hand. "What if I feel the same? No man should be as stunning as ye are. Any woman would kill for that thick, blond hair and your eyelashes. Never mind the gold bits that make your eyes shimmer like gemstones."

"Speaking of which—" he drew the opal out from beneath his clothing "—my stone adores you. Just look at how it's glowing."

"Twin to mine." She found the leather cord and arranged the pink moonstone on top of her clothing. "I knew it was shining because I felt it warm against my body."

"Darling. Sweetheart. How could the stones linked to us not be happy? I'm so delighted, it's a wonder I haven't cracked wide open."

Her lips were inches from his, full and inviting. Sam dipped his head and covered her mouth with his own. They didn't need to hurry. They had all the time in the world, but his body wasn't buying it. Swelled to fullness, his cock pressed hard against the laces of his pants.

He ignored it and concentrated on the sweetness of her mouth. When he licked along the seam between her lips, she opened her mouth to his tongue and sucked on it. The hand she'd nestled against his cheek moved behind his neck, and she tangled her hand in his hair, holding him tight.

Sam closed his arms around her and ran his hands the length of her body. When he got to the edge of her top, he pressed a hand beneath the loose-fitting garment, delighted to find nothing beneath but silky, heated skin.

She pushed her tongue inside his mouth, and he nibbled, bit, and teased. She tasted of the whiskey they'd shared, of sweet nectar, and promise. Her nipples hardened to points where they pressed against his chest, and he cupped the side of one breast, tweaking the sensitive tip.

Isla tugged her mouth from hers. "Not fair."

Wanting her spread through every fiber of his being. "What's not fair, sweetheart?"

"Ye still have all your clothes on, but we can fix that in a flash." Tossing a vixen's smile his way, she knelt and ran her hands down the front of his body, lingering over his startlingly erect cock, but not staying there.

He groaned in frustration, wanting her to keep touching him, when she moved lower and began on the laces holding his boots in place. Though he understood the boots had to go before he could step out of his breeches, any delay was maddening. He dropped to the floor next to her and worked on his other boot.

"If I would've thought ahead," he murmured, "I'd have been barefoot just like you."

Still grinning, she tugged his boot off. "Nay. 'Tisn't the same at all. All I need to do is pull my skirts out of the way."

"Really?" he countered, grinning back. "And all I need to do is unlace a few spots."

"Like here?" She placed a hand over his burning, aching cock —and began on his laces.

He yanked his top over his head and tried to get enough of a grip on hers to do the same, but she slithered out of his grasp and pulled his breeches down his legs, stripping them out of the way.

"These fit like skin," she complained, freeing his second leg with a firm tug. "Not that I'm complaining, mind ye. Ye've an ass like one of the angels."

"And how would you know about that?" he teased, making another grab for her. Isla rolled out of the way and to her feet in one, fluid movement. "Where are you going? I'm naked and you still have all your clothes on."

"Excellent powers of observation. Stay put, and ye'll get everything ye want." She moved closer to the fire, unwound the scarf from around her neck, and draped it over a chair. Next she turned away from him, and ever so slowly pulled the cream-colored sweater over her head. Her back was lovely, straight and shapely with hints of the curves of her breasts on both sides.

His throat constricted and his cock throbbed with unslaked lust. "Are you going to turn around?" he asked and rose to his feet.

"I told ye. Stay put. I want ye as badly as ye desire me, but we can fly together soon enough. 'Twill be all the sweeter for the waiting."

Sam blew out a tangled breath, and then another. "I want to touch you."

"Aye." She glanced over one shoulder at him. "Why do ye think I'm faced this way? So I willna be looking at that glorious cock standing out from your body. Such temptation would be impossible to resist."

"And you think I'm stronger than you? That I can stand here and watch you bare your body one piece at a time without reacting?"

Isla didn't answer, but fumbled with the laces at the side of her skirt. It tumbled to the floor in a pool of red wool, displaying the curves of her high, tight ass. She stepped out of the skirt and slowly turned to face him.

Sam forgot how to breathe. Her body was lovely beyond his imaginings. Coppery nipples tipped firm, well-shaped breasts. Hips flared beneath a delicate waist, and acres of legs supported the dark, magical vee between her legs, guarded by a coronet of spiky curls. Dark hair cascaded around her shoulders, beginning to curl as it dried from the heat of the fire.

He took a step toward her, and then one more. When she opened her arms, he raced into them and folded her against his body. The shock when her skin contacted his almost drove him into a climax. Her skin was dynamic, liquid silk flowing next to him. Slowly, almost reverently, he explored her back, curious how each vertebrae sat against the next. Her body fit perfectly with his, curves nestled into his muscled frame.

She tilted her head and he kissed her, wanting to be as close as he could get. Isla moaned and writhed in his arms, hips thrusting against his erect cock. Snaking a hand between them, she curved it around him, holding, touching, stroking. He wove threads of magic to slow himself down. He wanted to savor every single moment, which meant he didn't want to come yet. Even though he could come two—or even three—times, nothing was as intense as the first one.

Sam moved his mouth from hers and scooped her into his arms, carrying her to the bed. He'd turned it down earlier, so he placed her on snowy linen, fragrant from the laundry. Kneeling above her, he played his hands over the tight buds of her nipples and bent to suckle them as he reached lower, between her legs.

He teased the slick heat of her distended nub, but not enough to bring her to a crest. He wanted her frantic for him, so when he moved his fingers lower, deeper, exploring her core, he backed off when the tension in her muscles told him she was almost there.

Isla opened her midnight blue eyes. "Must I spell ye to get this—" she squeezed his cock "—inside me?"

"Do you want me inside you?" he teased, aching to thrust into her palm, her mouth, anything. Holding back was killing him.

"Aye." Her eyes turned to liquid need. "Verra much."

If she'd teased him back, he might have held out longer, but not when she looked at him like that. Straightening, he positioned himself so his cock nested at the entrance to her body. She still had her fingers curled around him, and she guided him inside.

Once he was past the entrance, he moved her hand away. She held onto his hips, using them for leverage as she tried to get more of him inside her. "Damn ye. Fuck me. Doona just sit there." She lapsed into Gaelic, but he understood well enough.

Sam lowered himself inch by inch into her scorching center. Her muscles snugged around him, and he tightened his own in return. Her eyes burned like twin coals, and her nipples grew even longer. Color painted across her chest and ribcage, and her face took on a rosy glow.

He pulled almost all the way out, twirled himself around her entrance, and pushed back inside half a dozen times before his body rebelled. Plunging into her hard and fast, he plumbed her depths. A climax burst from her, and she cried out, digging her nails into his hips.

He rode it out. He'd bring her off again, goddammit, before he totally lost it himself. Without magic, he never could've managed. The world narrowed until the only thing in it was his cock as it drove into her waiting body. Colors intensified, and her scent rose to claim him. Magic shimmered around them, so bright it was hard to look at. The gemstones suspended from their necks reflected light back at each other, adding to the kaleidoscopic effect.

Her vault tightened about him. "Soon," she breathed. "Verra soon. Ye'll join me."

Sam felt compulsion beneath her words and laughed. As if she had to spell him into release. The thing he'd been riding herd on as if his life depended on it for the last hour. But two could play the magic game.

"With pleasure," he panted. "Now. Darling. Come with me." He waited until he felt the rhythmic contractions of her climax begin before he let himself go. Semen boiled from his balls and jetted from him in gouts of almost unbearable ecstasy.

He remained above her, watching her, for long moments. Her flush deepened, and a soft, satisfied smile curved her mouth into the loveliest thing he'd ever seen. She let go of his hips and opened her arms. He let himself down atop her and turned them onto their sides.

She nuzzled his neck, purring with pleasure. "When will ye be making an honest woman out of me?"

"Tomorrow?" He pulled back to smile at her. "We can rustle up the Founder. He loves performing weddings."

"Och, nay. Hester would be flummoxed if we dinna have her do the honors."

Snorting laughter, Sam said. "How about this? We'll ask if both of them can officiate. Then they can sort out who does what?"

"Sounds perfect. Ye can tackle the Founder. I'll rustle Hester up."

"Luke will want to be part of things. I stood as his best man." Sam thought about his friend's wedding. "Will we want to consult the Tarot? To find the most auspicious date?"

Isla looked away, long lashes laying against her cheeks. "I may already have done that."

Pleasure filled him, mingled with delight that she was as anxious to join her life to his as he was to do the same. "Well? How does tomorrow work?"

"Sunset would be nigh onto perfect."

"Done. We'll announce it once everyone gets up. They'll have the whole day to prepare and fuss over us."

Isla trained her gaze on him. "I do love ye. If we take care of each and every day we're together, that love will do naught but grow over the years." She hesitated. "We might have talked of this afore, but ye do want bairns, right?"

"A houseful. Would that work?"

She nodded, and tears sheened her eyes. "I always wanted a family of my own, but it dinna seem possible."

"Funny, but I felt the same. I've wanted a family since the one I was born into rejected me. My life on the road was a hedge, a way to keep myself safe from commitments."

"Are ye certain ye're wanting to change that?"

He drew her close, tangling his hands in her unbound hair. "Very. I've been waiting for you my whole life. It wasn't accidental I rode to your aid. The goddess's hand was at work. I love you, darling. I'll care for you always. Sleep now. Dawn's nearly upon us, and we'll want a little rest."

"'Tis our wedding day." Wonder shone beneath her words.

"Yes, darling. Our wedding day." Her wonder kindled a fire in his breast, and happiness spilled through him. He'd devote his life to caring for and protecting the woman in his arms.

"Watch it. I'll hold ye to that." Humor sparked from her eyes.

"Stay out of my head, woman." He brushed his lips over hers.

Isla shrugged, the movement almost lost in the closeness of their bodies. "If ye wanted the sanctity of your thoughts, ye should've picked a wife without magic."

"True enough, darling. True enough."

With the woman he loved cradled against him, Sam summoned a small spell to give them both a few hours' rest. He wanted to be wide awake later to enjoy the many toasts and merriment that were sure to follow after the wedding. Gratitude mingled with love and longing. Isla made him whole, completed him in a way he'd never imagined possible.

"I love ye," she murmured just before she drifted away.

He kissed her forehead, eyelids, and chin. "Love you too, sweetheart," he whispered before surrendering his consciousness to the thick, luscious darkness swirling around them. He'd wake soon enough with Isla next to him, and life couldn't possibly get any better than that.

This is the end of *Blood and Illusion,* and the end of the Coven Enforcer Series, at least for now. I do hope you've enjoyed it.
Please leave a review. I'd very much appreciate it.
If you liked this series, you might enjoy *Highland Secrets,* first book of the Dragon Lore Series. A sample follows.

ABOUT THE AUTHOR

Ann Gimpel is a USA Today bestselling author. A lifelong aficionado of the unusual, she began writing speculative fiction a few years ago. Since then her short fiction has appeared in a number of webzines and anthologies. Her longer books run the gamut from urban fantasy to paranormal romance. Once upon a time, she nurtured clients, now she nurtures dark, gritty fantasy stories that push hard against reality. When she's not writing, she's in the backcountry getting down and dirty with her camera. She's published over 70 books to date, with several more planned for 2019 and beyond. A husband, grown children, grandchildren and wolf hybrids round out her family.

Keep up with her at www.anngimpel.com or http://anngimpel.blogspot.com

If you enjoyed what you read, get in line for special offers and pre-release special reads. Sign up for Ann's newsletter on her website or her blog.

Furious and weary, Angus Shea wants out, but no matter how he feels, he can't stop the magic powering his visions. The Celts kidnapped him when he wasn't much more than a boy and forced him to do their bidding. He's sick of them and their endless assignments, but they wiped his memories, and he has no idea where he came from.

Dragon shifters are disappearing from the Scottish Highlands, and the Celtic Council sends Angus to investigate. He meets up with Arianrhod, legendary virgin huntress from Celtic myth, in Fire Mountain, the dragons' home world.

Arianrhod prefers to work alone, mostly because she harbors a dirty little secret and guards her privacy for the best of reasons. She's not exactly a virgin, and she'd be laughed out of the Pantheon if the truth surfaced. Despite the complications of leading a double life, she's never found a lover who tempted her to walk away from her fellow Celtic gods.

Attraction ignites, hot and so urgent Arianrhod's carefully balanced life teeters on the brink of discovery. Angus is everything she's ever wanted, but he's far too close to her Celtic kin to keep her secret safe. Angus wants her too, but she's a Celt. He's hated them forever, and she's part of everything he's lain awake nights plotting to escape from.

Can they risk everything?

Will they?

If they do, can they live with the consequences?

HIGHLAND SECRETS, CHAPTER ONE

Angus Shea stroked beneath icy waters off the northern tip of Ireland, blending his energy with a pod of Selkies. The sea creatures cut through choppy waves in front, behind, and above him. He'd rather dive and play in the deeps with them—and if it were any other day, he would have—but he needed to keep an eye on the skies, so he edged toward the surface, pushing his head free.

Celene, a coal black Selkie he'd done more than swim with, drew close enough her lush pelt stroked his skin. He draped an arm around her, and she nuzzled his neck with her snout.

"Where have you been?" She spoke deep into his mind. Accommodating vocal chords were part of her human form, not her seal, and he'd never learned the Selkies' lyrical language.

"I spent a little time at my home in Scotland, but mostly I've ranged far from the Irish Sea."

"That doesn't tell me anything." She nipped playfully at his shoulder with her squared-off teeth.

"Prying ears are everywhere." He leaned into her warmth, enjoying a respite from the cold water.

"We could go where no one would hear."

He was tempted, so tempted he toyed with saying yes and taking a break from watching for the dragon he expected. Dragons interpreted time in their own way, and the damned thing might not show up today or tomorrow or even this week. If it showed at all.

How much could he tell the Selkie?

An answer crowded on the heels of his question.

Nothing.

Angus shuttered his mind, so the creature swimming by his side couldn't read it. Much as he yearned to talk with someone, anyone, about the impossibilities the gods tasked him with, prudence won out. Not that this assignment was worse than any of the others, but he'd finally figured out they'd never end.

I could say no. Tell them I'm done.

He cut off the bitter laugh that wanted out. Whoever had the balls to refuse the Celts risked swift and certain punishment. He could hear Gwydion, master enchanter, or Ceridwen, goddess of the world, laughing their heads off—before they cut out his tongue or killed him on the spot.

"You don't have to say a word." Celene went on, almost as if she'd peeked into his thoughts before he took care to protect them. Selkie laughter buffeted him, spraying him with a warm, rich melody mixed with salty water. *"I'm curious, but I miss your body."*

He missed hers too. She'd been his only break from solitude for more years than he wanted to admit. He cast another glance skyward. Though he tried to be subtle, he heard a smug murmur near his ear and knew he hadn't fooled the Selkie.

"You wait for an Ancient One." The tenor of her mind speech shifted as she shielded it from anyone who might be close.

Without stopping for him to corroborate, she forged ahead. *"We can take up the banner and watch for you. My kin will let us know."*

Angus picked his way carefully, as if he walked through a field of unexploded ordnance. "I appreciate the thought, but no one can know of my comings or goings, lass."

"We know more than you think." Celene batted him with a flipper. *"In truth, very little escapes us, but here isn't the place to share what I heard about your latest mission."*

Concern rippled through him. If the Selkies knew, who else might? Hell, he didn't know much beyond his assigned meeting place with the dragon, and they'd be heading into danger.

What else was new? Danger was so second nature, his adrenaline pumps barely flinched at anything these days.

"Come with me." Either Celene was oblivious to the turmoil rumbling through him, or she ignored it. She swam from beneath his arm and herded him toward shore. *"There's a secluded glade deep in marsh grass. No one will find us, and my kin will keep watch for the dragon. I already asked."*

The Selkies would do their best—and maybe today it would be enough—but they were no match for evil that had sunk its roots deep into the fabric of the Old Country and the rest of this world. It was why the gods stooped to using him—half-mortal, half-divine, or whatever the hell he was—to do their dirty work. Arawn, god of the dead, revenge, and terror, caught him skulking in the time-travel tunnels when he wasn't much more than a boy and trapped him, cutting off any possibility of return. To make certain Angus remained, the god altered his memories, so he had no idea where he came from.

Now almost twenty-five years later, Arawn and the others still came up with enough for him to do that a life to call his own was out of the question. The carrot they dangled was the truth about his birth, but they never came close to divulging it. The stick was his fear of what they'd do, if he told them he was done.

Over time, he'd stopped asking about his origins. He cared, but it wasn't worth the energy to run up against their stony faces and cunningly crafted half-truths that revealed exactly nothing. Despite his reservations about a quick dalliance with Celene—and maybe missing his rendezvous with the dragon—he was sick of his self-imposed isolation.

She chivied him into shallow water. Once she was certain he'd follow, she drew ahead easily. As if the other Selkies understood, the pod dispersed. When he peered through gray-green water for their multi-colored pelts, they weren't there.

By the time he clambered onto the rocky shore, Celene had shucked her skin. In human form, she opened her arms to welcome him. Long black hair shrouded her almost to her feet. Violet eyes gleamed in welcome. Her generous breasts peeked through the curtain of hair, their copper-colored nipples already pebbled with wanting him.

Angus had tucked his clothes beneath a rock before joining the Selkie pod. Because he swam nude, nothing was in the way as he plunged into Celene's offered embrace. God, how he'd missed the touch of another against him, skin to skin. Celene's body felt warm against his chilled one. She closed her arms around him and ran her hands down his back, lingering over the curve of his butt.

He hugged her in return. The scent of her, salt and mint, flooded his mind with images of their lovemaking, and his cock hardened between their bodies. He trailed his fingertips down her smooth skin, marveling at how different she felt from a human woman. Velvety and charged with electricity. Some Selkies walked among humans, even took permanent partners. Angus didn't understand how they eluded discovery.

Celene closed her mouth over the junction between his neck and shoulder, licking, sucking, biting. He moved a hand from her back to cup the side of her face and lowered his lips over hers. Desire engulfed him. Hot, urgent, desperate, he sank his tongue into her waiting mouth.

She grappled with his ass, pulling his body hard against hers as her hips writhed and breath hitched in her throat. Tearing her mouth from his, she gasped. "Too long. It's been too long."

Liquid heat trailed the path of her mouth as she licked her way down his chest, stopping to tease his nipples. He kissed the top of her head and wove his fingers into her long hair. Every nerve came alive with wanting her, but it ran deeper than that. Touch was such a basic need, and he'd denied that essential part of his humanity—along with every other comfort.

For what?

No matter how much he gave the Celts, they took every shred—and him—for granted. He wanted to get a job, blend in with humans. Something mundane like driving a cab, or flipping burgers in a grill, but his requests were denied. The Celts provided for him. So long as they housed and fed him, why would he need to clutter his time with anything as humdrum as earning a living? What if they needed him, and he was in the middle of washing dishes in some nameless restaurant? He could almost hear Gwydion's voice. See the master enchanter with a long-suffering look on his face—

He wiped his Celtic masters from his mind. This time was for him and Celene. No one else belonged in his head. Just because he'd chosen a semimonastic existence was no reason he couldn't give her everything she needed. Months had passed since they'd last been together, maybe as much as a year. He moved back enough to fill his hands with her breasts, rubbing her erect nipples before he bent to suck on them, remembering the little biting motions she loved.

A low, guttural moan escaped her, and she threaded her fingers through his hair. Holding him against her breasts, she began to sing as he loved her. A series of low, sweet notes rose in cadence and intensity as she lost herself in his touch. He'd asked her about the music once, and she told him it was how sea people vocalized their joy. The music filled him with unbearable hunger—poignant, mind-bending need for another person's touch.

Although he'd never done it before, he raised his voice and joined her song. The change was instantaneous. In that moment, he sensed her loneliness and isolation, twin to his own and recognized that both of them needed more kisses, more touches —even more than they needed sex.

"Lay on your belly." His voice rasped with wanting her. He tore tufts of marsh grass and arranged them to make her a bed on a sandy stretch between rocks.

She lay down, continuing to sing. Angus sang too, as he straddled her and ran his hands down her back rubbing tension from her muscles. He followed his hands with his mouth and strung kisses across her shoulder blades and down the line of vertebrae from her neck to the curves of her ass. Between their song, the feel of her skin beneath his fingertips, and his cock getting stiffer by the moment, waiting became almost painful, yet he held back, not quite sure why.

The rhythm and cadence of her song shifted as he alternated his mouth and hands across the sculpted planes of her back. The intense pressure in his balls receded almost as if he'd reached a peak, though he hadn't come. Maybe she sensed his need for warmth, contact, much as he'd sensed hers.

"Move off me so I can look at you." Celene flipped over to

face him, kneeling above her. Rose and gold splotched her pale skin, and a broad smile split her exotic, high-cheek-boned face. "Today was different. You sang with me. You've never done that before."

He shrugged, suddenly self-conscious. "It felt right. Even though I wasn't inside you, what happened between us felt right."

She cocked her head to one side and trained her gaze on him. "Are you sure you don't have sea blood?"

A flicker of annoyance at the Celts' staunch refusal to disclose anything about his birth narrowed his eyes. "I have no idea what I am." He ticked what he did know off on his fingers. "I'm not immortal, but I'll live well beyond human lifespans. My magic is closer to seer and witch than anything else, yet I'm neither of those. The covens acknowledge me as one of theirs, but only because the local witches are too kind to tell me to go away. The time-travel portals accept me." He shrugged again. "I don't suppose knowing more would make a hell of a lot of difference."

"You're not from Scotland, even though you live there." She stated it baldly, as fact.

He frowned. "Why would you say that?"

"Your speech. There's something about the lilt of Scotland that's impossible to rid yourself of. You don't sound Irish or British, either, at least not from the time we live in." Her nostrils flared. "Maybe that's it."

"Maybe what's it?"

"You could be from the past, and not just a few years back, perhaps hundreds—or even more. I'm not old enough to recall what human speech sounded like then, but some Selkies are."

"Fine." Frustration tightened his chest, like it always did when the mystery of his origins became a point of discussion. "My first memories are when the god of the dead dragged me out of a time-travel portal when I was fifteen."

"I'm sorry." She draped a hand over his hip, cradling it. "I've upset you."

He started to protest, but she silenced him with a look. "Don't insult me with a lie, Angus, but you don't have to talk about it, either. Such a pretty man." She stroked hair back from his face. "With your deep brown hair and amber eyes. Did you know they shade to dark gold when you're angry?"

She was trying to divert him with flattery, but he wasn't buying it. "You have no idea what it's like not knowing—" He shook his head, and the rest of his words died unspoken. It didn't matter what she knew or didn't know about him. She'd never be more than an occasional lover, and both of them knew it.

"It could be more," she said softly, obviously having been in his mind.

Angus took her hands in his and gazed at her. "You get more of me than anyone, and you see how pathetically little that is. There's nothing more to give."

"There could be," she persisted. "You could refuse next time they send you on—"

He bent toward her and laid a hand over her mouth. "I'm not free. Not now. Not ever."

"I don't understand." She pushed his hand away and closed very white teeth over her full lower lip.

He smiled crookedly. "Not sure I do, either. Every man has a life's work. No matter how I feel about it, this appears to be mine."

Even though it wasn't wise, he started to ask what she knew about his current assignment, but a flash of unusual energy drew his gaze skyward. He leapt to his feet. A copper-colored dragon circled to land not far from him. Maybe the Ancient One had seen him with Celene and decided to be considerate.

Not very fucking likely. Dragons were a force unto themselves.

"I have to go," he said. "Let me walk you to your skin, so I know you're safely on your way home."

A sad expression crossed her face, creasing the skin around her eyes into a network of fine lines. "It's right here." She scrambled to her feet and gripped both his upper arms, forcing him to look at her. "Thank you."

"For what?"

"Being you." She brushed her lips over his and moved to a marsh grass thicket. In moments, she'd dragged her pelt over her human body. Transformed into a seal, she waded into the surf.

Before it engulfed her, she turned to gaze at him. *"Be careful, and think on what I said."*

He didn't answer, just watched her head bob in the waves before turning toward his clothing. It wasn't far from the place Celene had led them. His body felt vibrant, alive, and he still tingled from her touch. He longed for a woman of his own, children, a home, before he stuffed the impossible so deep under wraps he couldn't mourn the loss.

Angus moved the large rock he'd placed over his clothes to protect them from the wind. He pulled a ragged dark blue fisherman's knit sweater over his head and stepped into thick, black woolen trousers. Settling on a log, he pulled on socks and laced up stout leather boots. Though the breeze was raw, he'd worn neither hat nor gloves.

Ready as he figured he'd ever be, he covered the fifty yards to where the dragon had settled up the beach. He didn't recognize this one, but he'd only met a bare handful of the hundreds living in Fire Mountain and on other worlds as well. When he drew near, he stopped and bowed his head respectfully, waiting for the dragon to speak first.

"I don't like this any better than you do," the dragon muttered. "Come close enough I don't have to broadcast our business to the world."

Angus walked closer. He could've suggested the dragon use telepathy since all the Ancient Ones were conversant in the technique, but he kept his mouth shut. The dragon was smaller than many he'd seen. Copper scales shaded to burnished gold on its chest, and dark eyes with golden centers whirled so fast they held a hypnotic quality. Lethal, six-inch-long red claws tipped its stubby forelegs. The dragon stood upright on hind legs tipped with the same sharp claws and kept its gaze averted, not saying anything.

What the hell? Every other dragon he'd met was proud, imperious, and quick to remind Angus of his inferiority. This one seemed young, but was it? After another long few minutes, Angus tossed respect—and caution—to the winds.

"What's your name? And what are we supposed to be doing? All Ceridwen told me was to meet you here."

The dragon opened its mouth, and a gout of flame landed scant inches from Angus's boots.

He frowned and drew his brows together. "If we're going to work together, I need to know what to call you." He sent a speculative gaze across the air between them. "If you annihilate me, they'll just assign you a new partner, and I'm a hell of a lot easier to get along with than any of the Celts."

"Tell me something I don't know," the dragon rumbled and belched smoke.

Frustration in its voice struck a note in Angus's soul, and he gestured with both hands. "You may as well tell me who you are and what we're supposed to do together." He infused his words with subtle persuasion. If the dragon didn't care for the Celts, either, they'd likely get along well enough.

"Why? What I should do is leave." The dragon sounded sulky —and scared.

"If you could, you'd already be gone." Angus was as certain of that as he was of anything. The dragon needed him for something, and whatever it was, the Ancient One wasn't particularly proud of it. "What happened? Am I some sort of punishment for you?" Tension settled like a steel bar across his shoulders, and he curled his hands into fists before he realized what he'd done.

"Oh I'd be gone, would I?"

The dragon ignored Angus's questions, and it mimicked his tone with eerie precision. It furled its wings and flapped them a time or two. Dirt swirled; small pebbles slapped Angus in the face. The creature belched steam and looked so distraught, he felt sorry for it.

"My life's not exactly a picnic, either," he ventured, on a hunt for common ground. "I'm a permanent mercenary, with no time off and no possibility of parole."

That got the dragon's attention, and it focused its whirling gaze on him. The golden centers of its eyes deepened with fiery motes that looked like little shooting stars. "Why would you want a respite from being a warrior?"

Good question.

"Because I'm tired. I'd like what most men have."

"What's that?" The dragon raised its brows, and its scales clanked against each other in a dissonant tinkling.

He shook his head. "It doesn't matter. The sooner you spit out whatever you need to say, the easier it'll be. The worst part about holding something you're ashamed of inside is it eats at you until you're nothing but a hollow shell."

Wings flapped, and those intense, whirling eyes shifted to the rocky beach. "I'm not *ashamed* of anything. I've been banished.

Ceridwen said if I worked with you—and we were successful—I might be able to return."

Angus kept surprise out of his voice. "Banished from Fire Mountain?"

Steam puffed from the dragon's open mouth. "No. Idiot. I could live with that. They've banished me from the Highlands. My home."

"What happened?"

"It doesn't matter." The dragon threw his words back at him. "We have to go to Fire Mountain, where I'm to find one of the First Born. Once we have him—or her—"

"One of the six First Born dragons?" Angus broke in, scarcely believing the dragon's words. "They'll never show themselves—unless it's in their best interest."

Another wing flap and a defiant head toss. "There are actually ten. One of them was my father."

"When's the last time you saw him?" The words slipped out before he could stop them. Dragon males frequently didn't hang about once mating was over with, but the trembling mass of scales in front of him likely didn't need to be reminded.

"Never. Mother said he was too immersed in battles on another world to return for our hatching."

Angus unclenched his fists and hunted for something soothing to say that wasn't an outright lie. Dragon energy poked past his wards and into his mind. He tried to block it, but couldn't.

"You believe locating a First Born is hopeless." The dragon sounded resigned. "I may as well throw myself into a crater at Fire Mountain. I'll never see the Highlands again—or my mate." More wing rustling and the dragon rose a few feet off the ground, clearly intent on leaving.

"Hold on." Angus loped forward until he was right beneath the dragon. "I didn't say that—or think it, either. I don't know enough to make any sort of judgment. How about if you start at the beginning? If we're going to work together, I deserve that much."

The dragon circled a few times, indecision stamped in its erratic flight pattern.

"I know what it is to be alone." He kept his voice gentle. "And to not have anyone who cares if I live or die."

Maybe it wasn't totally true. Celene might shed a tear or two, but she'd be the only one. He kept his gaze trained on the sky, relieved the dragon wasn't putting distance between them. Something about the creature's pain tugged at his heart and made it feel like a kindred spirit.

The copper dragon folded its wings and settled heavily to earth a few feet from where Angus stood. It straightened its shoulders and tipped its chin defiantly.

"My name is Eletea," the dragon announced, revealing its gender.

"Angus Shea, though you likely know that."

"Yes, I do. I killed a mage, who fancied herself a dragon shifter." Eletea's eyes whirled faster, as if she dared Angus to say something.

He crinkled his forehead as he dredged up what he knew about dragon shifters. "Don't mages take their chances when they show up seeking a dragon to pair with?"

She nodded once, sharply. "The mage seduced one of us into believing her. I saved him by killing her, but he turned on me. Reported me to the Dragons' Council, and they roped the Celts into deciding my fate, since the one I killed had Celtic blood." Eletea's scales rippled in the dragon equivalent of a shrug. "I don't understand why they're bothering. It's not like I went after one of the gods. They're immortal. The one all the fuss is over barely qualified as a Celt."

Angus kept his expression neutral. "Celtic blood aside, I thought mages only bonded with same sex dragons."

"That was another problem," Eletea said, sounding vindicated. "No one saw it but me, though."

Sensing the worst was out on the table, Angus settled on a nearby rock and invited, "Start at the beginning. We have time."

"No, we don't," Eletea protested. "We should've been at Fire Mountain yesterday." She hung her head. "I didn't know what I wanted to do, so I flew and flew and flew. I almost didn't land this afternoon."

Angus did his best to project optimism. "Let's open a time-travel portal and be on our way to Fire Mountain." At the dragon's reluctant nod, he went on. "I understand you have your own ways of returning home, but if you travel with me, you can fill me in as we go."

What he didn't say was it probably wouldn't matter when they arrived at the dragons' home world. First Borns wouldn't give them the time of day, whether they showed up early, late, or right on time. He held many concerns, such as what would a First Born do, assuming they could locate one? But he held those cares inside for now.

He could've dreamed the future. Instead, he summoned a spell to take them to a time-traveling portal. Once the undulating gray-pink tube admitted them, he gradually paid out questions.

Reticent and quiet at first, Eletea finally began to talk.